MORTAL WOUNDS

MORTAL WOUNDS

A NOVEL

SUE DUFFY

PROMISE PRESS

An Imprint of Barbour Publishing

Published by Promise Press, an imprint of Barbour Publishing, Inc., P. O. Box 719, Uhrichsville, OH 44683, www.promisepress.com

 Member of the
Evangelical Christian
Publishers Association

Printed in the United States of America

Sirens wailed in the desert night. Flashing lights sprayed their blues and reds against the monstrous ruin outside the city. A heaving cloud of sand and dust expelled from a powerful blast choked emergency personnel digging through the rubble.

It was three in the morning, and in the distance loomed the glitter of Las Vegas.

But here the desert was charged with chaos. Construction and rescue crews swarmed over the fallen Prince, shouting urgent commands to each other.

"Get a head count!"

"Hey! Get away from that wire!"

"Need a crane in here to secure those beams before they fall on us. Right now!"

"Get that camera out of my face!" Detective Tony Armbruster shouted at a newsman. "There's your story," he snarled, pointing to the steel and concrete wreckage that was the most spectacular gambling casino on the continent.

The Crown Prince was to open its crystal doors to the public in just three weeks. Publicity had been frenzied. The lavishness of the casino's interiors and its gallery of priceless art and antiques had been spread across the glossy front covers of magazines around the world. Headline performers and junkets aboard the new casino's private jets were booked for years to come.

"It ain't nothing now," declared a fireman to his buddy, "except a tomb. Come on, Joe, let's get in there."

Quickly, the hunt for victims began. The dogs went in first. Then rescue volunteers inched their way into the debris, their voices growing more muffled the deeper they ventured.

Suddenly, a low rumble began at the broken west wall and grew louder.

"Get 'em out of there!" someone shouted. "It's coming down!"

The men suddenly shot from the wreckage and dove into the fleeing crowd just seconds before the remaining walls of the great casino plunged to the ground with a thundering roar.

When the air cleared, a man's body was seen sprawled on the ground as if spat from the mouth of the collapsing Prince.

A crowd quickly gathered around the torn remains of a man whose security badge glinted in the harsh lights.

"Stand back!" Detective Armbruster commanded, pushing his way toward the body.

Just then, an older man in a red windbreaker stumbled into the small crowd and gaped at the dead man on the ground. Painful recognition pinched his face. Turning to no one in particular, he said, "I'm. . .the manager here. Someone. . .tell me. . .please. . ." The man began to shake violently and Armbruster helped him to the backseat of a patrol car.

"Who's in there, sir?" the detective asked urgently.

The man seemed not to hear the question. His eyes were vacant and fixed on the ruin before him. "I'm. . .Grayson Myers," he finally said in a halting whisper. "You must clean up this mess. . .immediately."

"Medic!" Armbruster called. "Bring a blanket to this man."

He turned back to Myers who appeared to be in shock. "Sir, we need to know how many people were in there. Try to think clearly."

Myers didn't respond.

"Sir! Please!"

Myers blinked his eyes rapidly and cleared his throat. "The guards. Seven. . .eight."

"And this man?" Armbruster pointed to the mangled body. "Do you know him?"

Myers gazed down at the bloodied form. "Mitch Rondo," he answered slowly. "Security chief."

"Thank you, sir. That will be all for now."

As a paramedic arrived to treat Myers, Armbruster turned back to examine the body. It was then that he noticed the empty holster strapped beneath the shredded jacket.

Detective Don Avery noticed it, too. "He saw something, Tony," Avery said as he crouched beside the dead man. "Or heard it, then pulled his gun."

Armbruster leaned over the body for closer inspection. As he turned the head to one side, he found what he was looking for. A clean bullet hole behind the left ear.

CHAPTER 1

Beyond the windows of the Oval Office, a light autumn rain fell on Washington, D.C. Greg Langston and Mark Bafry gazed somberly into the gray morning, only occasionally glancing at each other for reassurance. They'd been summoned by President Raymond Wellon after the casino explosion two days earlier. They watched quietly as Wellon reviewed a preliminary FBI report on the incident. With each page, his countenance grew more severe, his thick, dark eyebrows closing together forming an unbroken hedge over the rapidly scanning eyes.

Finally, Wellon looked up at the two men seated before him. "The FBI is calling it the work of a skilled demolitions man or team."

Langston and Bafry knew there was more to the report than that, or they wouldn't be there.

"About seven o'clock this morning," Wellon continued, "the *Reno Gazette* took a call from a man who claimed responsibility for this." The two men looked expectantly toward Wellon, who quickly added, "The caller identified himself and his Christian comrades, as he called them, as the Soldiers of the Cross."

Bafry squeezed his eyes shut. Langston stared into the president's drawn face.

Wellon suddenly picked up the report and slammed it against the desk, then leaned back in his chair trying to control his anger. Forcing calm into his voice, he began slowly, "Gentlemen, when we spoke last, these Soldiers of the Cross were burning down topless bars and X-rated flick houses. No one killed. Very few hurt." He paused. "But now!" The calm was gone. "Now we've got six dead, two more presumed to be, and cataclysmic destruction in that desert. These people have declared war!"

After an uneasy silence, Bafry spoke. "Sir, I can assure you—"

"Mark, you listen to me," Wellon interrupted sharply. "You dig into every crevice until you find these people. It's not enough that the FBI is on this. They don't know your organization like you do, and somebody in your ranks has got to know who these maniacs are. Hunt them down!"

Bafry straightened his slender body in his chair. A strand of wavy, gray hair fell loose over his forehead, and he hurriedly pushed it back. "Sir, please let me speak." His tone was respectful but firm. "You're well aware that after our last meeting, my people and I conducted an extensive investigation throughout every chapter in the country and uncovered no trace of any such activity. Christians United is in no way associated with whoever is doing this."

"Mark, you've got over three million people out there," Wellon said, his voice rising. "Do you want me to believe you've talked to every one of them?"

"We just about did, sir," Bafry said. "Look, this whole thing has been a blight against us all. We want them stopped as much as you do. Even Greg has—"

"Let Greg speak for himself," Wellon snapped. The president turned to Langston with something approaching deference. It was no secret that Wellon was one of Langston's devoted readers. Books on marriage and the family, political responsibility, and other volumes by Langston lined the president's personal library.

"What is this war you say has been declared, sir?" Langston asked.

Wellon gazed curiously at him and waited for him to expand upon his question.

"Is it a morals war?" Langston continued.

"Explain yourself," Wellon said, folding his arms and setting his mouth in a tight line.

Bafry watched with a glimmer of amusement as Langston, his old friend, slipped into his professorial mode. Bafry had sat in on some of Langston's classes at Highgate Christian College in Maryland and watched as Langston had led his students to cut and polish a passage of study or concept until it flashed with brilliance.

"What are these people trying to achieve?" Langston persisted.

"Isn't it painfully obvious what they're doing?" Wellon responded irritably. "They've always been quick to claim responsibility for their attacks. They're crusading against the 'dens of sin,' they say."

"Are they?" Langston probed.

"For Pete's sake, Greg," Wellon said, "what are you getting at?"

Bafry settled back in his chair, trying to guess where Langston's reasoning was headed. "If it's a morals war, I can understand the raunchy nude clubs and porno houses. They've destroyed a couple of those a month for a year now, and much of the public has even begun to applaud their efforts." Langston paused.

"Go on," Wellon insisted.

Langston seemed to be exploring a theory as he spoke. "In spite of the frequency of attacks, their work has been fairly low profile—small joints in Toledo, Savannah, Detroit, Ft. Lauderdale. Then this."

"A high visibility target," Bafry offered.

"Exactly," Langston agreed. "The group has left its humble origins and moved into the big time. And quite suddenly, too. Why?"

No one ventured an answer.

"Why a grand Las Vegas palace with lots of recent press?" Langston wondered aloud.

"Attention," Wellon answered.

"But they were getting that already," said Bafry.

"Maybe they weren't getting enough," Wellon said, turning to look out the window and shaking his head wearily. "So they blew up the biggest 'den of sin' they could find. And all the fine paintings and sculpture inside that place." His tone was now sullen. "It was more of a museum than a casino."

"So then. . .it was a great loss, right?" Langston suggested.

Wellon turned suddenly toward Langston as if seeing the first light of reasoning. "The others weren't great losses, were they?"

Bafry jumped in. "Like you said, Greg, lots of people even supported what this group was doing. They were cleaning up the dirt that our lawmakers let collect."

Wellon raised an eyebrow in Bafry's direction and seemed to struggle with whether a defensive response was necessary.

"You're right about the people's reactions, Mark," Langston

continued. "These Soldiers have become Robin Hoods of sorts."

Bafry and Wellon both nodded their heads in agreement.

"But now the people are outraged," Langston went on. "The Soldiers have overstepped their bounds and destroyed something the people wanted."

"Keep going," Wellon urged.

"So now, they are no longer Robin Hoods," Langston said. "They're enemies of the people."

"Is that what they want?" Bafry asked, knowing the answer wasn't at hand.

Wellon turned to him, and his eyes widened. "They want to be enemies of the people?" He turned this thought over in his mind.

"And, perhaps, more importantly, in the name of Christianity," Langston ventured.

The room grew silent, each man struggling to make sense of the strange scenario.

Finally, Wellon said, "I don't know where all this is taking us, if anywhere. But I do know that these madmen must be stopped."

Wellon turned to Bafry. "Mark, launch another search at once. Look at possible splinter groups, those who think your politics are too soft-pedaled. Look for discontents with an excuse for vengeance. Look for kooks! These people are nuts. And nuts eventually give themselves away. Be alert."

The rain had stopped by the time Langston and Bafry emerged from the White House. It was almost noon on that late October day, and the sidewalks were crowded with serious pedestrians intent on getting somewhere in a hurry. A blur of tan and black raincoats swept past the two men now buttoning their own coats against the blustery chill.

"It's a good thing you just happened to be in Washington today, Greg. I wouldn't have wanted to endure Wellon's wrath alone."

"He's afraid, Mark."

"Sure he is. Afraid he won't get re-elected next term. Christians United was largely responsible for getting him his job. If we're shamed, he's shamed. He can't afford that."

"And he's got Ramsdale snapping at his heels."

"Especially now," Bafry said as he and Langston walked slowly down the sidewalk. "Don't think for a minute that blast in Ramsdale's home state won't get milked for every drop of political juice it's worth. The senator from Nevada has a desert full of ammunition against Wellon now. I can hear it coming. 'Wellon and his religious fanatic buddies have gone too far this time.' "

Langston stopped suddenly and stared at Bafry.

"What's the matter, Greg?"

But Langston's thoughts were racing too quickly for words. He looked away for a few moments, then said, "Nothing, Mark. Just a restless imagination. Forget it. How's your appetite, old buddy?"

The two men crossed the street to the Amber Hotel where Gooley's Grill was quickly reaching a capacity crowd.

An hour later, they left the restaurant and walked into the unexpected rays of the sun as it appeared from behind a sprawl of clouds.

"Greg, I wish I could talk with you some more today, but—"

"But you and I have too many places to run off to, don't we?"

"That's right. I don't know if I'm busy doing good things or too busy to do good things."

Langston groaned in agreement.

Bafry looked closely at Langston, taking in the dark circles under his eyes, the weariness that seemed to have washed over him just then. "What's wrong, Greg?"

Langston stared at the ground as they walked. "Don't know, Mark. Something's gone out of me."

"What kind of something?"

Langston raised his head and squinted as if searching some far horizon. "Remember when we were in seminary together and how convinced we were that all we had to do was share what we'd learned with the multitudes and they would see God?"

Bafry took a deep breath and sighed. "We were too inexperienced to know what we were up against. And maybe a little too cocky about our inspired capabilities."

"But we were passionate," Langston insisted. "Filled to overflowing with hope for what we might do."

Bafry just listened as they walked. They were heading south on 15th Street toward Constitution Avenue.

"It's the passion that's gone," Langston said, "and maybe some of the hope."

"Hope?" Bafry asked in a troubled tone. "Hope in what, Greg?"

Langston caught Bafry's concern. "Don't worry, Mark. I'm not talking about my hope in Christ. That's the only constant in my life. No, it's hope for all of them." Langston pointed toward a large crowd of tourists gathered about the Washington Monument. He and Bafry were just crossing Constitution Avenue toward the great lawns surrounding the towering landmark.

"How many in that crowd know Him?" Langston asked.

"What do you want, Greg? Statistics? Promises that every knee shall bend one day?"

"That day will be too late for too many."

Bafry stopped walking. Langston turned to face him.

"It's not for you to know how many in that crowd are His," Bafry gently admonished. "It's never been for you to know. Just write your books and teach your classes. Let God count the returns."

Langston looked away toward the throng in the field. "I need more than that."

Soon, the two men said goodbye, and Bafry returned to his office. With the sun still shining, Langston chose to walk back to his hotel near the Capitol. His steps were quick as he passed between the Justice Department and the National Museum of Natural History. *Just get home,* he urged himself.

He crossed into a clearing and glanced up. The Capitol loomed before him like a sun-washed temple, and a vague unsettling swept over him. He stopped and looked around him. It was business as usual on the streets of Washington. Smartly suited men and women scurrying with their briefcases to important meetings. Joggers on the Mall. Vendors feeding lines of tourists on break from the museums and memorials.

He looked toward the sky, at the sun and clouds exchanging light and dark, and again he sensed a strange foreboding.

He moved into a stand of trees. The wind rattled through the barren limbs and stirred against his chest. The prompting inside was immediate and clear:

Watch. Stand firm.

CHAPTER 2

Standing on the steps of the Lincoln Memorial, Jake Gaddy recalled a day twenty years earlier. He remembered holding his dad's hand and watching other tourists climb toward the great statue. He had been only seven and concerned with nothing more than the ice cream melting down his arm as his dad tried to explain who Lincoln was. Just a few months later, his dad was dead. So was his mom, and all the years had done little to ease the pain.

As a cool breeze brushed against his tanned face, Jake squeezed his hand shut as if closing it over someone else's. After a moment, he pulled the hood of his running suit onto his head and ran toward the Washington Monument and the long Mall. Running always freed him from his hurts, at least for awhile. He'd entered the University of Virginia ten years earlier on a track scholarship, and, before he'd graduated, had broken three school records. He still worked his long, chiseled body every day, running with a couple of his students before class each morning.

In a few minutes, he was to meet Dominick Swain, the man who'd become his spiritual mentor. Some of his followers called him Father Dominick, but most people knew him simply as Dominick. He was waiting for Jake in front of the Capitol.

As he ran, Jake remembered his introduction to Dominick just a year earlier at the man's lakeside estate in Charlottesville. Jake, an assistant professor of engineering at UVA, had been invited by another faculty member to experience what Dominick called a celestial gathering.

How intellectually enlightened the group had seemed to Jake. He was pleased to find a few UVA faculty members as well as other area professionals active in the gatherings, and he'd returned to the estate many times.

As he neared the Capitol, Jake saw that something newsworthy was about to happen. On the steps was a growing contingent of reporters and camera crews. As he approached, he heard his name called. He turned and saw Dominick mingling with a group of tourists who'd been drawn to the sudden flurry of activity.

Jake waved to Dominick and hurried to join him. "What's going on?"

Dominick smiled broadly. A fine-featured man in his early sixties, he was elegantly dressed in loosely fitted gray pants and a three-quarter-length black cashmere jacket that cloaked his ponderous weight. "My guess is that one of the higher-ups is about to address the lesser-thans. I think. . .oh. . .look. It's Ramsdale."

All heads turned in the same direction, and the small tangle of tourists swept past Dominick and Jake for a closer look at Senator Linc Ramsdale, now descending the steps with three young aides.

"Come on, Dominick," Jake urged. "Let's join them."

"You go on. I'll watch from here."

Jake looked at him curiously.

"Go on," Dominick insisted. "That's your next president, you know."

Jake walked up behind the pressing crowd of reporters and listened.

"Senator, are there any new leads in the bombing?" The reporter from CNN fired his question before Ramsdale was even halfway down the steps.

"Good afternoon, folks," the senator called, sidestepping the question. His silver hair glistened in the sunlight, crowning an otherwise inglorious face. His nose was long and narrow, separating two hollow cheeks that lay flat against his skull. But his eyes burned with a fiery expression.

"Thanks for coming out this afternoon to chat with me," he said. His usual ivory smile and prairie-home congeniality was missing this day. Instead, he wore a grave expression that displayed personal turmoil.

The CNN reporter repeated his question, "Any new leads, sir?"

"Let me first say that the good people of my home state of Nevada will not stand for any delay whatsoever in apprehending those who attacked us two nights ago. It was premeditated and murderous, and I now call upon our president to do everything—I mean everything—in his power to flush these despicable creatures from their lairs!"

"Sir—"

Ramsdale charged ahead. "I'm sure you're aware by now of the phone call made to the *Reno Gazette* this morning and just who these murderers claim to be." Before anyone could respond, he blurted, "The Soldiers of the Cross!"

Jake was stunned by this recent news. He wondered if Dominick could hear what was being said. He turned to wave his friend closer, but Dominick was gone. Not far, Jake was sure. He'd catch up with him after the interview.

"Senator, is there a task force in place to identify the members of this organization?"

"Absolutely. The attorney general has assured me of that, and I personally will be involved in this manhunt."

"What reasons might there be for blowing up the casino?" asked another reporter.

"If it truly was the Soldiers of the Cross, I can only suggest it is their militant attempts to force their fanatical beliefs on this nation."

"Do you see this group associated with any others?" an NBC reporter asked.

"Repeat the question, please," Ramsdale said, and his eyes burned brighter.

The same reporter reworded his question for clarity. "Do you suspect this group is acting alone, or is it allied with any other groups?"

Ramsdale frowned and showed reluctance to answer. "I'd rather not respond to that question at this time."

The answer drew the desired response. The reporters all jumped at once.

"What do you mean by that, sir?" one asked.

"Are you aware of something that has not yet been revealed?" asked another.

"Do you think other Christian groups are involved?"

Ramsdale proceeded cautiously. "I know nothing of any such alliance, but. . .I'm told the president was in conference this morning with members of Christians United. Perhaps you should ask him that question."

"So you believe it was backed by Christians United?" asked a CBS reporter.

"I never said that," Ramsdale replied quickly.

"You never said what, sir?" asked the same reporter.

Ramsdale smiled broadly, and his eyes crinkled with amusement. "Now, as long as I've been on this hill, don't you think I know a trap when I see one? Nice try, son."

"Senator," a young woman reporter called, "is there any truth to reports that you were once associated with a Middle Eastern religious sect?"

The eyes suddenly flashed, and the senator's smile froze in place. "Excuse me?" he replied searching for the face of the questioner. The crowd grew still.

"Here, sir." The petite young woman raised her hand and repeated the question.

Ramsdale recovered quickly. "You know, I guess I should expect to be asked most anything. Just last week, some guy from a magazine in Los Angeles asked me if I thought teenagers should be allowed to have sex change operations without parental consent." He rolled his eyes and kept talking. "Now what do you think of that?"

Ramsdale didn't wait for a response. As far as he was concerned, the interview was over. Though the press continued to hurl questions at him, he just waved graciously and returned to the cavernous building.

Jake found Dominick strolling by the reflecting pool across the street. Together, they walked to a vendor for lemonade and sat on a shaded bench on the Mall.

"Was the press adoring or rabid today?" Dominick asked, stretching his portly frame across the bench. Wisps of his grayish blond hair played about his forehead.

"I'd say. . .accommodating," Jake answered. "The man's angry, and he wants everyone to know it. The reporters will see to that, I'm sure."

Dominick nodded in agreement.

"But have you heard that the Soldiers of the Cross have claimed responsibility for the casino bombing?" Jake added. "You've heard of them, haven't you?"

"Indeed, I have. Vicious bunch, aren't they?"

"They're certainly not the Deer Creek variety of Christian," Jake commented lightly.

"I'm sure that little town you come from is the picture of tranquility up there in the Blue Ridge Mountains. But even in a place like that, there's a simmerpot somewhere. Someone's got a back room where they hide their little secrets, their implements of destruction for the sake of whatever cause suits them."

"Not in Deer Creek," Jake said, with a spreading grin. "Papa would have found them out by now. He's the postmaster, you know. He knows everything about everyone around there." Jake envisioned his grandfather busily tending the tiny post office and chuckled to himself.

"Oh, yes," Dominick drawled, "the patron saint of Deer Creek Baptist Church."

The grin disappeared from Jake's face, and he looked sharply at Dominick, who quickly changed the subject.

"Do you think Ramsdale has a chance against Wellon in two years?" Dominick asked good-naturedly, regretting his careless comment about Jake's grandfather.

Jake didn't answer right away. He could still see his grandfather's face before him. It was the face that had held the world together for him after his parents' sudden deaths. His devotion to the old man was fierce, and he resented Dominick's remark.

As if reading Jake's thoughts, Dominick said, "Forgive my flip comment about your grandfather, Jake. I didn't mean to offend."

Jake pulled himself up straight. "It's okay. Forget it." He paused before adding abruptly, "And 'I don't know' is the answer to your question. You're asking the wrong guy. Politics interests me even less than the future of square dancing."

Dominick looked intently at Jake. "But you must be interested in such things, Jake," Dominick insisted. "Policies from the Oval Office could ultimately effect what research grants you and your engineering college might receive. Or whether your grandfather gets the best medical care available."

Jake looked directly at Dominick.

"You have to care about who wins the next election, Jake," Dominick said.

"You seem pretty sure Ramsdale will. Why?"

"At this point, there aren't any serious Republican contenders to take re-election away from Wellon. That leaves the Democrats to climb into the ring with the best they've got."

"But there are plenty of heavyweights in that party," Jake said.

"True. But no one more powerful than Ramsdale."

"Probably no one with more charisma," Jake conceded. "I mean, he's got all that down-on-the-range appeal and a big wholesome family working a ranch in the desert. The guy's a regular Roy Rogers."

Dominick laughed and quickly agreed, but added, "However, Wellon's got an impressive track record so far, a squeaky clean reputation, and the support of the Christian conservatives."

"How big is the Christian vote?"

"Bigger than you think," Dominick said. "Catholics, Protestants, even Jews joined forces to get their man of God into the White House. They'll do everything they can to keep him there."

"Is that so terrible?" Jake toyed with Dominick, knowing the man's spewing intolerance of such religions.

But Dominick merely sipped his lemonade and eyed Jake coolly. Ignoring the question, he asked, "Jake, what do you trust in?"

Surprised by the question, Jake turned quickly to meet Dominick's challenging gaze, then looked away. "I'm not sure about that."

"Haven't I taught you to trust in yourself?"

"I'm not real comfortable with myself, Dominick. You're trying to help me, I know. But I've got a ways to go before I know what's true about this life. . .or me."

Dominick's tone grew authoritative. "You're ready for a higher plain of awareness, Jake. Spiritual awareness. But first you need to understand how things work in places of power. Power unlocks the soul, Jake. This is the place of power." He swept his arm before him in the direction of the Capitol. "Soak it in."

Jake was silent as Dominick continued. "Right now your soul is trapped under the debris of childhood and the teaching of that quaint little church you came from. Little by little, though, we'll salvage the real Jake Gaddy."

Jake was now uncomfortable, and he knew Dominick was reading his reluctance to approach the subject of home.

"So, did Ramsdale handle the press with his usual finesse?" Dominick asked brightly.

"I'd say so. Even the question about the Middle Eastern sect."

Dominick lowered the cup from his mouth and turned toward Jake. "What?"

Jake chuckled. "Some girl asked him if he ever belonged to a religious group in the Middle East."

"And what did he say?" Dominick asked casually.

"He just sloughed it off. Said he was used to crazy questions, gave an example of another one someone once asked him, and that was it. He left."

Dominick watched as Jake finished his own lemonade and walked to a trash bin to deposit the empty cup.

Returning to the bench, Jake asked, "When do we meet the others?" Dominick had invited several friends to join him for the short stay in Washington.

Dominick seemed not to hear the question.

"I say, Dominick, when do we meet everyone else?"

"Oh, yes. . .sorry. Well, uh, I hope you won't be offended if I leave you all to entertain yourselves this evening. I have business to discuss with my attorney here in Washington."

"Fine by me. Will you be having dinner with us?"

"Not tonight. And I will need the van. I hope you won't mind taking a cab."

Dominick pulled a one-hundred-dollar bill from his money clip and handed it to Jake who resisted.

"Take it, Jake." Dominick shoved the money into Jake's hand. "You're my guest this trip, remember? I hope you've enjoyed these few days."

"We all have, Dominick. You're very generous."

"I handpick a few of my young friends to accompany me most everywhere I go. It keeps our fellowship alive, don't you think?"

Jake hesitantly agreed. He'd only known Dominick for a short time, and though he was intrigued by his teachings, he wasn't yet at ease with Dominick's notion of fellowship.

The gray van pulled onto Highway 50 and merged with traffic heading east out of Washington. It was early afternoon. Dominick had a three o'clock meeting.

He was happy to be alone with his thoughts. He smiled contentedly and injected a Dvorak CD of symphonic poems into the player. As "The Water Goblin" stirred the air with its haunting melodies, Dominick tapped his fingers against the wheel to the recurring three-note rhythm.

Near the Patuxent River, he turned off the highway and drove north for another twenty minutes. He turned again onto a twisting, country road and drove a little farther, seeing nothing but dense woods on either side. At a large wooden gate on the right side of the road, he slowed, pulled over, and stopped. Taking a key from his wallet, he got out of the van. The lock on the gate was rusty, but after a moment it gave way. Dominick swung the gate open wide and returned to the van.

On the other side, he stopped to relock the gate, then headed down the shaded drive. After a couple of sharp turns, he eased the van to a stop in front of a cabin that was perched on the steep bank of a wide creek. He got out and looked carefully about the property before approaching the cabin. No one was in sight. No dogs barked. No twigs cracked. He could proceed.

The front porch creaked with each step he took to the door. He found the key, which had been wrapped in masking tape and shoved into the dirt of a nearby planter. When he used it to open the door, a stale, musty odor engulfed him. He wrinkled his nose, stepped inside the one-room cabin and turned on the lights. Scattered about the room was rustic, antique furniture caked with dust. Family photos in mildewed frames hung on the walls.

A heavy oak table nested by twelve straight-backed chairs ran nearly the width of the room. Beyond was a line of appliances and countertops tucked beneath a long window overlooking the meandering creek below. From the small bathroom off the kitchen, Dominick took a towel and wiped off some of the chairs. Then he sat down and waited.

Half an hour later, Dominick heard a car approach. He watched from the front window of the cabin as a dark green Ford Explorer with heavily tinted windows stopped beside the van. When he saw the driver, a man wearing jeans and a Redskins sweatshirt, get out and walk toward the porch steps, Dominick opened the front door.

"It's okay," he told the man on the steps, who then signaled to someone in the Explorer.

From the backseat, another man got out and stretched his legs. He wore jeans, a brown leather jacket, sunglasses, and a wide-brimmed field hat.

Dominick waved, and the man took off his hat to wave it in return. Even in the deep shade of the clearing, the silver hair shimmered. The flat face broke into a pearly smile as the man approached Dominick.

"How are you, Linc?" Dominick asked his old friend.

"Not certain, Dom," Senator Linc Ramsdale replied hesitantly. The two men shook hands and went inside. Ramsdale's aide remained near the Explorer.

"I know the cabin is filthy," Ramsdale admitted, tossing his hat on the table. "But no one's going to see us here. That's why I bought the place. It's somewhere to hide when life gets too nutty around town. Anyway, please excuse it."

"Linc, have you forgotten that flea trap we slept in for a month in Jodhpur?"

"Yeah, but we were so high we didn't know a flea from a St. Bernard."

"Do you miss it?" Dominick pried.

"Miss the drugs? No. The freedom? Yes. Everybody's watching me now."

"But that's what you like, Linc. The spotlight. You've always wanted it, even at the commune in Burma. You wanted power then, too."

"And you don't?" Ramsdale shot back with unmasked irritation. "I know what you want, Dom. To be this nation's guru. The president's own Rasputin. You're looking for power of your own, Dominick, and—"

"Cool down, Linc, and remember why we're here."

Ramsdale glanced uneasily at Dominick then pulled out a chair. He ran his hands through his thick hair and sat down.

"This whole sordid affair is making me crazy, Dom. I don't know if I can continue. That mess in the desert was scary."

"It was necessary."

"Not for those security guards to die."

"Misinformation," Dominick admitted.

"I still don't know if I can stay with it."

"You're not. I am." Dominick pulled out another chair and sat facing the senator. "You won't have to know anything else until you read it in the newspaper or catch a glimpse on the evening news."

"But if something else goes wrong. . .if that woman and child are hurt in any way. . .I. . .I just don't know if I can let you do anything more."

Let? Dominick thought. *With or without you, old buddy, it's going to happen.*

He pulled his chair closer and locked eyes with Ramsdale. "If you want the Oval Office, you won't interfere," Dominick said coldly. "President Raymond Wellon will be charred merchandise after we get through with him."

Ramsdale slumped in his chair and stared at the floor.

"I guarantee you that nothing will go wrong with the plan," Dominick assured him. "It'll be a cakewalk for Peterson after Las Vegas. No traces at all, I guarantee it."

Eyeing Dominick cautiously, Ramsdale whined, "If someone ever connected me with this scheme, I'd spend the rest of my life in prison." His mouth trembled slightly as he leaned forward to rest his head in his hands. Almost under his breath, he added, "I don't think I can take any more risk."

Dominick banged the table with his fist as he rose to his feet and glared at Ramsdale. Ramsdale's body jerked as if he'd been struck, and Dominick shouted, "Winning the race for president is going to take a stronger man than the one I see before me—already sniveling in defeat!"

Jumping from his chair, Ramsdale growled, "Don't you dare speak to me that way. I'm a sena—"

"Yeah, yeah, you're a senator. And that's all you're ever going to be if you don't find some courage inside your spoiled, pampered self."

Dominick took a deep breath and returned to his chair. "Sit down, Linc," he urged calmly. "We don't need to do this to each other. The election is a couple of years off. We're going to approach it one strategic step at a time until Wellon's no longer credible. So relax. . .Mr. President."

The indignation on Ramsdale's face melted away, and a wistful gleam sparkled in his eyes. Dominick had seen it the day Ramsdale visited him at the lake house and told him he wanted to be president. He'd seen it nearly thirty years ago when the two men met at a seance in London. He remembered the young Ramsdale well. Even now, he could see the slim, dark-haired adventurer, lounging on a mat and smoking weed in a London flat filled with students.

"Ever think of Angela?" Dominick asked.

The question caught Ramsdale off guard. He stared hard at Dominick then down at the floor. "More than I should."

"Know where she is?"

"It's best I don't," Ramsdale said. Then he looked suspiciously at Dominick. "Why?"

"Just wondering how the press heard about your Middle East days."

Ramsdale wrinkled his brow. "How did you know about that?"

"A young friend of mine overheard your press conference on the Capitol steps today."

Ramsdale nodded slowly. "Yeah, it was a shock. But I deflected it pretty well, I thought." He looked pensive for a moment, then added, "But it wasn't Angela. No way."

"You can't be sure."

"Leave her alone, Dominick. I'm warning you. Stay out of her life."

Dominick raised a surrendering hand.

"I think about those days, Dom, and I wonder how we survived."

"Well, you had Daddy's big bucks supporting you. All I had was my paltry savings from the art institute. Art professors, even in London, didn't make much, you know."

"No, I mean it's amazing we didn't die of tainted opium or get our throats slit in the night. We wound up in some pretty horrible places."

Dominick nodded slowly, never taking his eyes off Ramsdale.

"Remember Cairo the year after I graduated from Notre Dame? That tent on the edge of town?"

Dominick smiled slightly.

"Angela and I used to lie awake at night watching to see who might slip in on us."

Dominick settled back in his chair and crossed his legs. "She loved you very much."

Ramsdale smiled gently. "She was a redheaded spitfire, wasn't she?"

"She was a force," Dominick said. "The first time I saw her she was teaching a transcendental meditation class at a flat across from mine in Chelsea. Writers, actors, and an occasional member of Parliament crowded into the room every week to learn from her. I think half of them were in love with her."

Ramsdale smiled wistfully.

Dominick continued. "But it was the young college grad from Nevada she fell for."

Ramsdale grew sullen. "She would have been better off with any of the rest of them."

"It was your call, Linc. You didn't have to run home to the ranch."

"My dad had just died. You know I had to go."

"You could have come back."

Ramsdale looked weary. "Dominick, why do we have to rehash this again? I'm living with my choice. Why can't you?"

"Oh, I have no problem with what you've become, as long as old entanglements don't trip you up."

Ramsdale looked sharply at Dominick. "Angela is not an entanglement. I'm happily married with three great kids. She's not in the picture."

Dominick raised a brow. "What would you call your little tryst in London?"

"That was over twenty years ago, Dominick. Just a fluke."

"Tell me about the. . .fluke."

"Why should I?"

"Because I'm your spiritual adviser, remember? Your key to the White House door. I deserve to know what lurks inside you."

Ramsdale sighed long and loudly. "I was there on family business and decided to make a nostalgic visit to Chelsea. She just popped out of that same music shop where we used to hang out, and I quite literally bumped into her." He paused.

"Go on."

Ramsdale's tone softened. "It'd been ten years, but she looked just like she did that last day. That gorgeous hair curled around her shoulders. She was even wearing the silver heart earrings I had bought her in Cairo." He seemed to drift away.

"And. . . ," Dominick prompted.

"And we went back to her flat for awhile. That's all."

Dominick looked relaxed and smug. "Just old friends, making a baby together."

Ramsdale gave him a stony gaze. "That's right, Dom. You got it. Now, let's get on with business."

But Dominick continued to search Ramsdale's face.

"Why do you keep looking at me that way?" Ramsdale asked irritably.

"Just remembering the Linc I once knew."

"The pothead?"

"No. The passionate spirit who loved so freely. What happened to that guy, Linc?"

"They bronzed him and packed him off to Washington. Now, can we get back to business? I've got to go."

"Sure, Linc." Dominick folded his arms and gazed coolly into the narrowing eyes of the senator.

"Now, when is this thing going to happen?" Ramsdale demanded.

"March."

"It'll be Peterson?" Ramsdale visibly shuddered at the name.

"Yes."

"You know what he's capable of, Dominick. Can you trust him not to harm the woman and child?"

"Completely."

Ramsdale relaxed a bit. "Let's be honest. I need you. You wreak havoc with the Christian political machine supporting Wellon, humiliate him before the nation, and I'll give you access to the masses. That's the deal, isn't it?"

Dominick smiled slowly. *If he only knew what the whole deal really was,* he thought to himself. *How can someone so short-sighted be president? He'll need me more than ever in the White House. And he won't mind what else I had to do to get him there.*

"What are you thinking, Dom?" Ramsdale asked.

"How very clever you are."

Dominick left the cabin first, pulling the van onto the narrow country road just before dark. Ramsdale and his aide left moments later.

No one in either car noticed the old, blue Grand Prix backed deep into the woods at the first turn in the road.

CHAPTER 3

Joanna's nightmare was always the same. . .

Currents swirl gently into the Bimini cove where the Gaddy boat is anchored. The sea is at rest. But inside the dark cabin, Joanna tenses at every sound—even the rhythmic breathing of her parents as they sleep, curled against each other in the forward berth. She turns quickly as a sudden breeze sweeps through the open doorway. It ruffles the covers over her parents, and she rushes to tuck them tightly against the motionless bodies, lovingly touching each tanned face.

It will come, she warns herself. *And there's nothing I can do to stop it.*

She climbs from the cabin to the upper deck and gazes into a moonless night that hangs like a black veil in every direction. And she listens. Waves slap lightly against the long hull of the power boat. An occasional wind rustles the fronds of unseen palms on shore. Distant wind chimes jangle a warning.

Then it comes. A droning vibration at first, then the advancing howl of a powerful engine, its growl growing deeper and louder. She races to the cabin door and down the steps. The roar grows fierce, and she leaps on top of her parents, spreading herself over their stirring bodies.

In one final motion, she raises her face to the porthole as the towering bow of a huge vessel plunges through the cabin wall. . . .

And it was over. Joanna's nightmare ended in that blinding flash of impact. It always did.

For twenty years, her parents' final hour had visited her repeatedly in her sleep, each time the dream compelling her to try harder to save them. But the ending was always the same. And once again, she was jerked from restless sleep in a cold sweat, heart pounding and tears stinging her eyes.

The wind howled outside now as Joanna sat up, struggling to clear her head of the awful vision. She was alone. On her own boat.

Just as she did in the dream, she climbed from the cabin to the upper deck and gazed into the surrounding night. But this night, this very real and waking night was bright with moonlight and stars shimmering overhead. Now she could see clearly—the palm fronds on shore swaying in the brisk wind, the abandoned cottage where the wind chimes now played their endless dirge.

She was there. In that Bimini cove she'd visited so many times with her family. The same cove where her parents had met their violent end. It was her first pilgrimage since the accident.

She raised her face to the heavens, fingers locked in tight fists, and cried, "Where were you?"

Three weeks later, Joanna Gaddy pulled her red Jeep from the parking shelter of her Biscayne Bay condominium into the head-on glare of a Miami morning. She was late for the boat. On Sundays, she and her friends cruised the bay waters of her childhood.

She turned onto Brickell Avenue and headed south. Overhead, the great banyan trees linked arms to form a fluttering canopy. She passed joggers and matrons walking their dogs past elegant homes nestled behind the massive trunks of the banyans. Joanna had almost found peace in this neighborhood where seawater lapped against secluded streets and where people lived like it was nobody's business.

She rolled the windows down, and at once, the salty rush of air pungent with both life and decay stirred up the past. She inhaled deeply, and moments that lived and people who died tumbled into view. It was why she was here, to pick up where her childhood had ended so abruptly. She remembered the knock on the screen door that morning twenty years ago. . . .

The babysitter, Mrs. Maynard, told ten-year-old Joanna not to peek at her cards while she went to the door. They were playing gin rummy at the kitchen table while seven-year-old Jake fished from the dock behind the house. The children's parents had taken the Gaddy boat on a leisurely cruise to Bimini and were due back that afternoon.

Minutes later, Mrs. Maynard called to Joanna in a shrill tone the young girl thought odd. "Joanna, go outside with your brother. We'll finish the game later."

Jake and Joanna were catching fiddler crabs under the dock almost an hour later when Mrs. Maynard appeared at the back door.

"Children, come inside, please." Her tone was no longer shrill, but still odd, Joanna thought as she raced her brother to the door where Mrs. Maynard slowed their playful charge.

"Wait just a minute now. Some friends of yours are here to see you, so come with me into the family room." Mrs. Maynard led them inside. At the sight of several neighbors, the minister from the family's church, and two uniformed police officers, Joanna jerked away from Mrs. Maynard and moved toward Jake. The two stood wide-eyed before the strange assembly.

Mrs. Torres, a close neighbor, coaxed them next to her on the sofa, and after softening her approach with irrelevant chatter about the fiddler crabs, carefully began her story. "You know how your parents like to anchor in a cove somewhere and spend the night?"

Only little Jake nodded his head. Joanna's fixed stare didn't waiver.

"Well," Mrs. Torres continued, "that's what they did last night. They were at that beautiful island you all like to go to, and while they were asleep, uh, another boat that didn't see them, uh, accidentally ran into them. Do you remember how you used to—"

"Are my parents hurt?" Joanna blurted.

"Well, they were, uh, flown to a hospital early this morning. But your Papa and Grandma Abby are coming down here today to take care of you. Won't it be nice to see them?"

"What hospital?" Joanna demanded, leaning into the neighbor's face. "Are they hurt bad?" Frantic tears sprang to her eyes. "I want to see them!"

Rev. Alex Summerill moved next to Joanna and Jake on the sofa. "Joanna, you won't be able to see your mom and dad for awhile. But one day you will see them again. God's taking care of them. And He's taking care of you and Jake, too. Your grandparents will be here this afternoon, and we'll all talk about this together, okay?"

Joanna heard more than she was told. "Why won't you tell me where they are?" she cried angrily. "My Papa will."

She suddenly grabbed Jake's arm and ran with him down the hall to her parents' bedroom where she locked the door behind them and flew to the phone. Ignoring Mrs. Torres's pursuit and anxious knocking at the door, Joanna grabbed her mother's phone directory from the drawer of the night table. It was the little book Joanna had covered in a shiny chintz of bright yellow daisies and given to her mother for Christmas two years ago.

Gaddy. Deer Creek, North Carolina. Joanna dialed the number.

Three rings. Four. Five. "Hello?" Eli Gaddy answered.

"Papa?"

"Joanna. Is that you, child?"

"Papa, what's happened to Mom and Dad? Please tell me. Please." She impatiently wiped tears from her eyes.

"My sweet darlin'," Eli consoled in a trembling voice, "don't you worry about your mom and dad. They're just fine where they are, and Grandma Abby and I are coming down there right now."

"Are they dead?" Joanna waited agonizing moments for the reply.

"Oh, Joanna, God has healed their wounds. You let Him heal yours. In His time, He'll bring you and Jake where your mom and dad are now, and you'll never be separated again."

As Joanna drove toward the marina, she heard Eli's words again. *Too bad it's not true,* she brooded as she turned into the marina and parked the Jeep. They were waving to her from the boat, this family she had assembled for herself. They were friends from the ad agency where she'd worked since graduating from the University of Miami, and a few close neighbors.

The boat was Joanna's, the only extravagance she'd allowed herself with the considerable inheritance from her parents' estate. Her father had prospered in his insurance agency, invested extensively in beachfront property, and left his two children with solid financial, if not emotional, support.

The sleek, thirty-six-foot Sea Ray was powered by twin Mer-Cruisers and slept six. Joanna named it *The Abbey* after her grandmother Abigail, in one sense. In another, the boat was her sanctuary, a soulful retreat, as the mountain cabin was Jake's.

Joanna knew every inch of *The Abbey*'s glossy white and navy hull, as well as its powerful engines. She could hold her own at the helm in any weather. She'd memorized the navigational charts and routes from Miami to the Bahamas. Especially to Bimini.

"Hey, Jo! Nice of you to show up!" hollered Sid Shake, known to most as just Shake, graphic artist at the Torrence-Jacobs Advertising and Public Relations agency, where Joanna had recently been promoted to account executive. "I was about to drive this baby off without you."

"In your dreams, Shake," Joanna shot back. "You couldn't paddle a canoe out of here." She grinned broadly at her stocky, long-haired friend who'd shown her around the agency that first day eight years ago. Now, he was thirty-six, single, and wore his dark hair in a ponytail that trailed down his broad back. She remembered how he was dressed that first day: beige linen pants that tied at the waist and a rumpled white dress shirt beneath his "I'm-a-Garfield-kind-of-guy" necktie. Their friendship was instant and platonic, though other men at the agency had taken a different sort of interest in the striking new female recruit.

Joanna, like Jake, had her mother's curly auburn hair, which only occasionally was allowed to cascade down her back. Most of the time she wore it loosely gathered at the nape of her neck by an artful clip from one of the Coconut Grove boutiques. Her build, like her father's and Jake's, was tall and lean. She'd always been strong, running or swimming with Jake in furious competition, yet delighting when her little brother took all the honors. Her delicate features and sensitive green eyes masked the bold force of her will.

Shake reached for the grocery bags Joanna carried on board and handed them to Pete Linstrom as he emerged from the cabin. Pete was short and wiry, middle-aged, and divorced twice. He was a copywriter from the Torrence-Jacobs agency, who also considered *The Abbey*'s mates his family and his weekend job manning the boat's lines.

Marlene Gold, Joanna's neighbor and closest friend from college days, had already taken her customary station in the galley, preparing chicken salad and fruit plates for the crew's lunch. Rachel and Alan Bloom, also neighbors, were helping with the food.

"Hey, guys, sorry I'm late," Joanna called into the cabin. "Ready to roll?"

A chorus of voices gave her the go-ahead.

"Okay, Pete, cast off," Joanna finally commanded. Pete tossed in the lines and hopped aboard as Joanna eased *The Abbey* from her slip and steered toward the channel.

Blustery winds picked up an occasional spray and hurled it at the seagoing party. Joanna welcomed the wet sting in her face as she coaxed *The Abbey* into the choppy expanse of Biscayne Bay. The thrill of acceleration gripped her, and she could have raced endlessly through the open sea, for wherever she was bound. Wherever that was. She didn't know.

"Hey, you, Captain!" Marlene cried from the galley. "Unless you'd like a nice chicken salad to walk in, you'd better slow this thing down."

"I hear you, Marlene," Joanna called back. "*The Abbey* just wants to play. Why don't you give that chicken stuff a rest and come up top. You're missing it!"

Joanna cruised north from Coconut Grove past her Brickell Avenue condo building, past the reflective shards of glassy architectural feats that housed banks, law firms, insurance companies, and ad agencies. The Torrence-Jacobs agency had just moved from its cozy bungalow offices in Coconut Grove, which most of the staff had preferred, to a suite on the ninth floor of what looked more like a mirage than a building. Not only did the structure's great walls of tinted glass wavily mirror and merge with the surroundings, but cut clear through the midsection was a giant circular hole in which the building didn't exist at all.

They were cruising slowly behind the unusual structure when Shake broke into his familiar routine, placing hands, mime-like, against imaginary walls. "Ah, yes. And somewhere in this direction we have the infamous transparent building that could. Could be here. Could be there."

Shake loved to perform. "To get to work each morning, I just pull in beside familiar cars, follow the arrow on the sign that says 'This way to building,' and keep walking until I bump into something."

"Shake, you're killing us," Alan moaned, having heard it all before. "You should be resurrecting vaudeville in Vegas."

"Yeah, right, and get myself blown to bits by the Soldiers of the Cross. Can you believe what happened?"

"The casino?" Alan said. "Pretty scary, isn't it? It's a fanatical holy war, according to Senator Ramsdale. Did you see him on the news last night?"

"Yeah," Pete answered. "He's out for blood. He's even accusing President Wellon of supporting those lunatics through that conservative political group. . .what's it called?"

"Christians United," said Shake. "But I don't believe that. That group's not harboring terrorists."

"How do you know?" Rachel asked.

"Gut reaction. I saw one of them on TV one night. The author guy, what's his name, uh, Greg Langston. He was talking about all the ways God communicates with us, and I liked what I heard."

Over the hum of the engines, Joanna had listened in on the conversation. She glanced curiously at Shake.

"What does an old hippie care about stuff like that?" she teased, without smiling.

Shake grinned at her. "Enough to know you should look into it yourself."

Joanna cut a defiant eye toward him. "I don't do fairy tales anymore." She grabbed the throttle and gave *The Abbey* more power, angling the bow straight into the wake of a passing boat, causing everyone on board to grab for support.

"Easy, Joanna," Shake said gently. "Easy now." He stared at her until she met his eye, then he gave her a knowing smile, which wasn't returned.

They soon approached Bayfront Park in the heart of downtown Miami. In a few hours, the Saturday night revelers would be coming to life and to the park. They came to taste the international flavors of a city on the cultural border of many nations. There was food, music, dance, and apparel from the Caribbean, the Middle East, Asia, and Europe.

It's sure not Deer Creek, Joanna mused as they cruised by the park. *No narrow little minds here.*

"What do you say we haul over to the port and check out the cruise ships," Rachel suggested.

There were five ships docked when they arrived. Two were preparing to sail for the open sea. Colorful flags and tourists waved from decks high above the water. The playful crew of *The Abbey* waved back as Joanna spun in her own wake midway down the channel and retreated back to its mouth. She'd never been comfortable alongside the monstrous vessels. They were threatening to her and her *Abbey*. She sped away to Key Biscayne, where they would anchor for lunch.

There was a spot near the last bridge to the key that had always drawn Joanna. It was a secluded beach, hidden from the causeway by sprawling mangroves and palms. Clear, blue green water pooled along the shaded dunes, free of churning currents. Years ago, the Gaddy family had proclaimed it their private beach.

Joanna cut the engines in her approach and searched for the vision of a young auburn-haired girl and her mother on a bright yellow float. Many times, *The Abbey* and its lone captain had come to this place and drifted into another time. As Joanna would coast silently toward the shore, she would hear her mother's squeals as her father would swim beneath them and overturn the float. Then Joanna would cling to his neck, tasting the salty drops as they fell from his hair, knowing she was safe, and loving him with an intensity only little girls have for their dads.

But today, the clamor of her friends preparing to drop anchor dispelled the vision. She set the hook and tied it off at the forward cleat, then, without waiting for the others, plunged into the crisp cool of the water. When her long, silken body surfaced far from the boat, there were no strong arms to hold her head above water. *I don't need them anyway,* she told herself. *I can take care of myself.*

"I thought the captain was supposed to be the last to leave the ship," Shake teased as he swam up beside her.

"Just had to get in, Shake. I knew you'd catch up." She pushed his head under and stroked toward shore. The others followed, all except Marlene, who was overweight and uncomfortable in a bathing suit. She always preferred to remain on board in tee shirt and shorts and prepare the food. Besides teaching Gothic literature to high school sophomores, she also conducted easy-gourmet seminars for people like Joanna, who usually preferred to nuke their food in a prepackaged frozen container.

After a romp in the water with a Frisbee, they all returned to Marlene's lunch on board. "My compliments to the chef," Pete offered later through a mouthful of carrot cake.

"Same here, Marlene," Alan agreed. "Yours is always the finishing touch. That last sweet morsel to top off the day. And you know where to deposit any leftovers you may ever have, don't you? Rachel, give her our new address again."

"I think I can find my way back to that house where we all wasted a whole weekend painting for you guys," Marlene snapped playfully.

Joanna felt the vibrations of family every time she gathered with these special friends. Special because they let her be. They let her quietly rummage through her hurts, though each had tried to dislodge her from them. She remembered the times they'd tried.

"Joanna, move on," Marlene had gently prodded several years ago. "It was so long ago. And so much time lies ahead. Get going in that direction."

"Accept a date every once in awhile, for Pete's sake," Pete had enjoyed saying one afternoon as the group gathered for dinner at Marlene's. "All kinds of guys want to take you out. Just choose one and go. You're not funny, are you?" He had raised an eyebrow. With that, Joanna had tackled him to the ground and smeared artichoke dip across his face.

"Lighten up, Joanna," the Blooms had implored. "Climb out of those books you're always reading and go see the world."

But it was Sid Shake who had waited at the marina one Sunday afternoon three weeks ago. Against his objections, Joanna had left alone the day before, heading for the Bimini cove where her parents were killed.

When *The Abbey* returned late that afternoon, Shake had watched from the shadows as Joanna had lowered the fenders and secured the lines. Only when she had completed her tasks had he approached her. His sudden appearance had startled her.

"Did you tame the demons?" he had asked tenderly. She had stared hard at him for a moment, struggling with a response. Without answering, she had gone to him and laid her head on his great chest as he held her gently. She finally had broken away, and with only a tremulous smile and a wave of her hand she had walked to the Jeep and driven home.

Joanna shook her head to clear the memories.

It was four o'clock by the time *The Abbey* backed into her slip at the marina. A storm was moving in quickly off the Atlantic. As the darkening sky rumbled, Joanna and Pete secured the lines to the dock while the others cleared out the cabin. Then everyone exchanged hasty farewells. After a final check on the lines that would have to hold firm during the storm, Joanna bade one more farewell.

"Hold tight, girl. I'll be back."

A solid sheet of water advanced across the bay as she turned from *The Abbey* and raced for the Jeep. Suddenly she stopped and listened. The rain had begun to roar, like the sound of a powerful engine. She turned to face the bay, to wait for the impact.

Am I going mad? she cried silently as the downpour overtook her.

CHAPTER 4

For fifteen years, Greg Langston had taught the Scriptures to third and fourth year undergraduates at the rustic campus perched above the banks of the Susquehanna River. On this October morning, he arrived late at his office in the old, fieldstone cottage that once housed the first caretaker to tend the college grounds. He'd been home from Washington for three days and still didn't feel sufficiently rested. This was his first day back on campus, and he looked forward to the peaceful flow of routine.

He'd grown weary of traveling, preferring to seclude himself with his students, his family, and his writing. But the popularity of what he wrote created a demand for him to speak, and he was called to address audiences all over the nation. Declining such offers ran counter to his ministering nature, and so the reluctant celebrity went wherever he was called.

Hoping to capture the vigor of a new day, he paused at the front door of the cottage to inhale the fragrant vapors off the river. He turned to survey the pastoral beauty of the campus, the expansive lawn that sloped toward the water, the towering trees that were now bare, and the brick and stucco buildings clustered in village fashion about a square that was centerpieced by a plain wooden cross.

The caretaker's cottage, which he had renovated himself, was quietly withdrawn from the clamor of the campus. It, and the home he'd built for his family in the woods outside town, balanced his high-performance life with a restorative solitude. He pinched off the withered heads of chrysanthemums springing from the ground on either side of the front steps and went in.

"Good morning, Greg," Avis Benfree chimed. She was happy to see her boss again. "I've gone through two message pads since the debate last week. I hope you're ready for the feedback."

Langston smiled a return greeting, but cringed at her news. "I'm ready for a nap. Thought I'd never get out of Washington this time, and I was more anxious than ever to leave."

"Why is that?" asked Mrs. Benfree, who had been Langston's secretary for nine years and an old classmate of his at the University of Maryland.

Langston paused to consider whether he should tell his trusted aide about his sudden call to the White House. He decided it was best not to involve her. "You know Washington's always wired. And this casino bombing has made some people really nervous."

It was answer enough for Mrs. Benfree. "How was the atmosphere at Ellis-Dohn?" she asked cheerfully. Campus Crusade for Christ and Ellis-Dohn University in Washington had invited Langston to debate the credibility of the resurrection of Jesus Christ as presented in the Bible. Arguing against him was an Ellis-Dohn professor of philosophy and acknowledged agnostic. After the debate, the floor was opened for questions from the audience.

"Charged, as usual," Langston answered casually while sorting through the mail that had piled up during his absence. "You know how religion stirs the tempest. Well, there was a tempest that wouldn't quit somewhere in the back of the auditorium. He kept firing some pretty abrasive questions at me, and I'm used to that. But this guy had a real edge to his voice. Never could see him for the lights. One of the monitors finally got him to cool down and—well, look at this. A letter from Rod and Janis. Did you see this, Avis?"

He diverted his full attention to the letter which he tore open and began to read. It was from his former, and favorite, graduate assistant, Rod Nettles. He and his wife, Janis, had moved to New York and the mortgage banking business seven years ago.

"Sure did," Mrs. Benfree replied, "and I got a call from Janis this morning. They want you to stay with them while you're in New York next March. Want me to cancel your hotel reservations?"

" 'A new condo overlooking Central Park with a live doorman in uniform,' " Langston read aloud as he strolled to the doorway of his office and flipped on the lights inside. "Wall Street's been good to our young friends, Avis." He finished the letter then called over his shoulder. "Yeah, sure, Avis, tell the Hotel Internationale 'Sorry, another time.' "

Later that morning, he left for his eleven o'clock class. "The Life and Times of Paul" was one of his favorite courses. His students found the vitality of his teaching exactly what they were looking for when they enrolled at Highgate. Many came solely to study under him.

Anyone unfamiliar with Dr. Greg Langston would have no difficulty finding abundant references to his work at any library in the country. His advancements in family counseling had spawned a considerable following in the Christian community, as reported in both Christian and secular journals. But it was his books and the volume of their sales that had created an uncommon stir in the publishing industry. He was a prolific and passionate writer on the subjects of marriage, parenting, career development, and political responsibility.

At fifty-seven, Langston had also become a speaker and debater of national prominence. He was willing to enter the fray on such issues as separation of church and state, the relationship between pornography and crime, censorship and freedom of speech, creationism versus evolution, and other provocative issues. Many thought it was his increasingly frequent appearances at well-publicized debates in cities like New York, Philadelphia, Boston, and Washington that had created the most interest in him.

Weekday mornings, however, usually found Langston in his usual energetic stride across campus, exchanging hearty greetings with students and faculty. On the speaking tour, he was often tense and overwhelmed by the heavy schedule. Only when he returned to his family and beloved students at the homey campus did he fully relax and bask in the simple life.

But not this morning. Instead of taking the path to his classroom, he hurried down an overgrown trail to the river. At the water's edge, he dropped his weary body onto a flat boulder beneath the spread of an oak tree and stared into the swirling currents. They were like the ones inside him, sucking him down to a numbing cold.

"What's happening to me, Lord?" His plaintive cry hung in the air. "Why do I want to just quit? All of it."

Each time he'd ventured beyond the rallying spirit of the college, he was overwhelmed by the growing number of those living in open defiance of God's laws. And now, the treachery of those who claimed to be God's people, these Soldiers of the Cross, were compromising everything the church was trying to teach.

He lingered awhile longer, letting the meditative quiet calm him a bit, then hurried to meet his class. Some students were looking for him out the windows as he approached the building. He waved and wondered if they could see his despair.

Citizens of Rockledge were always invited to audit classes at Highgate Christian College. No charge. No requirements or exams. They could attend as many classes as they wished, as often or as little as they wished. Langston's classes were particularly popular with the local community. People admired him for his contributions, certainly, but even more for the person that he was.

His humility was famous. He was one who endured his prominence. His students came for the deep, soothing voice that proclaimed the truths of the Almighty in simple, everyday language. They came because he understood their misgivings and doubts.

The teacher was a comfortable sight to his students. His weathered face spoke of the only luxury he allowed himself—fishing with his young son. He'd played football in college and all five feet, ten inches of him was still rock solid. A little more rock had appeared about the waistline over the years, though, and the sandy brown hairline had moved north and divided.

Though he worked out to maintain strength and stamina, appearances were irrelevant to him. "As long as my socks match and my underwear's clean I'm good to go," he'd countered his wife's frustrated urgings to update his wardrobe. His daily uniform rarely deviated from khaki pants and a white, sometimes yellow, button-down shirt. Cold weather brought out a couple of worn sweaters and the same "Highgate" parka he'd been wearing for a string of winters.

Langston swept into the classroom, apologizing for his tardiness and noticing a couple of visitors toward the back. He was used to seeing the auditing extras in most of his classes and recognized the elderly woman from a course he'd taught last semester. But the other visitor was a man he'd never seen.

"Mrs. Albans, it's always nice to see you in my classroom," he began. "And, sir, we're happy you could join us as well."

The man nodded and smiled slightly.

"Would you care to introduce yourself?" Langston asked the visitor.

"Herbert Long," the man answered in a low, barely audible voice.

"Are you from Rockledge, sir?" Langston inquired, leaning forward to hear.

"No," the man answered.

Langston waited for him to continue, and when he didn't, he encouraged the man. "Is this your first time on campus?"

"No," the man replied simply.

Langston waited again for the man to expand on his answer, but nothing else was offered.

Wrapping up the stilted exchange, Langston said, "Well, we're glad you could visit us today."

He opened the class with prayer. Every head bowed but Long's.

Langston read the passage from Acts they would study that day and moved into his notes. As he later opened the floor for discussion, he scanned the room, seeking out each of his students. Eye contact was very important to him in communicating with them. As he surveyed the classroom, something in Herbert Long's face caught and held Langston's attention. There was a faintly smug lift to the eyebrows and an almost teasing grin.

As he taught, Langston continued to observe the man without being obvious. Long was in his early sixties and considerably overweight. His graying blond hair was combed straight back, curling at the collar. His clothing was casual but expensive. And there was that strange grin again. Langston's curiosity peaked.

"Mr. Long, would you mind reading the first five verses of this passage for us, sir?" Langston asked cheerfully.

"I'm sorry, but I have no Bible," Long said.

Odd that he would come to a Bible class with no Bible, Langston thought. "Here, use mine." Langston offered his worn and ragged copy to the man.

"That's all right, Dr. Langston, I'm not in good voice today. Touch of a cold, I think." The man's voice was low and tight. Langston thought it somehow familiar, too, but dismissed the notion and dug back into the lesson.

After class, Langston was approached by several students wishing to continue the discussion of the Acts passage. He always obliged his students, but this day he declined in order to search out Herbert Long. He walked into the hallway, spilling over now with students, but Long wasn't there. Langston slipped through a side door in time to see the man climb quickly into a gray van and drive away. He noted the Virginia license plate.

Another day and Langston would have lingered over the man's puzzling behavior, but he had two more classes to teach before hurrying home to Roxanne. He needed her to tell him that the despair that threatened his work would soon disappear.

It was a thirty-minute drive from the college to the Langston home on ten acres of rolling wooded land. He and Roxanne had lived in a five-room bungalow near downtown Rockledge for most of their married life. Unable to conceive a child, they were alone in the small home and content. But the faster the books came and the more frequent the demands for personal appearances, the more vivid grew Langston's dream of space and privacy.

Adopting their infant son, Jeremy, had quickened Langston's plans for a new home. He liked to say he was midsentence in teaching Noah's heroic efforts to build the ark when the house in the woods first appeared in his mind. He had told the story many times:

"Conjuring an image of the contractor, Noah, high above the dry ground, tarring up the final seal on the vessel that would sail him and his family into a new world, I suddenly saw this tall, wooden house with something like a captain's walk around the top, and me at the railing watching for the first drops of rain. The day didn't end before I placed a call to a real estate agent to start looking for that dry ground where I would construct my own great escape."

He would add apologetically, "That's sappy enough to gag you, I know. But it's true."

Langston turned off the two-lane highway he'd followed from Rockledge and entered the unpaved lane to his house. His new Chevy truck was a good match for the rough terrain. The cleared path to his house didn't offer a smooth ride, but it might as well have been hard-packed with gold for the pleasure it gave Langston on his approach to

The Ark, the name his students had given the unusual house.

Rounding a stand of plump cedars, Langston caught the first sight of his home and the architectural feature that had, ironically, drawn the attention he sought to escape. Where the tall, cedar-sided walls of the house ended just above the second floor, a narrower structure began its own ascent. Fashioned like the top of a lighthouse, Langston's "navigation room" was enclosed by glass and surrounded by a deck and high railing. It was the high, pointed roof of this structure that Langston saw capping the tree line ahead.

He pulled into the yard, passing the stocked pond that stretched in front of the house like a reflecting pool. He parked on a bed of crushed gravel and looked up at his home. Its umber wooden siding blended with the forest surrounding the home. The "navigation room" afforded the only view into the distance. It was there that Langston went to get his bearings, to quietly consult the Mapmaker before taking off in any direction. Only now, the energy to go, to try to make a difference on any front, eluded him.

"Dad!" Nine-year-old Jeremy Langston called from the other side of the pond. His voice lifted Langston like no other sound could. Langston climbed from the truck to greet his family. Roxanne Langston hurried along beside her son, already spotting the shadow that had begun to overtake her husband's countenance more frequently.

"Well, it's Boone and Crockett come a-callin'," Langston greeted. He marveled at his good fortunes making their way around the pond in a footrace, and wondered why their eager love couldn't keep him from slipping into despondency. They were joy and peace, bundled and delivered to him from on high each day. Shouldn't that be enough?

Roxanne hadn't changed since the day he'd met her in a sophomore humanities class at the University of Maryland. The energetic, petite blond pursuing a degree in education had charmed the laid-back Greg Langston, who didn't have a clue where he was headed.

Jeremy was Langston's very breath. The wriggling, freckle-faced boy with the buzz cut reached Langston breathless and sputtering excitedly as he hugged his dad about the waist. "Dad, how 'bout we target practice this afternoon up at the barn?"

Langston wrapped his arms about his son and squeezed, then leaned over and kissed the soft blond curls on top of his wife's head.

"That sounds good to me, son," Langston said, but with an obvious lack of enthusiasm.

Jeremy crinkled up his nose and studied his father. "You sure, Dad? It seems like you're pretending that it sounds good to you when you really don't want to."

Langston put his arm across the back of his son's shoulders and started walking him slowly toward the house. "Jeremy, at what point in your life did you decide to become a psychotherapist? And how long have you been practicing on your dad?"

Jeremy giggled. "Mom and me can read you real good," he said with a triumphant grin. "You're easy."

He grabbed his dad's hand and started running. "Come on, Dad. Sweat it out!"

Langston dropped his briefcase to the ground and sprinted after his son. Gears shifted inside him, and his tense muscles glided into a stride that, for the moment, freed him from every burden. When they reached the heavy oak front door, he grabbed up his son and hauled him upside down through the doorway, dropping him onto the living room sofa.

"See, I told ya," Jeremy squealed, righting himself and springing to his feet. "You just needed to play. So now can we go shooting?"

"Don't nag, Jeremy," Roxanne said, coming through the doorway carrying her husband's briefcase. "Why don't you get your homework done early and give your dad some breathing time. Then you can do something together later."

Jeremy frowned and sighed dramatically.

"We'll do the barn tomorrow, Jeremy. Maybe tonight we'll go into town and look at that hunting bow at Albert's."

"All right!" Jeremy pumped his fist and bounced from the room.

In the kitchen, Roxanne scrubbed potatoes at the sink while Langston sorted through the mail on the counter. "I got a letter from Rod and Janis," he said, settling onto a tall stool near his wife.

"Well, finally. I was beginning to think those two had forgotten their small-town friends." She set the potatoes aside and started peeling carrots. "How are they?"

"Doing well enough to afford a new apartment on the Park. They want me to stay with them while I'm in New York."

"Oh, you'll have a wonderful time. Tell them 'yes,' Greg."

"I will. But I want you to come. Isn't there any way?"

"Honey, if it was any day but that Monday. Opening day at the school's new library? How can the head librarian fail to show up? And Jeremy's solo in the chorus's dedication recital? There's just no way."

Roxanne saw the shadow return to her husband's face. She rinsed her hands and dried them, then went to him and kissed him full and long, feeling his embrace tighten around her. "I love you so much," she whispered. They held each other quietly, each feeling the heartbeat of the other.

"I just don't want to go at all," Langston said, still holding his wife. "I couldn't care less about their awards. If the publisher wasn't pushing me on this, I'd tell that committee to just mail it to me. What's a dead-wood plaque to me?"

Roxanne pulled away to look at him. "You're far too cynical for your own good, Dr. Langston. Learn to accept your laurels graciously, then just put them away where you never have to look at them again."

"It's such a waste of time, Rox. All that media hullabaloo over the stars of prime time basking in the light of their ratings. Praising authors like that guy who just wrote the book promoting extramarital affairs. I don't want to be there."

"Your publishers need the publicity. And what's good for them just might be good for you. Go graciously."

"Rox, they'll be deifying people who parade immorality. And you want me to be gracious?"

"I want you to be different," she answered. "And tell them why you're different. They don't have to like you. But they have to listen."

"Nobody listens, Roxanne. That's the trouble."

"Okay, now we've tipped over into another matter, haven't we? The what's-the-use syndrome."

Langston shrugged and stared at the floor.

"Greg, look at me." Roxanne squared herself in front of him. "What it's all about is a message spilling from one person to another. That's all. God places a message on your heart, you write about it and speak about it. That's all He's called you to do. What happens to those who read it and hear it is up to them and Him, not you. You will not save the world by yourself. You won't save one person by yourself. Only God can do that."

She rocked back on her heels and studied him. "Now, if you

think you should be doing a better job than God, I can understand your frustration."

Langston grinned. "You always drill right to the core, don't you, Rox?"

"If that's where it hurts, then yes. That's what He called me to do." She leaned over and nuzzled his cheek, then returned to the sink.

"I guess my anguish and I have been dismissed, is that right?" Langston sulked.

"Why don't you see if Jeremy needs help with his word problems?"

"I hate word problems, Rox. And who cares if a car traveling fifty miles an hour passes one limping along at thirty headed in the opposite direction?"

"I guess an attitude like that has no place in our son's education, so skip the homework for now. Maybe you could nail the latch back onto the south gate. We noticed it had come loose again on our walk this afternoon.

"That I can handle," Langston said, relieved by the prospect of an unstressful, physical task. He rose from the stool and headed for his workshop off the kitchen.

"Oh, by the way," Roxanne called to him, "there were men in the woods today."

Langston stopped short at the door and turned around. "Where?"

"Beyond the south gate."

"What were they doing?"

"We couldn't tell. They were in the distance walking away from our property."

"How many?"

"Two."

"Did you call to them? Did they say anything?"

"No and no. We just watched them leave. I don't know if they saw us or not."

Langston considered this for a moment. They had never had any trouble in the two years they'd lived there. Hunters had once wandered onto their property, and the couple had to install a wire fence to mark their land. There had been one disagreement with a neighbor over the placement of the fence.

"They were probably more surveyors sent by Mr. Brison,"

Roxanne said. "He's determined to prove we encroached on his land with our fence."

"You're probably right. I'll give Mr. Brison a call in the morning and see if he sent anyone out. Meanwhile, just be alert. Maybe you two shouldn't walk so far from the house."

"Greg, this is our home, all of it. I won't live in fear of walking my own land."

"I'm just asking you to be careful. People get stranger all the time. I had a guy in my class today who—" Langston stopped. He recalled the way Herbert Long stared at him, the peculiar grin on his face, and his reluctance to speak.

"What's wrong?" Roxanne asked.

"Just thinking about a visitor to the class today. Rather odd fellow." He paused. "Anyway, just be careful."

Langston walked out of the kitchen trying to ignore an unsettling inside. But it persisted. He turned and went back to his wife. "Call me immediately if you ever see anyone out there again."

CHAPTER 5

"Mornin', Jake," Mitty McGill called from behind the cash register. "Out of Oreos?"

Jake's grin was slow and sure. "You know Papa can't go a day without those things, Mrs. McGill. We've got ants as big as coons camped around his chair living on fallout from his lap."

Mitty's old face crinkled in amusement. Jake and Eli Gaddy were two of her favorite people, and after thirty-six years of selling groceries, feed, and seed from the weather-beaten old store on Deer Creek Square, she knew everyone there was to know. But no one could compare to Jake. He'd first captured her heart as the big-eyed little boy who visited every Christmas and summer vacation with his parents. There was a tenderness about him that touched her long before he was orphaned.

After he moved to his grandparents' home, Mitty watched him grow to great physical strength on the local playing fields. After each football game and track meet, Jake's name was repeated with pride throughout the valley. In the teachers' lounge at school, it was Jake's percentile-busting grades and science fair awards that were cheered. But what you saw when you looked at Jake Gaddy was a gentle, humble spirit. There was something else, too—a terrible yearning not everyone could see. But Mitty saw it. No matter the victories, Jake was never content. He seemed to always be searching for something he couldn't identify.

"Your grandfather needs a housekeeper out at that place. Why don't you ask May Burkett to spend one day a week cleaning and cooking for him? She could put up enough food in the freezer to last 'til the next time she came. And that old man wouldn't have to eat so many Oreos." She giggled from deep inside as she drew a pencil and paper from the drawer. "Here's her number, Jake. Call her before Eli comes down with something awful, you hear?"

Jake snapped to attention. "Aye, aye, Capt'n. But will she work for free?"

"Heavens, no." Mitty looked surprised.

"Well, Papa doesn't part with much cash, you know."

"He always pays his bill here, and I know he's got the money for housekeeping. You talk to him, Jake. He listens to you." She paused as if struck by a sudden pain. "I swear, ever since you and Joanna left home, he's like a lost puppy roaming around looking for attention. Is Joanna coming home for Christmas, too?"

Jake's smile dimmed. "No, ma'am. She's gone to Colorado to ski this year." Jake hoped his disappointment didn't show. It would be his first Christmas without Joanna. "But Papa and I are flying down to see her for a few days in February."

"Oh, how nice that will be. You give Joanna my love, and tell her everyone up here would sure love to see her."

"Yes, ma'am. I'll do that." Jake paid for the Oreos, kerosene, bran cereal, and coffee while Mitty opened yet another subject.

"Did you and that pretty young doctor ever get back together?"

Jake's expression clouded again. "Uh, no, Ma'am."

"Well, that's a shame, because she seemed to think you hung the moon."

Jake managed a faint smile. "Not for long, I'm afraid. Anyway. . ." He was anxious to leave now. "I've got to get home. My errands have taken longer than I thought, and it's getting dark. Papa will be standing on the front porch watching for The Sidewinder."

"Is he still calling the cars out there by name?" Mitty giggled.

Jake relaxed, eager to push life's disappointments aside. "Yep. And Joanna's red Jeep is Jezebel."

Mitty was still giggling when Jake waved and closed the door behind him, setting the bells on the Christmas wreath to jingling in the still, cold air. Jake paused to close his eyes and inhale. It felt good to breathe in a frosty breath, to hold it long enough to let it sting and invigorate, then release its vaporous plume in relief. The store had been stifling. The conversation too pressing.

Jake hurried across the snow-covered town square toward his old Ford pickup parked on the other side. He'd driven the truck since he was sixteen. But rarely did he approach it without a flicker of recall from a certain day many years ago. The truck had been Eli's, what was left of it after Jake had backed it over the bank and into the creek behind the house. Jake shook his head, remembering his adolescent recklessness. He'd wanted to give his grandfather a scare that day by throwing the truck into reverse and racing toward the bank—planning, of course, to hit the brakes a second before reaching the edge. But it had rained that morning, and the grass along the bank was still wet. The brakes had locked, and young Jake and the truck had spun sideways and skidded mightily into the creek.

Jake suffered no injuries beyond acute regret, but the truck was a mess. Promising to pay Eli back for the extensive repairs, Jake had worked odd jobs all over town, squeezing them in between track, football, schoolwork, and his usual chores at home. After a year, the debt was paid. It was then that Eli surprised Jake with the title to the truck, newly christened The Sidewinder.

"You certainly made it what it is today, son," Eli had drawled, "so I reckon it ought to be yours."

Jake topped the grassy rise in the middle of the square and stopped. He looked out at the lights twinkling in the trees that lined the sidewalks, at the villagers greeting each other as they passed unhurriedly on their way, and realized that this was home. The Charlottesville duplex he rented within walking distance of his classes was where he lived. But this valley town of just a few thousand residents stored his history.

Deer Creek curled contentedly in the lap of the Blue Ridge. It was the kind of town whose natives seldom left. They worked in the textile mill, alongside cousins and uncles, farmed the same soil their great-great grandparents had tilled, and gathered often in clans of thirty and forty at a time, rarely venturing beyond the mountain passes to see what the rest of the world was doing. It didn't matter.

The town square, a rustic hub of shops, small businesses, and churches, fanned into a web of shady lanes where the comfortable homes grew lovelier with age. But Jake was glad his great-grandfather Mitchell

Gaddy had chosen to build the family home away from town. Picturing the old place with its rose trellises on either side of the long, sagging front porch and the wide sweep of land before it, Jake started quickly for the truck. He'd just reached the door when he stopped abruptly and drew in a sharp breath.

The first four notes of "Joy to the World" had suddenly pealed from the tower across the street. The penetrating tones swarmed over him and burrowed deep into old wounds. Unlike the soothing images he'd indulged in just moments before, chilling sensations of grief and despair flooded through him, and he was helpless to stop them.

It had been his and his mother's favorite Christmas hymn, and she'd taught him to play it on the family piano when he was six. She even taped one of his performances of the song, and throughout the following year would occasionally pop the cassette into the car's player as they rode together, praising him for his skills and encouraging him to start formal music training.

Jake was a born pianist, his new teacher had said. He had learned quickly and demonstrated a passion for the music, especially his mother's favorite hymn, no matter the season. But when the choir sang the hymn at the memorial service following his parents' deaths, the triumphant notes, for Jake, had turned to daggers, the lyrics to lies. If the torn and lifeless bodies of his mother and father were "wonders of His love," Jake could believe in no such god.

He flung open the door to the truck, annoyed with himself for indulging in tired old pain. It had been twenty years. Why couldn't he forget? But he knew the answer. He'd worn grief like a secret badge of shame. He believed God had taken his parents away because he hadn't deserved them. All those years growing up, he'd believed himself unworthy. Each day he'd stroked his wounds raw, intensifying the pain, prolonging it. He was desperate, now, to stop it.

Jake quickly started the engine and shifted to reverse. In his hurry to leave, he nearly backed into Mr. Inman's new Pontiac that was cruising slowly behind. Jake hit the brakes and waved an apology to the old man who'd taught him freshman English at Boulder County High School. The man waved back and motioned for Jake to roll down his window.

Groaning behind his forced smile, Jake lowered the glass.

"Merry Christmas to you, Jake!" Mr. Inman called from the driver's seat. "Will you be home long?"

"About a week, sir. That's all Papa can stand me." His cheer was weak, and he just wanted to get away.

"I'm sure Eli is thrilled to have you home, son. Come to church with him tomorrow night. It would mean so much to him."

What an odd thing to say, Jake thought. He had no response.

Mr. Inman filled in the awkward silence. "He's not well, Jake."

Jake was shaken. He didn't know of any new developments in his grandfather's condition. The diabetes seemed to be under control, and Dr. Wetherington hadn't called Jake since the day Eli fell and broke his wrist. That had been two years ago.

"What do you mean, sir?" Jake asked cautiously. Mr. Inman had always had a flair for the dramatic, unlike the engineering professors he was used to at UVA.

"No cause for alarm, Jake. But he's much weaker than he used to be."

Jake had noticed Eli's difficulty in raising the stubborn metal door on the tractor shed but thought nothing of it. Now, he was embarrassed that he, of all people, wasn't aware of failing health in the one he loved more than any other. Had he neglected his Papa? Was it his fault? Again?

"Maybe I shouldn't have mentioned it," Mr. Inman said. "I can tell I've upset you. I'm sorry."

Jake recovered. "No, sir. Don't be. I'm glad you told me." He paused and looked beyond Mr. Inman, not focusing on anything. Then he added, "I haven't been home much lately."

"Well, you've got a big job up there, and we're all very proud of what you've become, Jake."

Jake looked puzzled.

"Dr. Jake Gaddy. I've kept up with you, son. I knew the day you received your master's, the day you taught your first class at Virginia, and when you got your Ph.D we all celebrated, Jake," Mr. Inman chuckled. "Eli made sure of that. And I would have done the same, if you were mine."

Jake was clearly embarrassed. He remembered that Mr. and Mrs. Inman never had children. He also remembered what a special interest

Mr. Inman seemed to have in him all through high school. He was the one who insisted Jake should apply for a scholarship to UVA, then helped him fill out all the forms.

"Thank you, Mr. Inman," Jake offered shyly. "And, you're right. I should go to Christmas Eve services with Papa."

"That's just great," Mr. Inman said as if achieving a victory. "See you there, son."

Jake watched his old teacher drive slowly off and marveled at the influence others had on him. As much as he strived to live life his way, he was still vulnerable to the persuasion of certain others.

He thought of Dominick and guessed what Eli would think of the man teaching Jake to forsake the faith of his fathers. *But it's not my faith,* Jake thought. *And Papa doesn't have to know about Dominick.*

It had begun to snow as Jake left town and headed out State Road 94 toward home. As he drove, he pictured Dominick before his flock and heard the smooth resonant voice proclaim confidently: "God is energy, the spirit that holds all living things together. We, through our very existence, are gods. Our powers are unlimited if we only tap into the energy within."

I'm no god, Jake laughed to himself. *Sorry, Dominick, but you missed the mark on that one.*

Jake gazed out the window and saw a man taking feed to his barn. *Dumb animals,* he thought. *They don't have to do anything for themselves. Don't even have to think. I wish I didn't have to think.*

Again, Dominick's words came to Jake. "There is no need for salvation for sin. Man is inherently good."

Jake looked back at the farmer. It was Lee Adams, home from prison. In a drunken rage, he'd set fire to a neighbor's barn a few years ago. The neighbor was still inside and barely escaped with his life.

Inherently good? Jake pondered. *Wrong again, Dominick.*

But much of what Dominick taught intrigued Jake enough to keep him exploring a realm of spirituality that both fascinated and, sometimes, troubled him.

Dominick's words kept coming to Jake. "Man isn't doomed to eternal hell. Neither is he bound for some heavenly roost. Man is destined to perpetuate his own greatness through reincarnation—his soul passing from one age to another."

They were words Jake had lapped up those first few months with Dominick's family of followers. Hungry for truth, he'd challenged Dominick to answer the questions that had plagued him all his life: Who, or what, was the real God? Where could one find this god? One night on the back terrace of Dominick's estate where a few followers had gathered, Jake announced with conviction, "If my parents' lives were no more significant than to be extinguished like swatted flies, then I have no right to be here at all." Dominick focused on Jake's pain, and with firm yet delicate strokes began to paint a new picture of Jake, one the subject came to believe in.

Dominick created self-worth for Jake from a metaphysical palette of alluring colors. Under Dominick's guidance, the new recruit began to explore what Dominick assured him was the essence of God. Though apprehensive, Jake allowed Dominick to lead him into exercises of channeling into the astral plains, of meditation over assorted crystals and icons. And slowly, Jake began to believe there might just be a redemptive, higher calling for himself, somewhere within Dominick's realm of authority.

All this came back to Jake as he approached the apple orchards bordering the Gaddy home. When he turned into the long, graveled lane to the house, he saw the lights from the Christmas tree blazing in the wide front window, and the lingering thoughts of Dominick and his teachings made Jake squirm.

The front door flew open wide, the aged screen door sailed outward with a screech, and Eli was down the steps and loping toward the truck. Jake couldn't deny a penetrating sense of guilt at cheating on his grandfather's faith, and that Christmas tree in the window was cutting him like a sword.

"Where in tarnation have you been, son? I only wanted bran flakes and Oreos."

Jake suddenly laughed. There was no tonic like Eli Gaddy. "Got 'em," he said. "Now, have you got dinner ready, old one?" He loved to call Eli that.

"Don't you 'old one' me," Eli growled, throwing a light punch into Jake's shoulder. "You're just half the man I used to be."

"Now, Papa, don't make me have to hurt you." With that, Jake dashed out of Eli's range and through the front door, laughing at the volley of empty threats Eli was hurtling from behind. Eli followed him into the kitchen, and Jake knew his grandfather was watching him as he stopped and examined the day's collection of Christmas cards stacked on the kitchen table. He withdrew one and laid it aside, then set the grocery bag down on the counter.

"I thought you'd be interested in that one," Eli said, moving toward the counter. As he removed the few items from the bag, he watched Jake from the corner of his eye. Jake opened the card and read it quickly, replacing it on the pile when he finished. He looked up to see Eli's hopeful expression.

"She just got carried away by the season, I guess," Jake said with stiff resignation.

"May I see?" Eli asked softly, pointing toward the card.

"Sure. It's addressed to you, too."

Eli pulled thick glasses from his shirt pocket and sat down at the table to read: "Merry Christmas, Jake and Mr. Gaddy! I think of you both often and wonder how you're doing. It's a working Christmas for me at the hospital. My internship doesn't recognize holidays, so I'm here for the duration. Jake, I'd like to hear from you. Just tell me how you are. And have a wonderful Christmas with your family. With love, Carol."

Eli folded the card and looked at Jake who was busying himself with the groceries.

"Turn around, son."

"Papa, I need to put these groceries away and start dinner, since there's nothing ready to eat." There was an edge to his voice that Eli didn't like.

"Dinner's in the oven, Dr. Gaddy," Eli corrected. "Now turn around and look at me."

Jake obliged, knowing what was coming.

"Now, I don't know what happened to you and Carol. You've been about as vague as you can be with me, and I'm not going down that road again. But I hear a young lady trying to reach you." Eli held up the card. "And I know that at one time, she loved you very much. I thought you loved her, too."

Jake was silent. He did love her, but she'd shamed and ridiculed him for dallying with Dominick's spiritualism, with what she'd called the occult. "Don't you know how dangerous that is?" she'd scolded. But her protests only drove him from her and deeper into Dominick's teaching. He needed to know what was right with him, not wrong with him. Carol's Christian God had condemned him as unworthy when he was only a child, Jake believed. And he'd fought his whole life to prove Him wrong.

Unable to reveal his secret life in Dominick's cult and the real reason for the breakup with Carol, Jake responded the only way he could. "Papa, I don't want to talk about this. Please don't ask me anything else about Carol. Okay?"

Eli just shrugged and shook his head.

Dinner conversation that evening was strained. "You did a respectable job on the roast beef," Jake allowed.

"Thank you. Mitty told me to use onion soup mix on it. Right nice flavor, I think."

"Yes, sir, it is."

Jake's formal tone troubled Eli. "Look, I'm sorry if I upset you, Jake."

Jake looked full in Eli's somber face and shook his head. "Everyone's sorry to upset me today," he said wearily, remembering the conversation with Mr. Inman. "I must be the thinnest-skinned jerk around."

"What are you talking about?"

"Nothing, Papa." He paused, then added, "Uh, would you like for me to go to Christmas Eve service with you tomorrow night?"

Eli brought a fork full of mashed potatoes to a halt in front of his mouth. He stared blankly at Jake for a few moments before putting the fork down again. Jake hadn't attended a service at Deer Creek Baptist Church since he was in high school. Eli suspected his grandson's offer was spontaneous and rooted only in peacemaking.

"You know I'd love nothing better, son. But only if you truly want to go."

"I do," Jake lied.

Eli decided not to press the issue. "That'll work fine with me." He got up from the table and moved toward the sink. "Now, I think I'll do up these dishes and get on to bed. I'm awfully tired tonight."

Jake suddenly remembered Mr. Inman's observations. "Why are you tired? You're not feeling badly, are you, Papa?"

"Goodness, boy. I'm sleepy, not dying."

"Okay, okay. Just asking." Jake decided to probe a little. "But you would tell me if you ever had a problem, wouldn't you? Pains, or weakness, or blurry—"

"What's gotten into you?" Eli snapped. "There's not a thing wrong with me except I got this six-foot-two nanny trying to mother me."

"That old Eli tonic," Jake smirked.

"What's that?"

"You're deaf, too. Go on to bed, old one. I'll clean up the dishes. They need to be done right."

The next afternoon, Eli prepared dinner early so the two men would have plenty of time to dress for church. Jake didn't need the time. Eli did. He starched and pressed his white shirt to perfection, then insisted on doing the same to Jake's.

"Papa, I'm going to run this kerosene up to the cabin. Be back in a little while."

"See that you are. We need to leave at six on the dot, okay?"

"Okay. See you."

Jake nearly shot from the back door of the house, anxious to be free of the Christmas hymns playing on Eli's radio, the tree with its glaring lights, and the hypocrisy of the coming evening. *I'll make my appearance, go through the motions, and Papa will be happy,* Jake thought as he hurried up the trail to his private retreat. The cabin he and Eli had built so many years ago was the safest place on earth. No one watched him there.

"Jake!"

He stopped and listened to the far-away cry.

"Jake! Come back!"

Papa! Jake raced down the mountain, picturing his grandfather collapsed on the floor. He threw open the back door and ran hollering into the house. "Papa! What's wrong?"

"It's Joanna, son," Eli called calmly from the top of the stairs.

Jake's heart was pounding.

"I thought you were hurt," he growled at Eli.

"Sorry to disappoint you. But your sister wants to wish you a Merry Christmas. I've already talked to her."

Jake drew a full breath and let it out slowly as he picked up the phone in the kitchen. "Hey, you little snow bunny."

Eli hung up.

"Merry Christmas, Jake. Are you and Papa all right?" Joanna's tone was soft, almost wistful.

"Well," Jake began dryly, "our three-legged stool is missing a leg."

Joanna groaned. "You're not going to make this easy for me, are you?"

"We just miss you, Joanna. But Papa and I understand."

"Do you really?"

"Oh, sure we do," Jake said, affecting a syrupy drawl. "It was an opportunity you just couldn't turn down. An all-expenses-paid vacation to Vail at Christmastime? A gift from a grateful and very important client? Why, sugar, you simply had no choice."

Joanna sighed and waited for the rest of it.

"After all," Jake continued, "who'd want to spend Christmas with a couple of deadheads in Deer Creek?"

"Jake, you're being cruel."

"Oh, yeah?" He was silent a moment. "Well. . .you're right about that. Cruel and selfish. I'm sorry. Just not in a good mood."

"What's wrong?"

"Oh, nothing. Just wish you were here."

"Well, if I could, I'd leave here today. The skiing's great and everyone's getting along, but I belong somewhere else. It's our first Christmas apart, you know."

"Yeah, I know," Jake was growing weary of the gloomy conversation. "But, hey, wait 'til you see the old man in his new Hawaiian print shirt and sunglasses."

"His what?"

"I even bought him a bathing suit for the trip to Miami."

Joanna laughed. "What color?"

"Lime green, the brightest I could find. Load the camera." Jake's voice and mood had brightened thinking about his and Eli's upcoming trip to see Joanna.

"And let me guess. . .you're giving it all to him tomorrow when it's eighteen degrees outside."

"You got it. Can't you just see him?"

Joanna was quiet for too long. Jake knew she was struggling to respond.

"Well, I've got to get dressed for church," he said, too cheerfully. "I promised Papa I'd go with him tonight."

Joanna sniffed quietly and said, "You're going to church, Jake?"

"I am." Jake didn't want to discuss it. "And we'll be late if I don't get going."

The conversation came to a quick close when Eli called for Jake to hurry up.

Riding into town, the two men briefly discussed Joanna's ski vacation and the few days they planned to spend with her in Miami. After that, they grew strangely quiet. Jake gazed at the snowy fields, shimmering like blankets of iridescent foam under a full moon, and remembered Christmases as a little boy. He would hunt for wild turkey with his dad and grandfather. They would rise early, climb into Eli's truck and stop for breakfast at a local diner. Then they'd walk the fields and woods all day in search of Christmas dinner.

But all too soon, the hunting party was reduced to just Jake and Eli. The memory of that first Christmas without his parents would never become a blur to Jake. It seared into him even at this moment.

As they drew close to town, they could hear the bells of Deer Creek Baptist Church heralding this expectant night and all who came to celebrate it. The tiny white lights in the trees lining the town square looked like thousands of fireflies caught in the entangling limbs.

Jake and Eli parked the car and walked to the front steps of the church where a crowd was funneling inside. Immediately, their names were called by one after another who were happy to see Eli—and shocked to see Jake entering the church.

Standing next to his grandfather as they greeted a host of well-wishers, Jake was reminded of Eli's popularity in the community. He was an elder in the church and son of one of its founding fathers, as well as the town's longest serving and most beloved postmaster. This was his church, his people. *What am I doing here?* Jake thought. *I'm a heretic. I don't belong. I don't believe!* He wanted to flee.

"Jake, it's so nice to see you here." The sweet voice that stole into his troubled thoughts was Mrs. Inman's. Her husband beamed silently by her side. "It's been so long since we've seen you at all."

Jake knew she meant, "and especially in church."

"It's nice to see you, too, Mrs. Inman."

She smiled and reached for his hand. "You know, Jake, there's no better time to come home than at Christmas."

What does she mean? Jake thought, but didn't have time to respond. The organ struck the opening chords to "Hark the Herald Angels Sing," and Eli motioned for Jake to follow him inside.

As they walked down the aisle, Jake wished Eli didn't prefer to sit up front. Too many heads were turning to look as they passed. Though the faces smiled pleasantly and nodded, Jake knew what they were thinking. It had been ten years since he had last entered the sanctuary. At seventeen, he'd not only graduated a year early from Boulder County High School but with high honors and a full scholarship to the University of Virginia. The Sunday after graduation, he was honored during a special service for graduates.

There's no honor in being a hypocrite, he thought. He quickly took his seat beside Eli and concentrated on the program, choosing not to meet the eager eyes trying to make contact.

The organ continued to play familiar passages of Christmas hymns that stirred no response in Jake's heart. Reverend Willingham walked to the pulpit and raised his hand for prayer, and Jake stared at the floor.

A young woman Jake knew from high school stepped from the choir and sang "O Holy Night." With all eyes locked on the young soloist, Jake allowed himself to look about the sanctuary. He knew most everyone he saw. They sat contentedly in the glow of the old church with its towering stained glass windows arched into the high walls, its crimson cushions and carpeting, its white paint layered thickly upon every surface. The hymnals smelled of aged refrains and rested so naturally in the hands of the congregation.

Everyone stood to sing. Jake took the hymnal Eli offered and turned to the announced page. He only pretended to sing.

Just do it for Papa, he told himself.

He sat still through the minister's message of birth and rebirth. He heard Rev. Willingham speak of the Savior who came into the world to redeem it and make it holy.

There's nothing holy about this world, Jake argued in his mind. *Just a bunch of misguided souls duped into believing they're good enough to please a god somewhere.*

When Rev. Willingham finished, he raised his hands, and the

lights dimmed. Candles were lit and the communion table laid with its elements.

As the cups and bread were passed, Jake heard the words: ". . .this is my body, broken for you. . ."

No, not for me, he cried to himself.

". . .this is my blood, poured out for you. . ." *What good is spilled blood?*

While those about him bowed their heads in reverence, Jake lifted his in defiance. He stared at the cross which seemed to quiver in the flickering light of the candles. He locked on the vision of a man hanging there. The man was pierced and bloodied—like the two bodies pulled from the wreckage of the boat. They're all dead.

Jake could stand it no longer. He slipped from the pew and hurried out the side door of the church.

He walked through the parking lot and into a thicket of trees. His feet sank in the snow, but he kept going until he came to a small clearing. There, he sat on a log and stared up into the dark twisting limbs above him until he began to tremble from the cold and the snow now packed inside his shoes.

"Who are You?" he cried softly. "Why do You hide from me? Do You not see me search for You? If You are truly the God of the cross, let me put my hand on Your side."

In the stillness, Jake waited for something to happen. Things happened when he was with Dominick and the others. Frightening things. But now, he waited for something else. He didn't know what. After a moment he heard something behind him and whirled quickly around.

"Jake? Where are you, son?" It was Eli, pushing branches aside as he stumbled along the dark path.

Jake hurried to him. "It's okay, Papa. Nothing's happened. Nothing at all. Let's go home."

CHAPTER 6

In the predawn hour before Atlanta awoke to a frigid January morning, a man in a dark warm-up suit slipped inside the small, vacant office building across the street from the Strathmore Clinic for Women. For someone who had compromised the security systems of embassies, banks, and airlines on three continents, the break-in was effortless.

From a first-floor window of an empty office, the intruder could see directly into the lighted lobby of the clinic. With binoculars, he watched as a young woman at the front desk chatted with a security guard. He noted the times the guard left and reappeared at the desk. Then he studied the roofline, walls, and windows of the five-story brick clinic, making a series of sketches on a legal pad.

As the man drew the intersecting lines of retaining walls and stress points, he tugged at his left ear. Since the accident, it was his habit to massage the mutilation, just as an animal licks its wound. It was no longer painful, and he didn't care that people stared. He didn't even try to conceal the ear, wearing his straight black hair in a short military cut. But the failure the disfigurement embodied gnawed at him constantly. He'd been reckless that night in Bimini and would never escape the consequence of his mistake. But there would be no more mistakes, he'd assured himself.

The security guard left the front desk again, and the girl was alone. The double glass doors to the clinic allowed a clear view down a wide hallway running front to back. No one entered the hall for a full twenty minutes. Then a young man in a blue smock emerged through the swinging doors at the back of the hallway and approached the desk. He handed the young woman a stack of papers, then left in a different direction than he had come.

From across the street, the man noted that the first floor of the clinic was well lit, but most windows on the upper floors were dark. He saw that only seven cars were parked in the lot next to the clinic.

He knew that in a couple of hours, the six o'clock shift would arrive. At ten, he would casually enter the clinic. He would approach the front desk and ask for directions to the business office, which he knew to be at the back of the building on the first floor. For now, though, while it was still dark, he would replace the locks and security wiring on the back door of the office building and return to the motel for a nap.

At ten o'clock that morning, Laurie Jean Webb was reviewing the appointment schedule for the day when a dark-complexioned man in a navy sport coat approached the desk, asking for directions to the business office. She immediately noticed his mangled left ear and tried not to stare.

"Just follow this hallway, sir, through the double doors. Take a right at the water fountain, and it'll be the second doorway on your left." She smiled brightly at him, receiving only a slight nod in return.

Once through the double doors, the man hurriedly scouted as much of the first floor as he could. He opened doors and peered into offices, excusing himself when confronted by anyone, claiming a "deplorable sense of direction." He particularly noted the location of storage closets and their contents, determining the likelihood of a concealed object remaining so—for as long as it took.

Over an hour later, Miss Webb was surprised to see the man just now returning through the double doors. "Sir," she said as he passed her desk, "did you have any difficulty finding the business office?"

"No," he replied bluntly. Then he realized she must be curious about his length of stay. Not wishing to arouse suspicion, he added, "I found a lounge back there and decided to do some reading. My sister is interested in your services."

"Then why not take her one of these?" she said, reaching into a box beneath her desk. She handed him a glossy brochure and said, "It's our latest one."

The man took the mauve-tinted brochure, noting its smooth, heavy stock and fanciful graphics. The heading on the cover, encircled by a pastel garland of roses, was simple and direct: Easy Steps to an Abortion.

Three weeks later, the same man arrived at the Drake Family Planning Clinic in Chicago. He walked to the receptionist's desk and asked for directions to the business office.

CHAPTER 7

For months now, Dominick had been encouraging his newer follow-ers to raise their spiritual consciousness to a new plateau. To reach "oneness with the deity of the universe." Jake participated willingly. One January evening at Dominick's lake house, he rowed alone to the middle of the dark waters where all horizons disappeared, and he waited. In his hands were the crystals meant to entrap "the powers" that swirled about him. Dominick had been vague about the nature of these powers, but Jake trusted his teacher to bring him to the brink of truth and goodness.

That night on the lake, no answers came.

But when Dominick encouraged his followers to make contact with a spirit guide, an actual being from another realm, something in Jake leaped to the surface, tripping an alarm.

"There are forces about us, awaiting our call to join us," Dominick enticed his flock. "These forces can take us farther than we ever imag-ined, out of our very bodies and into the astral plains."

Get out! The prompting from somewhere inside Jake was urgent and clear. It confused him, and he tried to suppress it, but it only grew stronger. Each time Dominick led the group in contacting their spirit guides, Jake withdrew further.

Observing Jake's discomfort, Dominick approached him one evening.

"Jake, my boy. A few of us are taking a brief holiday in New York next weekend. A friend of mine has a fine old home in Brooklyn near the Verrazano Bridge, which he graciously allows me to use. He and his wife live in Rome most of the year. Have you ever been to New York?"

"No, I haven't," Jake said.

"Then you must come. Every American should touch the pulse of the nation. We'll tour the museums, see the shows, and dine on the finest fare in the land. My treat as usual. What do you say?"

Jake weighed his growing uneasiness with Dominick against the tempting invitation dangling before him. Perhaps a change of environment would alter his perspective. He pushed his apprehensions aside. "Sure, I'll go," he agreed.

They drove from the UVA campus in Charlottesville to New York in Dominick's gray conversion van with all the trimmings—VCR, CD player, and a small refrigerator filled with drinks and gourmet foods. Francie Jeffers and Marcus Ruff were also along for the weekend. Francie was a graduate assistant in the psychology department at UVA. Marcus was finishing his doctorate in archeological studies. Both had known Dominick much longer than Jake, and both had been with Jake and Dominick in Washington. Jake was beginning to wonder why he'd been initiated into the inner circle closest to Dominick. It occurred to him that the older man had indeed become the center of Jake's uncertain universe.

From the backseat of the van, Jake studied Dominick's form. His grayish blond hair was combed straight back with no part, curling at the nape of his neck. He sat tall in his seat, the sharp features and strong jaw suggesting strength; but his body was soft and round. At sixty-one, he dressed himself in the young, casually elegant fashions of the Mediterranean coast he loved to explore. *Smooth,* Jake thought of him. *Scholarly, entertaining, and masterfully smooth.*

Father Dominick. The name was a curiosity to Jake. He claimed to have studied at various religious institutes, though he never specified which ones, nor the nature of degrees, if any, earned. Jake decided that adding "Father" to his name washed him in a reverent authority crucial to the master-follower relationships he sought. On the college campus, he eased into good graces with such openers as, "I love to exchange mind-broadening ideas. And I don't mind grilling a box-load of steaks to go with them. So let's just have a good time."

His lake parties were enormously popular, until some guests, Jake had observed, began to squirm from the frequent allusions to the metaphysical properties of life. The more Jake studied the man seated in front of him, the clearer he saw the path his adoption into Dominick's family had taken. There had been a sifting process. Remove the unreachable and isolate the intrigued. Jake had been isolated. And now, he was being coddled. He would be manipulated just so far, he told himself.

When they reached New York, another of Dominick's guests joined them. Steve Michon had dropped out of UVA his junior year and moved to Manhattan, where he'd worked odd jobs ever since. His light brown, receding hairline and wire-rimmed glasses made him look older than his twenty-five years. He was a little shorter than Jake and heavy, with a lumbering gait that made him seem sluggish. But his laugh was quick and infectious.

"Too many years ago, Steve here let a little thing like tuition get in the way of his destiny," Dominick had scolded by way of introduction. "If he ever decides to accept a loan from me, he can return to the classroom and our little family in Virginia. But he doesn't want to owe anybody anything."

Jake noticed Steve's discomfort over Dominick's remarks and wondered how far Dominick would go to secure allegiance from his "family."

The house in Brooklyn, a handsome two-story Georgian of tan brick with maroon shutters, faced the harbor. Its interiors were expansive with a wide curving staircase and Oriental rugs scattered over the glossy wood floors. Antique furniture and artifacts from around the world filled the house, giving it a museum-like quality that Jake found stifling. He longed for the little cabin on the mountain in Deer Creek.

All the bedrooms were upstairs. Francie and Marcus took a room apiece, Jake and Steve shared one, and Dominick occupied a suite of rooms on the back of the second floor. That part of the house seemed to have been sectioned off as a possible rental apartment and could be accessed through an outside stairway at the rear of the house.

The first evening in New York was thrilling to Jake. He'd never seen such a city. Dominick treated the party of five to dinner at Windows on the World restaurant atop the World Trade Center. Their table was almost level with a cloud line hovering over the city, and here and there through the white puffs Jake could see planes flying beneath them.

Later, they saw a Broadway show, then closed the evening with coffee and dessert at the Plaza Hotel.

The following morning, Dominick herded them back into the van for a day of sightseeing. They parked in a garage in midtown Manhattan and walked north along Fifth Avenue to the Guggenheim Museum. Dominick gushed over the swirling, futuristic lines of the Frank Lloyd Wright structure and the avant-garde, contemporary art exhibited inside. Steve had a different perspective.

"Hey, Jake," Steve said in a hushed voice, "does the twelve-foot orange paper clip hanging from the ceiling do anything for you?"

Jake glanced up at the twisting, neon configuration suspended above him and smiled. "What's the matter, Steve? You don't appreciate fine art?"

"Some of this stuff is all right, I guess. Those tin foil goats are kind of cute. But what do you say we find a Coke machine?"

"If there's one in here, it's probably on exhibit. Come on, we'll find a vendor outside."

After visiting the Metropolitan Museum of Art, Dominick led his entourage down Fifth Avenue toward Rockefeller Center. They were passing St. Patrick's Cathedral when Jake stopped to admire its architecture.

"Come on, Jake," Dominick urged. "We don't need to spend time here. There's so much else to see."

But Jake was enchanted by the lofty spires and intricate stonework. "Just a minute, Dominick. This building is magnificent." And before Dominick could say another word, Jake crossed the street and stood before the cathedral. As he approached the front doors, Dominick rushed up beside him, caught his arm and, much too vigorously, pulled him away. Jake was startled and annoyed by his action.

"Sorry to insist, Jake, but we just don't have time. Now come along."

Jake stared into Dominick's face seeing something he'd never seen there before. Fear, near panic. The man's usually cool composure was gone.

Jake withdrew his arm from Dominick's grip. "What's wrong with you, Dominick? I just wanted a quick look inside."

"There are things in there that will hurt you, Jake. You just don't understand."

"What do you mean?" Jake watched fury flash across the man's face.

"It's all a lie," Dominick hissed. "Just an elaborate hoax meant to keep you from the real truth. I can't stand here any longer, Jake. Please come with me now."

Jake saw that Dominick was trembling and feared he might collapse. Reluctantly, Jake followed him across the street, hanging back to meet Steve's curious stare.

"Tell you later," Jake whispered to Steve's unspoken question.

Jake avoided Dominick on their visit to Rockefeller Center, not to pout but to gather his thoughts and consider what had possessed the man to behave as he did. Standing before the gleaming statue of Prometheus, Jake pushed the incident from his mind, not wishing to spoil the pleasures of the day. But Steve kept shooting him probing glances.

Dominick hailed a cab and took everyone to Chinatown. They strolled past bars, restaurants, and curio shops from which the music and language of another land filtered onto the crowded sidewalks. Jake wondered how much of it was the Chinese version of America—or the other way around. Jake thought that the curious alphabet lit in neon against the storefronts, the robes and costuming of people on the streets, and the temples to Buddha tucked here and there were more reminders of a culture than evidence of one.

While Francie and Marcus browsed in a jewelry store, Jake and Steve puzzled over a menu posted outside a restaurant. Steve had cornered Jake there, anxious to know what had taken place on the steps of the cathedral. Jake told all there was to tell, then said he didn't want to dwell on it.

They had returned to studying the menu when Steve poked Jake in the arm and motioned toward Dominick, who was slipping into an alley without a word to anyone. "Wonder where he's headed," he said, pulling Jake toward the entrance to the alley.

"Leave him alone, Steve. I don't think he's feeling well."

But Steve kept coaxing Jake farther into the alley. "Aren't you curious about the old man? Come on."

Jake tagged along to humor Steve. He liked the big guy built like a bear, who worried about his thinning hair. "I've got to do something about this stuff falling out," Steve had told Jake while sharing the bathroom mirror that morning at the house. "Someday I'll have to plant those little corn rows of hair across my scalp."

They were about to turn the corner where the side alley opened into a courtyard when Steve stopped abruptly and jumped backwards, pulling Jake with him and motioning for him to be quiet. He'd spotted Dominick standing in a back doorway talking to someone unseen. Jake and Steve stood still and listened. They heard Dominick's voice clearly, but only a few phrases from the other. It was female and heavily accented.

"You're sure he'll come?" Dominick asked.

"Yes, he'll. . .12:30. . .you be here."

"I'll take a cab. Look for me."

"You come 12:30. . .sure. . .or he not wait."

A door closed, and Steve and Jake sprinted back up the alley disappearing around the front of the building just seconds before Dominick reentered the alley heading toward the street. When he approached the young men on the sidewalk, they were lost in the same menu.

"Still trying to figure it out?" Dominick asked.

"We've decided that 'hot dog' is easier to pronounce," Steve said. "Know where we can get a good one?"

After a late lunch, they returned to the garage for the van and drove back to the house in Brooklyn to rest. Later that evening, they ate dinner at an Italian restaurant a few blocks away in the Bay Ridge area.

"How about running with me, Steve?" Jake suggested a couple of hours after dinner. He was already changing into a sweat suit. "After three hot dogs and a mound of spaghetti, you could use it."

"Maybe. But I've got a better idea. It's 10:30 now. Let's stick around and see if Dominick slips out of here about midnight."

"You think the '12:30' we heard meant tonight?"

"Sure. When else? We'll be gone by that time tomorrow afternoon."

"It could be any time, Steve. Dominick comes up here a lot. It could be 12:30 next Friday."

"It's tonight, I'm sure. And you and I are going to follow him."

Jake laughed. "Down a dark alley at midnight in Chinatown. Sure we are." Jake laced up his shoes and headed for the door. "Last chance, Sherlock. Coming or not?"

"No, but I'll be ready to go when you get back. Wear something dark."

Jake rolled his eyes and left.

After his run, he'd realized there would be no sleep until he went with Steve to Chinatown, and he was pulling on a blue sweater and jeans when Steve raced back to the bedroom at 11:30 that night. He had been alert for movement in or out of Dominick's rooms all evening. Francie and Marcus had gone to a movie, and the house had been quiet until now.

"He just left," Steve announced excitedly. "I heard the back door at the top of the outside stairs open and shut. There's got to be a cab waiting somewhere near the house. It's not out front. Hurry up, let's go."

"Should we leave a note for the police to find?" Jake asked. "Just so they'll know where to look for our bodies."

Steve ignored him and fumbled through his pockets for the keys to the van.

"He's going to be real concerned about the missing van if he gets back before we do," Jake said, with a worried frown.

"No problem. He tossed the keys to me and said we could use it if we needed to, then pretended to go to bed early."

"Steve, you have a different agenda from the rest of us, don't you?" Jake grinned at him.

"I just can't believe you let a man you know nothing about teach you what to believe," Steve said on their way out the door, "and you're not the least bit interested in checking him out."

They climbed inside Dominick's van, and Steve pulled hurriedly out of the driveway.

"My eyes are open, Steve," Jake said, with a slight edge to his voice. "I'll see what I need to see."

They drove quickly into Manhattan, giving up on spotting the cab Dominick took. They were pretty sure where to find him, though.

Steve turned onto the same garishly lit street in Chinatown, just in time to see Dominick climb from a cab and enter the front door of the building next to the alley they'd followed him down that afternoon. It was twenty minutes past midnight.

Parking the van proved a challenge, but Steve wedged it in front of a delivery truck he guessed wouldn't be used until much later that morning. They walked quickly down the street, mixing with the Saturday night crowds, then crossed to the side opposite the building

Dominick had just entered.

"Now what?" Jake asked, without enthusiasm.

"It looks like a hotel or apartment building. Let's just go in."

"And. . ." Jake wanted a little more of a plan. "What if we bump into Dominick?"

"Well, I don't know. You come up with something."

"Steve, I didn't want to come in the first place."

"But now you're here, and you've got to be just a little bit curious about what Dominick's up to, aren't you?"

"Okay, here's our story. We just happened to have a hankering for Chinese food at midnight and drove twenty miles to get it. Then we saw our old friend Dominick who we just said 'good night' to, and decided to follow him into the building just to say 'hello' and marvel together at the incredible coincidence of it all. How about that?"

"Sounds good. Let's go." Steve was in the street and moving. Jake could only catch up and hope they didn't run into Dominick. He'd seen anger flare in his spiritual leader once today, and that was enough.

Just inside the door of the building was a small landing with steps going one flight up and one down. A long, uninterrupted hallway extended the length of the building on each level. There were doors spaced regularly down both sides of the halls. There was no front desk or attendant. Each door was marked in Chinese numerals.

From the noises drifting into the halls—children's voices, blaring television sets, and bursts of animated exchanges between males and females—Jake and Steve knew it was an apartment building. "Now how are we going to find Dominick?" Jake asked with a lingering trace of irritation.

"Walk slowly and listen at each door," Steve replied simply and climbed the steps to the top floor. He started down the hallway, pausing at the first door on the left. Jake hung back and watched, reluctant to follow Steve's lead.

Steve stopped at all eight doors in the upper hall without hearing a familiar voice. He returned to Jake, motioning toward the lower level. "Let's go downstairs. He's got to be in here somewhere."

"Maybe he entered the front door and exited the back, knowing he was being followed by dangerous creatures of the night."

Steve looked hard at Jake.

MORTAL WOUNDS 73

"All right," Jake gave in, "if it will hurry things along, I'll check one side, you take the other." He moved down the stairs and stopped at the first door on the right. No sound at all. Then the next door. Still no sound. Behind the third door, two men were talking rapidly and perhaps arguing, though it was hard to tell not knowing the language. At the last door on the right, a young child was crying and attendant adults were cooing gently to make it stop. Steve reached the back of the hall about the same time and shrugged in surrender.

"End of mission, Jake. Happy?"

"Relieved. Let's go."

Halfway down the hall they stopped short. At the second door Jake had checked, there was now a voice. Its words were sharp and staccato, pitched high with an insistence that riveted Jake and Steve to the floor. "Dravian, we hear you. Come close. Come close. We're here to receive you. Mighty Dravian."

The voice grew to frenzied pitch then dropped suddenly to a monotone cadence. Now it was a voice that was lulling and composed, and unmistakably Dominick's. Without moving anything but their eyes, Jake and Steve searched each other's faces for reaction, bound to every word coming through the door. "We lift your name and entreat you to come. There is work. The legions are ready. He must be nailed to oblivion. His reign be frozen in the astral stone."

Then a woman's shrill voice cut into Dominick's. "Our legions march, oh, Dravian. Come lead us!"

Another male voice joined Dominick's and the woman's. "March, oh, Dravian. He must be destroyed. The lamb of liars must be destroyed. Join us, enter our ranks, and empower us to serve."

Jake and Steve had leaned within inches of the door, so captivated by the voices on the other side that they didn't notice the young woman approaching from the back of the hallway.

In a burst of Chinese, she demanded to know what they were doing. When they jerked their startled faces toward her, she then demanded loudly in English: "What you do here? No business here. Get out!"

"Shh, ma'am," Jake begged. "We're okay. Not going to hurt anybody. Friendly." He flashed a nervous grin.

The young woman, whose baby was still crying down the hall,

called loudly to her husband as Jake and Steve tried to calm her down. Seeing their efforts fail, they were about to run from the building when the door behind them opened wide.

Dominick stood in the doorway, his face flushed, his demeanor off-balance. Jake noted the purple silk lounging robe over his shirt and slacks and suspected an intimacy going on inside that he sure didn't want to witness.

Dominick recovered instantly. In Chinese, he addressed the young woman and her approaching husband with a warmly inflected voice, sending them back to their apartment still muttering and looking back at the two young intruders.

Jake and Steve hung suspended in silent misery as Dominick searched their faces for an explanation. He seemed to be struggling with which emotion to display when he finally said coolly, "I'm impressed. You let your curiosity take you where you've never been before. That's exactly what I've taught you to do." He opened the door wider. "Come in and see."

As Jake and Steve passed through the doorway, they were enveloped by candlelight from a massive iron candelabrum at the center of the small room. The only other furnishings they saw were eight or nine plump pillows tossed haphazardly about a hemp rug, a vinyl-covered lounge chair, and a table with a glass pyramid on top.

Seated on pillows opposite the door were a man and woman they had never seen before. Dominick introduced the woman first. Her name was Cecelia Mour. She was about fifty, Jake guessed, with pale skin made paler by the overuse of dark eyeliner and deep blue shadowing. She was dressed elegantly in a navy business suit. Her blond hair was pulled tightly into a knot at the back of her neck. She smiled graciously and offered them cushions, but they declined, too stiff with anxiety to bend.

The man was slightly younger and not as welcoming. Even in the soft glow of the candles, his image was rough and malevolent. His eyes locked tight on Jake and Steve as they stood before him. Beneath his close-cropped dark hair, his taut, angular face was also dark. His nose was long and narrow.

"My name is Cort Peterson," he said, rising from the floor. He was much shorter than Jake, but the fitting lines of his knit warm-up suit showed him to be powerfully built. Then Jake noticed his ear, or the remains of it. It was the left one. Just a jagged ridge of bony tissue sheared close to the head.

"And this is Jake Gaddy and Steve Michon," Dominick announced motioning to each one in turn.

Jake caught a flash of recognition in Peterson's face.

"Gaddy?" he asked, turning to Jake.

"Yes, sir. Jake Gaddy."

Peterson blinked quickly and seemed uncertain of his next words. "Where, uh, are you from?"

"Deer Creek, North Carolina."

"Oh." Peterson seemed to uncoil from some brief tension. He turned to speak to Steve when Jake added one more thing.

"But I was born in Miami."

Peterson turned suddenly and glared at Jake. He didn't speak. He just studied Jake's surprised face with an intensity that made the situation even more uncomfortable. "What are you doing here?" Peterson asked abruptly.

"I think our young friends were just exploring and happened to see me, isn't that right?" Dominick's forced congeniality headed off any further interrogation from Peterson.

"These are old friends of mine, boys," Dominick continued, motioning to the man and woman. "We knew each other in Egypt. Occasionally, we find ourselves in New York at the same time and enjoy a few moments of catching up. Isn't that right, Cecelia?"

The woman nodded and smiled pleasantly. "Perhaps the two of you would like to sit down now," she suggested, tossing a couple of cushions their way. "We find it restful and more conducive to channeling our energies. Would you like to join us?"

Steve raised an eyebrow at Jake. "No, ma'am. We won't be staying."

"Of course they won't, Cecelia," Peterson interjected sharply. "They're too ill-at-ease. Are you ill-at-ease, boys?"

Jake grew restless and tired of being called a boy. "Dominick, we apologize for our behavior," he said, casting an accusing glance at Steve. "It was a spontaneous decision to follow you. We were just curious and foolish. And now, we'll be leaving."

"Nonsense," Dominick cheerfully objected. "You were overcome by the mysteries of this grand city, that's all. Actually, I'm glad you're here. You must feel the spiritual radiance in this room. Perhaps you're ready to meet the ones who guide us and lend us their powers. Don't you agree, Cort?"

Cort Peterson seemed suddenly amused watching Jake and Steve fret. "I'm not so sure, Dominick. Give them time. Let them age a bit more before you lead them into something they can't handle."

Jake bristled. "Mr. Peterson, I hope you don't feel threatened by our presence." Peterson stiffened. "But you're right. We shouldn't be here. There's probably something going on that's way over our heads."

Jake turned to Steve. "The fun's over. Let's go." Dominick made no move to stop them.

But when Jake reached the door, he turned suddenly to Dominick. "Who is Dravian?" he demanded firmly. "And the lamb of liars?"

Dominick started to speak when Peterson cut him off. "Perhaps one day we'll introduce you to Dravian. And he will show you the lamb, who was, and will be no more."

Jake glared at Peterson, then glanced reproachfully at Dominick as he and Steve rushed from the room and out of the building.

"Good work, Cort," Dominick said harshly. "You've just destroyed a year's campaign to bring Jake Gaddy under my wing."

"You don't need him. He's trouble, and I don't like him."

"What you like or dislike is irrelevant. And by the way, what came over you when Jake told you he was from Miami? I've never seen you so off guard."

"You're imagining things, old man."

"You did seem to come a bit undone, Cort," Cecelia remarked.

"You're both fogged from the wine. And I still say that boy's trouble. Drop him, Dominick."

"I'll do no such thing. I'll need a bright, capable boy like him in Washington."

"You're awfully sure old Ramsdale's going to make it, aren't you?" Peterson said smugly.

"You'd better hope he does," Dominick shot back. "You might want him to save you from the electric chair some day."

CHAPTER 8

The wind off the gorge whipped against the letter in Jake's hand. It was from Steve. Jake had read it twice already, not wanting to believe it. But the words were clear:

> *That nonsense Dominick was talking about at the farm is going to happen. . .they'll be coming for you. . .cut out of there, Jake.*

But Jake sat still on the rocky point overlooking the valley below. The brisk wind penetrated his jacket as he gazed upon the town of Deer Creek.

On the west side of the square stood the Baptist church, with its lofty spire and magenta-splashed windows. Somewhere in its parking lot, at this moment, was a 1968 white Chevrolet Caprice, a relic referred to by its owner, Eli Gaddy, as Clay Baby because of the indelible band of red clay stain ringing the lower half of the car.

It was not yet time for Sunday evening service, but for years Eli had arrived an hour early to join Rev. Willingham in a private session of prayer.

An involuntary smile stole across Jake's face as he suddenly pictured his grandfather, the merry widower of Deer Creek, slinging flour and sugar all over the church kitchen last June in a bumbling attempt to produce a better tasting "communion cracker."

Jake looked back at the letter and thought again of the farm in

Connecticut, wondering why he'd ever gone. After the trip to New York, he'd decided to break off entirely with Dominick's group, though he hadn't yet announced his decision to its intimidating leader. Now, he regretted his delay in ending the relationship and recalled the recent weekend at the farm.

Dominick had invited his followers to his country home in Connecticut for what he called a sabbatical. He graciously implored Jake to come, asking him to forget the whole incident in Chinatown and apologizing for Cort Peterson's offensive behavior. Dominick excused Peterson as an inescapable acquaintance from long ago who kept reappearing in his life. Jake wondered why the manipulative power Dominick wielded so effectively over others was inadequate to dispense with an undesirable acquaintance.

Feeling indebted to Dominick for his many kindnesses, Jake had reluctantly accepted the invitation, though only for a weekend. He vowed to himself that this would be his last communion with Dominick Swain.

Set in a patchwork of farmlands, the comfortable old home had been a gift to Dominick. He inherited it from an elderly follower who, suffering from congestive heart failure, expected to move permanently into a realm Father Dominick had assured him would be altogether pleasant. The rambling farmhouse, barn, tractor shed, smokehouse, and other outbuildings sat on two hundred rolling acres. It reminded Jake of home, and he wished he were there instead.

During his three-day visit, Jake often ran the vast fields surrounding the farmhouse. After a few days, he knew every rut and molehill on the property.

Steve was also a guest at the farmhouse. He'd found a friend in Jake and enjoyed exchanging thoughts with him. They had agreed in New York to hold each other's misgivings about Dominick's teachings and techniques in confidence and to never speak of the night in Chinatown to anyone.

After dinner on the last night of Jake's visit, Dominick gathered everyone in the living room. Confident of his followers', even Jake's, devotion, he unveiled something that caught his flock by surprise. Standing before them in the dark, wood-paneled room, he announced, "We can no longer be content with the progression of our souls alone. We are only elements of something greater. We are responsible for uniting as one, all powerful, to rule when the lies of others are finally exposed."

No one spoke. No one understood.

"Millions of people are doomed because they either believe lies about what God is or they believe nothing at all."

Steve and Jake began to squirm.

"Well, the time has come to expose the lies." He paused, then continued almost mournfully. "I'm growing old. Before I leave this world for another, I must show the world what God isn't. Maybe then they will see what God is. What truth is."

Still no one spoke.

Suddenly the man's demeanor changed. He squared his shoulders and raised his voice. "What is the greatest lie?" he challenged his followers.

"That Jesus Christ is the living God!" shouted a young woman who had been well coached by Dominick.

A chill shot through Jake. The lamb of liars? Had Cort Peterson been referring to Jesus Christ?

"What did this man Jesus teach?" Dominick continued.

"That man is sinful," replied another follower. "That by sacrificing Himself, Jesus paid man's penalty for sin. That to be forgiven and go to heaven, one must believe and obey Jesus only."

"That's the lie!" screamed Dominick, and his face contorted with rage. His audience jumped at the sudden outburst.

Jake and Steve exchanged cautioning glances.

"We must expose the liars. We must expose the intrusive Christian militants who bomb and kill for power."

"Are you talking about the Soldiers of the Cross, Dominick?" asked a young man sitting next to Jake.

Dominick smiled broadly. "That's exactly who I mean. The very ones who carry out the orders handed them by Christians United. The very ones who rule in the White House."

"You don't believe everything you hear on television, do you, Dominick?" Steve asked with an admonishing grin.

Dominick glared at Steve, then puffed out his expansive chest before declaring, "I will prove the Christian liars are also murderers. I will make the nation hate them."

"How?" The question came from a bewildered Jake.

Dominick smiled broadly. "Who is one of this country's most lauded authors of Christian propaganda?" Dominick quizzed.

Several names sprang simultaneously from the group. Only one was repeated triumphantly by Dominick. "Greg Langston! And which Christian celebrity has been chosen to address an audience of this nation's most powerful publishers and broadcasters in just three weeks?"

"Greg Langston?" came an uncertain reply.

A foreboding crept over Jake. The twisted face before him was the same one he'd stared into at the door of St. Patrick's Cathedral in New York.

Vigorously nodding his head, Dominick continued. "And if you were to select a person whose admission of guilt would most certainly bring down the Christian hierarchy, who would that be?"

"Greg Langston!" came the collective shout.

Steve slipped a firm grip on the back of Jake's arm and darted a wary eye in his direction.

"But how would you ever get him to admit something like that?"

Dominick stared into the face of the young woman asking the question. Then he spoke from a distant text. "To the one who shows no mercy, no mercy will be given."

Jake was startled. Did the man know he was paraphrasing the Bible?

"The man who lies to his brothers deserves no brothers," Dominick railed in a booming voice. "Nor wife, nor son."

The room was still. What was he saying?

"This man can be forced to admit that the lying Christians United is behind the bombings because his love for his wife and son is great." Dominick's tone was menacing.

Jake rose suddenly to his feet. "Say exactly what you mean, Dominick!" he commanded sharply. Everyone turned in surprise. No one ever talked to Dominick in that manner.

Dominick was momentarily stunned by Jake's anger. For many awkward moments, he seemed genuinely hurt and unsure how to respond. But slowly he regained his composure and turned a cool, leering eye on Jake.

"What do you think I'm saying, Jake?" he asked.

"Something deranged and threatening!" Jake answered sharply.

"Are you suggesting we would harm this man in some way?" Dominick toyed with Jake.

"No. You are. Prove me wrong, Dominick. I've trusted in you as a good and decent man."

"The good and decent man is the one who brings his brothers into the light of the truth. Who dispels the tired old myths of the ancients, the guilt imposed by lying mortals. Only then will we ascend to the godhood in each of us. Isn't that what you want, Jake? Isn't that why you're here?"

"I'm not here anymore!" Jake shot a warning glance at Steve, then ran from the room.

Reaching the top of the stairs, he heard footsteps behind him. It was Steve. "I'm with you, buddy. This has gone too far. Grab your things, and let's get out of here."

They never stopped on the way out the front door.

After returning to the university, Jake had been too distracted to focus on the needs of his students. As spring break approached, he asked for an additional week, claiming the ill health of his grandfather and his urgent need of Jake's help. He reasoned that it was only a half lie and quickly left Charlottesville. He'd been home nearly a week when the letter from Steve arrived.

In spite of his outrage at the things Dominick had threatened, Jake never believed the man would harm anyone. He and Steve had dismissed Dominick's threats as just more dramatic oratory to wow his adoring fans.

But now the letter. From on top of his mountain, Jake wanted to cast the crumpled paper to the wind, to ignore the warning. But Steve said they were coming. To Deer Creek. That Dominick was afraid they would interfere.

And now he had put his grandfather in danger of a madman's paranoia.

He couldn't delay another moment. He climbed off the rocks and hurried down the trail toward the old Gaddy homeplace at the foot of the mountain. He and his thoughts both raced, *Should I warn Papa? Tell him everything? How do I stop Dominick? I'll call the sheriff after I talk to Papa. He'll watch the house after I leave.*

Once inside the house, he started for his room to gather the things he would take with him. Halfway up the stairs, though, he thought of his sleeping bag at the cabin and decided he would need it. He turned and ran down the stairs and out the back door. He hurried back up the mountain to the little roughhewn shelter with the lopsided tin roof that he and Eli had built fifteen years ago. He had always loved the fairy-tale look of the place. The simple structure had been wedged in between the trees, appearing to have fallen from the sky entangling itself in the limbs. "It's my boy's refuge in a confusing world," Eli had explained to those concerned about Jake spending whole weekends alone at the cabin. "Let him be."

It was almost dark when Jake arrived at the cabin. He took the key from the dogwood tree and unlocked the door. Inside, he removed Eli's lantern from its peg, lit it, and placed it on the desk, looking quickly about the room. Everything was in order. The cane rocker stood in front of the stone fireplace. The twin bed with no headboard stretched under one window. A mahogany dresser displayed the last picture taken of Jake, his sister Joanna, and their parents on its sagging top. A bookcase along one wall was stuffed with volumes on religious sects, psychology, early American history, and biographies of Olympic athletes.

This cabin was the closest he'd come to finding peace in his life, and he hated to leave it. *Where do I go?* he wondered. *Joanna's? I can't drag her into this. I'll try to reach Steve.*

He found the sleeping bag, then quickly sorted through clothes and books for anything else he might need. He was so deep in thought that he didn't hear the three men moving slowly through the trees behind the cabin. He'd just turned to lay an armful of clothes on the desk when the door burst open and two men lunged across the room at him.

Jake reacted instantly. He grabbed the closest thing to him, the old lantern, and swung wildly, bashing the first attacker in the forehead.

The second man went for the tackle, diving at Jake's legs and bringing him hard to the floor. But still Jake fought—until a knife appeared in the hand of the one he'd struck with the lantern. The enraged man slashed at Jake, cutting him deep along the left forearm. He would have struck again, but a third man sprang forward yelling, "Stop!"

"But look what he did to me," the injured man whined, pointing to the purple, splotched lump rising on his head.

"You're not hurt, you moron!" said the third man. "Not as bad as he is." He pointed to the bloody gash on Jake's arm. "Dominick said not to—" The man caught himself, but not before Jake suddenly understood. It was happening just as the letter said it would.

After binding Jake's arms and legs, they wrapped his wound, then searched the cabin. They bagged up all papers, books, tapes, and anything else that might divulge information about Dominick Swain and his cult. They untied Jake's right arm and forced him to write a casual-sounding note to his grandfather, something that would buy them time to get well up the road with their bleeding charge.

The kidnappers were too rushed and careless to bother straightening the room or wiping the blood spilled from Jake's wound off the floor—and too imperceptive to notice signals in his handwritten note. They retied his hands and gagged him with one of his own undershirts. Then they rolled him inside his sleeping bag, secured it with wide leather straps, and hauled him and his belongings down the mountain.

Just before they reached the waiting van parked in a thicket of wild shrubs off the road, a car approached. They dropped to the ground with their wriggling bundle to escape the oncoming headlights and watched as an old white Chevrolet with red clay stains slowly passed.

CHAPTER 9

It was a radiant Sunday afternoon in Georgetown. Bright sunlight and a crisp March breeze off the Potomac drew people outdoors, and the sidewalks were full. Light traffic moved slowly along the shady streets lined on both sides with handsome Colonial homes. Senator Linc Ramsdale's three-story home stood tall on one corner. It was narrow across the front but ran deep along the side street. A latticework breezeway connected the stately house to a side-entrance garage behind it.

A shiny, black sports car with the top down and music blaring turned the corner in front of the Ramsdale home and pulled into the driveway behind the house. The teenage driver put his arm around the girl next to him and kissed her while waiting for the garage door to open, then he drove inside and parked next to a dark green Explorer. When he got out, the boy glanced into the street at the cars driving past the house.

"I get so tired of people driving by and gawking at our house," he complained to the girl.

"Well, you'd better get used to it. If your dad's going to run for president, they'll be lined up."

"Yeah, well, I still hate it. There was an old Grand Prix that must have driven past here ten times yesterday while I was waxing my car. It gives me the creeps."

"Who was driving it?" the girl asked.

"Couldn't tell. The windows were tinted just like Dad's Explorer.

Hey, maybe its another politico coming to check on the competition."

The garage door closed just as a blue Grand Prix turned the corner and parked down the street.

By dusk the neighborhood had grown quiet. Lights glowed from inside the homes, and few cars passed the Ramsdale house. The Grand Prix remained parked nearly a block away. The driver sipped coffee and watched.

At eight o'clock, the Ramsdales' garage door opened. When the Explorer backed out, the Grand Prix came to life and followed it down the street, through town to New York Avenue and Highway 50.

An hour later, the Explorer pulled up to the wooden gate at the river cabin. Soon after, the Grand Prix parked in the woods across the road.

"Dominick, I want to know what's going on," Ramsdale demanded as he entered the cabin.

Dominick leaned forward in his overstuffed chair near the door to the cabin.

"Why haven't you contacted me?" Ramsdale continued. "It's been three weeks since I heard from you last."

"Relax, Linc," Dominick said soothingly. "Don't be anxious. I've just had some family matters to tend to. A few wayward sheep to round up."

"What do you mean?"

"Just a few kids I had to persuade to keep their mouths shut. That's all. Absolutely nothing to worry about."

Ramsdale nervously paced about the cold, musty room while Dominick sat calmly with his hands folded in his lap. "I don't like having to track you down," Ramsdale scolded. "Why do you have to be so irritatingly independent? You need me, remember? So act like it."

Dominick's face spread into a patronizing smile that infuriated Ramsdale.

"Stop grinning at me like that! And where's Cort?"

With a heavy sigh, Dominick said, "Linc, why don't you sit down?" Ramsdale eyed him coldly.

"Please, Linc. You're not looking much like presidential material right now."

"I want to know where Cort is, and I'll sit when I'm good and ready."

Dominick threw up his hands as if dealing with an unruly child. "He'll be here any minute, Linc. Try to compose yourself before he arrives. His temper's a lot worse than yours."

"That's what worries me. What if he loses it with the Langstons? I swear, Dominick, I don't want those people hurt!"

Headlights blazed across the yard, and both men turned to watch them approach the cabin. Ramsdale's aide, standing guard on the porch, approached the car with a drawn pistol.

Dominick threw open the front door of the cabin and called to the aide, "It's okay. He's the one we're expecting."

Cort Peterson swaggered through the door to the cabin, and Ramsdale braced himself. "Hello, big shot," Cort said to Ramsdale and dropped into a chair at the table.

"Always a pleasure to see you, Cort." Ramsdale bristled and remained standing. "Killed any small children lately?"

"None that you would care about."

"Stop it!" ordered Dominick. "We have work to do."

"Can't stand it that I took your woman, can you, Linc?" Peterson said, ignoring Dominick.

"You raped her!" Ramsdale snarled. "I sent you to find her and the child, and you raped her!"

"You would prefer it was rape and not consent, wouldn't you, Linc? Did you really think she would have no other man after you?"

Ramsdale looked broken. "I only wanted to know that she and the child were cared for. And you took advantage of her!"

"Oh, so, it's not rape then. I just took advantage of her, is that right?"

Ramsdale wouldn't look at Peterson.

"Well, you must not have been too concerned," Peterson persisted. "You dropped her flat. Because you were a big shot, and you couldn't let your voters find out you had an illegitimate son somewhere."

Dominick caught Ramsdale's arm before he could land the punch to Peterson's jaw. "Mr. President," Dominick hissed sarcastically, "better get hold of yourself before you do something you'll regret." He jerked harder on Ramsdale's arm.

Ramsdale broke free of Dominick's grip and, avoiding Peterson's sneer, said, "Let's get on with this Langston thing. I want to know every last detail of the operation."

An hour later, Ramsdale and his aide left Dominick and Peterson at the cabin and returned to Georgetown.

"Where's Gaddy?" Peterson demanded once Ramsdale was gone.

"We have him. He's en route to the farm. Don't worry."

"What about the other one?"

"Steve?" Dominick hesitated.

"Found him yet?" Peterson asked.

"No, but I'm not worried about him. He's afraid of me. Besides he's very weak."

"And the girl?"

"We have her, too," Dominick answered wearily. "At an old mine in Colorado. Now, did you get the timers?"

"Yeah, this afternoon. UPS, can you believe it? Packed in a carton of cheeses and smoked sausage."

"How long will you give yourself?"

"Twenty minutes. I should just be pulling onto I-85 in downtown Atlanta when it blows."

"And Chicago?"

"I'll have a man there at the same time. They'll blow together. Then you can make your little phone calls to the newspapers." Peterson settled back contentedly in his chair. "What will you say?"

Dominick took a long breath as if preparing for a dramatic oratory. "That the Soldiers of the Cross have openly declared war on evil in this nation. That we were proud to destroy the casino and now the two abortion clinics. That more attacks will follow if such clinics are allowed to continue their murderous operations. So on and so forth."

"And the house of Wellon will come tumbling down."

Dominick smacked his lips. "The nation will be outraged at the barbaric Christians. President Wellon, the darling of the Christian political machine, will be branded a murderer, and his re-election campaign will fall into ruins. Then Linc will march right over him at the polls next year."

"How do you expect the Christians to react?" Peterson asked.

"Oh, they'll fiercely deny any complicity in the bombings. They'll be horrified at the tragedies and sputtering their grief, trying hard to convince the nation they had nothing to do with them. But who will believe them?"

"No one."

"Members of their ranks have already been proven guilty in courts of law for savage attacks on abortion clinics. And we're even going to make the almighty Greg Langston publicly condemn his own Christian brothers and sisters for such attacks."

"Just days before two more clinics blow! BOOM! Wellon will have to flee the country," Peterson predicted with amusement.

Dominick settled back in his chair and folded his arms behind his head. "But I'm a little concerned about Linc."

"Don't worry. He'd have to have a conscience to react. No threat there." Then Peterson frowned. "You're not thinking of telling him about the clinics, are you?"

"Of course not. He's about to have a breakdown over the casino and Langston. No, he'll find out like everyone else in the country. But I'm still concerned. He's showing weakness, almost panic."

"Will he suspect the clinics were our doing?"

"Right on the heels of Langston's, uh, confession? Yeah, the thought will definitely hit him. I need to be around when that happens just to make sure he doesn't do anything stupid."

"Can't stick around too long, Dominick. They're flying in for us that night. We'll have to get out of the country fast."

"There'll be plenty of time to escape," Dominick assured him.

"And when everything settles down," Peterson droned, "you can make your triumphant return and take your throne as exalted spiritual leader of the White House, while I continue to live on the run."

"Would you prefer a home in the suburbs with a poodle and kids?" Dominick chuckled. "Face it, Cort, you love being the hunted. It tests your wits and lets you live in those dark burrows of the world that always fascinated you."

Peterson stretched langorously as if basking in Dominick's appraisal of him.

"Even in Cairo, when you and Linc and I lived at the commune," Dominick continued, "you weren't satisfied with our search for spiritual light in the desert. You were drawn to the bowels of the city where you kept your perverse little secrets."

Peterson gazed about the dimly lit cabin and said, "Now, you have joined me."

As the two remaining cars at the cabin pulled away from the gate and sped down the dark road, headlights came on deep in the woods.

When Dominick and Cort reached Washington, they headed in different directions. Only then did Dominick notice the car in his rearview mirror. As it followed him into a turn, he glanced to see it clearly illuminated by the overhead street lights. An old, blue Grand Prix. There was something familiar about it. He tried hard to remember where he'd seen it before.

It followed him to the hotel. When he turned into the driveway, he stopped and watched the car continue down the street.

Whose car is that?

CHAPTER 10

The early morning traffic on Brickell Avenue swept Joanna along with it. Mondays always held a strange expectancy that something was about to unfold.

She laughed to herself as she approached "the building that could," remembering Shake's pantomime. *Yes, it's strange,* she thought. *But so is Shake.*

On the ninth floor, she breezed into the polished chrome and glass offices of Torrence-Jacobs Advertising and Public Relations firm. "How was the weekend, Joanna?" asked Paula Rodriguez, the motherly receptionist who'd taken a personal interest in the young and single account executive. "I hope you weren't out in your boat during that big blow we had yesterday."

"Just missed it," Joanna replied absentmindedly as she sorted through her messages. "But I did go back and spend the night on *The Abbey.* It was calm after the storm."

"What about that swank party on Star Island you were invited to Saturday night?" Paula inquired.

Joanna grimaced. "Same old let-me-impress-you circuit riders. They must spend their lives roaming from party to party. Just empty stuff. I left early. Has Harvey Weinstein at The Claremont called yet?"

"You didn't take a date?"

"Paula, can we cut to Weinstein here? And no, no date. Nobody to choose from, you know that?"

"You're just too particular, Joanna. You should go out with that guy from Channel Eight. He adores you."

"He adores himself. Now, what about Weinstein?"

"Haven't heard from him. But that Landers guy from Nova Men's Stores has called twice. Wants to see copy for the new radio spots. I said you'd call as soon as you got in. He was real pushy."

"Always is. I'll have to force myself over there this morning. If Weinstein calls, find me. I can't go any further with his ads until I know who's headlining in the Beaumont Room next month. Thanks, Paula."

Joanna passed the glassed-in offices lining the hallway to her own. People waved to her from phones, keyboards, and drawing boards. Torrence-Jacobs was a small agency on the rise, with new offices, an increasing number of lucrative accounts and an expanding staff. A senior copywriter promoted to account executive, Joanna now managed five accounts—a hotel on Miami Beach, a men's clothing chain, a car dealership, a mortgage company, and a plumbing fixtures distributorship. She thrived on the manic pace of her work, nurtured by the momentum.

She opened the door to her office and switched on the lights. It was like no other office at the agency. Her desk was a coarse-grained oak table from her grandfather's attic. The chair was an Early American wingback she'd set on casters. A braided rug on the floor spread its autumn colors—something Miami never saw—around the room. It had been a going-away gift from neighbors in Deer Creek, to remind her of the colors of home.

Her condo wasn't furnished that way. Her lifestyle wasn't Deer Creek. But she was vulnerable here, where hard-edged tactics and threatening competition could erode one's confidence and control. For that reason, she sought comfort and balance from the familial retreat she'd fashioned inside this room, stopping just short of admitting that she longed for something she'd left behind in that simple little place in the mountains.

She had just dropped her briefcase on the desk when Jason Landers called for the broadcast copy she'd promised. Pete had worked late Friday night to finish it. She pulled it from the file, slipped it inside a leather presentation binder and headed for the lobby.

"Paula, I need to discuss this copy with Landers face to face. He's not going to like the style, and I'll have to convince him he really does. Back in a couple of hours."

She was climbing into the Jeep when her mobile phone rang.

"This is Joanna Gaddy," she answered.

It was Paula. "Joanna, your grandfather just called for you. He says it's urgent that you call him."

Fear suddenly tightened her throat, and she swallowed hard before answering, "I'll call from here. Thanks."

Joanna hastily dialed the number to the old house in Deer Creek. Eli answered on the first ring. "Joanna?"

"Papa, what's the matter?"

"Joanna, I need you to come home right away. Tonight." His voice was shaking.

"What's wrong, Papa?"

"Something's happened to Jake."

Joanna caught her breath.

"He's been kidnapped!" Eli blurted.

"Been what?!"

"He didn't come home from the cabin last night," Eli explained, "and Martin and I went to see about him. There was blood on the floor, and this crazy letter about Marian Farley was—"

"Marian Farley? Papa, this isn't making sense. Slow down and start again."

Eli struggled to piece the story together. But only when he read the letter Jake left behind, did Joanna finally hear her brother's call for help.

CHAPTER 11

A careless wind hurled the cold into Eli's weathered face as he climbed the steep trail to the cabin. He'd just called Joanna to come home.

He stopped and leaned heavily against a tree, straining to hear above the raspy heaving in his chest. At seventy-nine, he struggled to maintain the gritty strength of earlier years, but diabetes had claimed his health and weakened his sight. Still, he labored on to that spot where surely Jake would return.

"Papa, I want a place just for me," Jake had said. "Up here on the mountain where no one's watching."

From the day Jake and Joanna had arrived in Deer Creek, people had watched. Here, where families were rooted as deep as the forests, brother watched over brother. When death came to one clan, it came to them all. And so it did when the news reached Deer Creek that the only child of Jefferson Eli Gaddy and Abigail Blythe Gaddy had been killed with his wife in a boating accident off Miami. The whole community grieved over the tragedy as Eli and Abigail left to retrieve their grandchildren from the midst of the horror. Jake was seven, and Joanna ten when their grandparents brought them from Miami to the old Gaddy homeplace at the foot of the mountain.

Both children were helpless to understand the tragedy. Joanna grieved openly at first, accepting the sudden rush of comfort from others. But all too quickly she threw up an impenetrable wall around her grief, letting no one touch where it hurt, camouflaging her wounds with an aggressive air of self-sufficiency.

But Jake wanted answers. His was a searching grief. Had God done this? Had he not been a good boy? Was it his fault? Eli and Abigail bathed the children in the Word of their Christian faith, praying that God would answer Jake's questions and soften Joanna's heart. But the children resisted. "He's not a God of love," Joanna declared angrily. "How could He be and do what He did to Mom and Dad?"

"Maybe He's not anything at all," Jake added hopelessly.

As Eli approached the cabin, visions of Jake swept before him. The sleek build of the runner, the short tousled curls of auburn hair dipping over his forehead, the questioning innocence in his wide-open brown eyes, and the broad toothy smile that always welcomed Eli to the cabin.

It was Jake in the doorway, waving Eli inside to the billowing warmth of the fireplace. It was Jake, skinning a rabbit or cleaning fish for the supper he would prepare for his grandfather.

It was Jake's music Eli seemed to hear now as the visions passed away. Strains of Debussy, Ravel, and Benjamin Britten's *Four Sea Interludes* spilled through the woods and splashed in the winds, only to evaporate once Eli stepped inside the cabin. There he saw it all again—the sheriff's men and their dogs pawing through Jake's clothes, and searchlights slashing the night.

Eli looked down at the rough pine floor still stained with blood. The antique lantern found on the floor with one of its glass panes crushed had been rehung on the peg near the door. The old man moved slowly toward the sagging dresser. He reached for the framed picture on top and clutched it tightly, remembering what had happened the night before.

Eli had returned from church about seven o'clock expecting to find Jake home from the cabin. He'd spent the weekend there with his books and music.

The old man entered the house calling Jake's name and singing the last refrain of a hymn sung in church: "Amazing love, how can it be, that thou, my God, shouldst die for me." It had been one of his Abby's favorite hymns and was sung at her funeral just four years earlier.

When Jake didn't answer, Eli climbed the creaking stairs to the second floor of the house where he was born. "And he says I'm going deaf," the old man muttered.

"Jake, where are you?" He would repeat the question many times in the coming days.

Eli found Jake's room the way he left it on Saturday morning. Eli opened the window and called toward the barn. No answer. He noticed Jake's Ford pickup truck still in the yard and recalled the conversation they'd just had about it.

"You spend more time under the hood of that old thing than behind the wheel," Eli teased. "Why don't you take some of your stock-pile of money and buy a new one, at least one built in the last decade."

"Now, you're one to talk," Jake shot back with a grin. "I wasn't even born when that thing you drive was glued together."

"Glued. . . I don't think so. That's a Chevy," Eli declared. "Tough as I am. Me and that car will outlast you all." Actually, Eli was pleased to see his grandson take little or no interest in material things. Jake had used his inheritance to pay for graduate school and little else.

Hurrying down the stairs, Eli searched the kitchen for signs of use. The dishes were still stacked neatly in the drying rack. No crumbs on the counter tops. Even the Oreo bag was closed. Jake always left it open. "Jake, you know those things go stale and all that good stuff in the middle dries out," Eli would complain. "I hate that."

Eli was beginning to wish he'd found the bag open. Jake was never this late coming home from the cabin. Then Eli noticed that the letter he'd left for Jake on the kitchen table that morning was missing. It had arrived the day before, addressed to Jake and postmarked in New York. Since Jake rarely received personal mail in Deer Creek, Eli was curious about the letter and intended to ask about it later that evening.

Eli called his closest friend. "Martin? Eli. I need your night eyes, buddy. Can you meet me at the house right away? Jake's not home from the cabin, and I need to get up there."

"Be there in two shakes," Eli's old friend replied.

Martin Tansley had always been there. The two men had been as close as brothers since Miss Livermore's first grade and would almost pass for twins, even in their seventies. Both were just over six feet and full-statured. Not round and blubbery, just solid. Both men sported a full thatch of hair, though Martin's hadn't bleached with age like Eli's. "I swear you dye that stuff," Eli loved to tease.

"You old fool. You just can't stand it because I'm better looking than you are," was Martin's usual reply. He was the king of asphalt in those parts until selling his trucks and equipment to a son-in-law a few years earlier. He had paved over as much of Boulder County as was absolutely necessary and not a square yard more. He had provided driveways for homes and parking lots for shopping centers, churches, schools, and hospitals. And that was enough, he'd determined.

When an investor from another state wanted to uproot a patch of woods near town to build a tri-county theater complex, he asked Martin to do the paving. Martin refused, saying, "Now, Mister, we like our old trees a far sight better than the prospect of our young people watching raunchy sex scenes and violence on the big screens you want to bring in here." The investor hired an asphalt contractor from another county and built the theaters anyway. Martin retired a couple of years later.

The high beam from Martin's spotlight streaked ahead of the two men as they trudged up the twisting path.

"I don't know why he has to spend so much time up in that old shack," Martin grumbled. "He should be at home with you. You're old."

"I'm younger than you!" Eli snapped. "Smarter, too. I'd have known that was soap powder I was baking with and not flour. I swear, Martin, that was the most tomfool thing I ever saw anybody do."

"That was evil, what you did. Putting that stuff in my flour can. The whole congregation could have wound up in the hospital over that stupid little trick."

"Maybe you won't be bragging so hard now about how you can bake up Josie's recipes better than she could, God rest her soul. And her not here to defend herself. I did it for your dear wife."

"Yeah, yeah. It was still evil, and I still say Jake should spend more time with you."

"Look, Martin. You know how troubled he was when he got home last week. I still don't know what's the matter with him. He just won't talk to me like he used to."

"Well, he doesn't need to be brooding all alone up on this mountain. And I'm still disturbed about those people I saw him with that time in Asheville—I told you how he pretended not to see me. How can you not see a bright yellow truck as big as all outdoors with someone who looks like me leaning out the window hollering at you? I was blocking the whole intersection, and not a soul in that car even looked my way. It was weird."

"He told me they were just old friends from college," Eli explained, pausing to catch his breath. "That he'd run into them while he was visiting that girl he used to go with. You remember Carol. . .uh. . .Italian kind of name. . .uh. . .Gramelli, I think. He even brought her home with him once."

"Yeah, I remember her. Real cute. Going to be a doctor, wasn't she?"

"A pediatrician. She likes kids. Wants a whole houseful, she told us."

"No wonder Jake quit dating her."

"Now, Martin, that had nothing to do with it. He said she was always at the hospital and didn't have time for him."

"Well, she wasn't in that car. And he sure didn't want to see me."

Eli was mulling over the conversations he'd had with Jake lately when they finally reached the cabin. There was no light inside. No smoke from the chimney.

"Jake!" Eli called. No answer.

The door was closed but not locked, they discovered. Jake always locked it when he left. Eli pushed it open as Martin trained the spotlight inside. Both men gaped at the mess. Jake might leave the Oreo bag open, but his room at the house and the cabin were always in order. Clothes and empty desk drawers were scattered about the room. The old lantern Jake treasured, the one that had hung on the back stoop of the house when Eli was just a boy, was on the floor with one of its panes shattered. As Eli bent to pick it up, he saw something dark spotting the floor. He pulled a finger through it, brought it to the light, and saw blood.

"Dear God!" Eli cried. "What's happened to my boy?"

"Now, just hold on, Eli," Martin said grabbing his friend's arm in support. "Let's look around before we get panicky."

Martin was about to pick up one of the drawers.

"Don't do that!" Eli blurted. "There might be fingerprints."

"Fingerprints!" Martin said incredulously. "Now, Eli, get hold of yourself. There's no crime here. Jake's just taken off and forgotten to tell you. The place is a little messy. But so what? And that blood's got to be from Jake breaking this lantern and cutting himself. That's all."

"But his truck's still at the house. How's he going anywhere without it?" Eli clamped his hand around the back of his neck and shook his head slowly. "Martin, you just don't know the kinds of things he's been saying lately. I don't know what to make of them, myself. Something about somebody with a plan he doesn't like and how he's got to stop them if they go any further. I mean real confusing stuff. He just mentions things offhandedly without explaining them. Like he wants to tell me something then changes his mind."

Just then Eli noticed the bookshelves. "Martin," he whispered, motioning toward the wall near the door. "His books."

Martin stared at the empty shelves, only then realizing that something was very wrong.

"The letter," Eli mumbled.

"What letter?" Martin asked.

"Jake got a letter from somebody in New York yesterday. I left it out for him in the kitchen, and it was gone when I got home from church. That letter has something to do with this; I just know it. We've got to find—" Something caught Eli's eye.

"Give me some light," he demanded rushing across the room toward the dresser. Throwing open his heavy jacket to pull the thick reading glasses from his shirt pocket, he reached for a sheet of paper propped against the wall behind the dresser.

When Martin saw what Eli was about to grab, he warned, "Don't touch it!"

Martin directed the light onto the legal-size sheet of yellow paper as it lay on the dresser, and they both saw Jake's blockish script. Eli read aloud. . .

Papa,

I'm sorry this is such short notice, but I've decided to take a quick trip with some friends who came to see me while you were at church. Ask Marian Farley to help you at the post office this week. I'm sure she won't mind leaving her husband a few hours each day. I'll call as soon as I can and let you know where I am.

By the way, I cut my hand this afternoon on that Buck hunting knife you gave me for Christmas. I'll tend to it. Don't worry. Really stupid of me.

Sorry for the mess and the lantern.

Have to go now. I love you, Papa.

Jake

The two men stared at each other in speechless alarm. Forgetting about the letter from New York, they raced for the door. They hardly spoke during the long, stumbling run down the mountain, stopping only once to force air into their lungs.

Martin reached the back door to the house first and held it open for Eli whose breathing was so labored he could barely climb the steps. Once he could speak, Eli grabbed the kitchen phone and called the Boulder County Sheriff's Office.

"Hello! This is an emergency!" Eli announced into the receiver. "My grandson's been kidnapped! It had to have been within the last few hours and there's blood on the—my name? Eli Gaddy. Yes, the postmaster. My grandson, yes. Jake. Jake Gaddy. What'd you say? He's twenty-seven. Yes. Yes, he's visiting me. Last time I saw him? Saturday morning. What's that? Now we've done just about enough talking on this phone. My boy's gone! You get here quick!"

Flashing blue lights are not a common sight in the tranquil valley town of Deer Creek. So, when two patrol cars cut a strobing blue streak down State Road 94, through the center of town, every phone rang at once. Alarmed residents wanted to know what was happening. A few followed the official cars and watched them turn into the long, graveled drive to the Gaddy home.

They came to a halt before the pale yellow, two-story home with its sweeping front porch and rose trellises at either end. Squinting against the blinding glare of headlights, Eli and Martin burst through the doorway, spilling their story and motioning the officers toward the trail to the cabin. The two men supplied as much information as their breath would allow during the climb. Eli wasn't sure his worn body would make the trip again, but adrenaline pumped him beyond what he could normally endure.

Sheriff's Deputy Bruce Hobbs was the first to enter the cabin, followed by two other officers. He'd been told about the blood, the lantern, the clothes in disarray, and some kind of letter. He and his officers searched for evidence of a crime. He read the letter, then turned to Eli and addressed him with a skeptical air.

"Sir, this letter indicates a willingness to leave with these friends of his. I don't understand your alarm, except for the blood, and there may be a reasonable explanation for that."

Eli drew a steady breath before he spoke. "I understand that you haven't been in this area very long, Deputy Hobbs, and I guess that's why these things Jake has said don't mean much to you. But pay attention to me. Jake told me to ask Marian Farley to fill in for him at the post office this week. He said that her husband wouldn't mind her leaving him a few hours each day." Eli paused to let that information sink in. "Deputy Hobbs, Jake doesn't work at the post office! And Marian Farley's been dead for six years!"

Eli drew in a long breath and kept going. "She was an old girlfriend of his who married another guy. Driving back from their honeymoon, they hit a deer in the road and ran off the side of Signal Mountain. They've been buried side-by-side in Rosewood ever since! Those are signals, Hobbs. And there's another one.

"Jake said he cut himself this afternoon on the hunting knife I gave him for Christmas. I saw him accidentally drop that knife into Lake Tawanee while we were fishing last summer! Now, are you going to do something to find my boy, or do I have to call up the FBI or someone else who knows a crime scene when they see one?!"

A day later, Eli's angry words still rattled about the cabin. He leaned back in the chair at Jake's desk and closed his eyes. Those few hours the night before had struck like a sudden and ferocious thunderstorm, and at once were gone, leaving behind no sweet cleansing, but a terrible haunting.

Eli rubbed his eyes and gazed out the window. He whispered into the chilled air, "Lord, lead me to him."

CHAPTER 12

Old wounds burst open and bled. Now it was happening to Jake, and the familiar pain of loss clawed at Joanna as she raced for the Florida Turnpike. It was just after noon on Monday. Immediately after Eli's call, Joanna took emergency leave from the agency and asked Shake and Pete to look after *The Abbey*.

The rush from Miami was a blur. Though Joanna's first impulse was to fly, she sensed a need for the Jeep and packed it with haste. Speeding north up the turnpike, she saw faces merge with the pavement ahead. Remembering the anguish in Eli's voice on the phone, she could see his kindly old face strained and searching for help. She saw Marian Farley's tragic face, the one that sprang before her when Eli read the letter. Jake had grieved bitterly at Marian's death. The two had talked of marriage at one time, but Jake had resisted too long. "You don't know what you want," she had told him. "I can't wait for you to sort things out, as you say." Jake had loved the girl. Joanna knew he would never have used her name in such a way unless he was desperate to sound an alarm.

"I'm coming, Jake," she whispered.

She had just seen her brother and grandfather the month before. They had visited her in Miami for only the second time. Eight years earlier, when her Grandma Abby was alive, Jake and her grandparents had come to watch her graduate from the University of Miami.

Knowing she wouldn't see Eli and Jake at Christmastime, she had persuaded them to travel to Miami in February, promising that Eli wouldn't suffer from the heat the way he had during the June graduation visit. Their last time together sprang vividly to mind. . .

Joanna had met them at Miami International that afternoon in February just as the rain began to pour for the first time in weeks.

"So this is the sunny south Florida paradise you've been bragging about, huh, girl?" Eli teased as he hugged her tight.

"Now, Papa, give it a chance this time, okay?" Joanna pleaded.

Jake jumped to help her. "Don't forget what they say down here, Papa: If you don't like the weather, just wait a minute. Right, Joanna?" He winked at his big sister as he squeezed her to him and kissed her cheek, tasting salt from the faintest tear. *She tries so hard to be tough,* he thought to himself.

Joanna felt Jake's eyes heavy upon her and briskly steered them toward baggage claim. "You two are going to dine fine tonight!"

"Is that so?" Eli said. "Been taking those cooking classes from, uh, what's her name?"

"Marlene Gold. No, Papa. It's better than that. The teaching chef, herself, is preparing the meal, with the help of a few friends."

"Oh, is that the ship's crew we've heard about?" Jake asked. "Shake somebody, and Pete and—"

"That's somebody Shake," Joanna corrected. "Sid Shake. And Pete and Rachel and Alan. And, of course, Chef Marlene. They couldn't wait to meet you and impress you with how great it is to live in Miami. Tonight's dinner is the kickoff."

"Well, I'm anxious to meet them, too, darlin'," Eli said. "Think I can get a little nap in before we have to leave for dinner?"

"Oh, they're already there, at my apartment. They're cooking in my kitchen. Someone should use it, don't you think?" She poked Jake lightly in the stomach.

"Oh, don't do that," he groaned.

"What's the matter?" she asked.

"Air sickness," Jake answered, cutting his eyes toward Eli and grinning with the assurance that it was a sore subject with his grandfather.

"Oh, no. Did he puke pretty good, Papa?" Joanna giggled.

"Well, it'll be a while before they can use that plane again," Eli grumbled. "It's so embarrassing, and he refuses to take Dramamine. Makes me so mad."

"That stuff knocks me out, Papa," Jake said, laughing at his grand-father's obvious distaste over the whole thing.

"If he could just make it to the bathroom," Eli said, wrinkling his nose. "But nooo. Got to wait 'til he knows for sure it's coming up, then it's too late. And those little paper sacks don't hold enough, you know. It's a terrible thing what he did to that poor woman across the aisle."

Joanna and Jake bent double laughing at their grandfather, who saw nothing funny about it.

"Come on, Papa," Jake said, pulling Eli toward the incoming luggage, now circling in review. "You get your sense of humor back, and I promise to take something before we fly home."

"You sure will, or you won't be sitting next to me."

Jake and Joanna grabbed the luggage and steered Eli to the over-hang outside. The rain was still heavy, but the heady scent of dripping wet tropical air and the poignant reunion with her family made Joanna giddy and exuberant.

"I'll run for the car and bring it around, Jake," she almost sang as she dashed through the rain wishing to remove the umbrella from over-head and let these quenching moments of joy soak into the depleted reservoirs deep inside her.

That evening at Joanna's apartment was one she would never forget. Her two families were together in one room, alive and vital, celebrating nothing but the sheer pleasure of each other's company. Joanna's eyes glistened as she looked from one animated face to another. *No one will hurt them tonight,* she promised herself.

The room was filled with a festivity that had rarely visited Joanna's "outpost," as Jake described her faraway home. The apartment was spa-cious and bright. A vaulted greatroom and adjoining balcony drank in the shimmering lights from Biscayne Bay three stories down. Joanna had selected the watery blues and greens of the tropics for her furnish-ings—unlike the muted earth tones of her country-cottage office. A sectional sofa and two club chairs hovered about an oversized, white marble-top coffee table where samplings from every food group were now spread. An antique secretary and sideboard from Deer Creek bal-anced the breezy room with their dark mahogany formality. The room was eclectic, like the dinner guests gathered there. Two, in particular, were gauging their differences.

"Now, I think it's okay that you've got yourself a ponytail, young fella," Eli said to an amused Shake, who glanced about the room to see if anyone else was listening. Joanna was but wouldn't have dreamed of interrupting. "I mean, George Washington had himself one, and Thomas Jefferson and some of those drug agents you got down here—and no one's ever questioned their manhood. So I think you're doing just fine with that thing down your back."

"Thank you, sir," Shake said, with a tight grin and eyes about to water from the laughter he was struggling to contain.

"Uh, Papa," Jake cut in, having also overheard his grandfather's remarks, "let's go see what else Marlene's cooking up."

"Well, if you don't think we'd be in the way."

"Not at all. You need to spread yourself around, you know. Let everybody hear what you think of them."

Shake couldn't hold it anymore.

"Now you made this young fella laugh, Mr. Smart Aleck," Eli snapped at Jake. "How come I'm not laughing?"

"Aw, now Mr. Gaddy, all young people are smart alecks, you know that."

"Well, you're not, Mr. Shake. I think you're a fine young man, and I've enjoyed talking to you. By the way, is that your real name?"

"Papa! We really do have to go to the kitchen. Now." Jake hustled his grandfather away, turning to mouth "Sorry" to Shake, who grinned and raised his hands in mock surrender.

When the evening was over, the crowd gone, and Eli asleep for the night, brother and sister took a rare opportunity for privacy and slipped out for a taste of the tropical night. They left the five-story condominium building by the back entrance, following a trail of Malibu lights that were strung like hooded pearls along the path to the water's edge.

On a bench overlooking the bay, Joanna and Jake settled into an easy flow of conversation. Theirs had always been a gentle communion nurtured by a fierce devotion to each other. In the aftermath of their parents' deaths, it was the sight of their protective young arms wrapped tightly about each other that had squeezed the heart of the Deer Creek community.

"Those two young'uns got a grip on each other that beats all I ever saw," Mitty McGill had observed. "Together, they're like a lone survivor."

Over the years, though, their grip had slipped. They couldn't see into each other like they once had. "I still miss you, Jake," Joanna said.

"I know," Jake replied softly. "Ever think of moving back? We'd be closer."

It took her awhile to answer. "I have an identity that I like now, Jake. A life of my own design, free of. . ." She paused again.

"Free of what, Joanna?" Jake probed. "What's so bad about life back home?"

"I am home, Jake. For the first time, I have a home of my own, and no one trying to stuff me into their mold."

Jake was quiet.

"After Mom and Dad died, I didn't know who I was anymore. Everything that defined me disappeared except for you, and I know I smothered you. I was so afraid I'd lose you, too."

"Joanna, you don't have to explain—"

"But you don't understand," she interrupted. "I wasn't anyone's favorite daughter anymore. Remember how Dad called me that just to hear me whine that I was his only daughter?"

Jake smiled and nodded slowly.

"Then he'd say, 'But if I had a hundred daughters, you'd still be my favorite.' Then, all of a sudden, I wasn't his daughter at all. In an instant, it was all gone—parents, friends, school, our house. Do you know I drive by the old place sometimes and stare at it from the street as if it were an ancient ruin."

Jake watched her intently as she spoke.

"I think, how dare these people live in our home, defile it with their presence. If I believed that God, whoever He is, was capable of a merciful act, I'd beg Him to let me go inside just once and find us all there again." She took a deep, quivering breath. "That's pathetic, isn't it?"

"Why do you do it?" Jake asked.

"Because it's the only place I belonged. I wasn't a graft in someone else's home."

"Papa and Grandma Abby didn't think of us as grafts, Joanna. They took care of us like their own children."

"But I don't want to be taken care of. I never again want to see looks on faces that say, 'Poor little thing, what a shame about her and her brother. Let's all pitch in and do what we can to help them.' I'll not be pitied, Jake. And I'll not be told by the simple-minded of Deer Creek that God is good, when we both know He isn't."

Jake didn't respond.

After a long silence, Joanna asked, "What are you thinking, Jake?"

"That I can't make you stop hurting, and I wish I could." He paused and glanced at the full moon overhead. "But I can't even help myself. They've got me so confused about who's running this universe that—"

"Who is 'they'?" Joanna cut in.

Jake was suddenly guarded. "Oh, well, no one in particular."

"But you said 'they,' " she persisted.

Jake rallied. "Everyone says 'they,' Joanna. 'They' don't make cars the way 'they' used to. That's the 'they' I mean."

Joanna knew her brother too well to miss the subtle tension beginning to coil inside him. It had always been a challenge to reach the deeper recesses of his thoughts. She could see him beginning to freeze her out.

"How's school?" she diverted quickly.

Jake seemed to welcome the change of subject. "Predictable. Teach class, grade papers, run track, go to bed, and do it all over again."

"You mean you're bored already? You just got the teaching post you've been working so hard for all these years. How could you be bored with it?" Joanna hoped her response hadn't been too shrill.

Jake stretched his legs out before him and laced his fingers behind his head.

That's a good sign, Joanna thought with relief. *Relaxed body language.*

"Do you remember when we used to dig for the periwinkles on the beach?" he asked pensively.

"Yeah, but what's that got to do with—"

"Everything," Jake answered quickly. "We wanted to catch those things real bad. To pry open the little shells and discover what was inside, but they were hard to get hold of. They clawed their way straight down through the sand with a speed you couldn't match with your finger."

"Oh, yeah." Joanna smiled and nodded, remembering her own frustrating efforts.

"But you kept trying," Jake continued, "shoving your finger inside one bubbling little hole after another, until one time you'd get lucky.

You'd get all excited and pop open the shell and find the same stupid little piece of slime that's in all of them. Never anything different or better. So why bother?"

Joanna looked blank. "Are we comparing your job to periwinkles?" she asked bluntly.

"Jobs, philosophies, gods," Jake answered.

"Gods? Jake, have pity on a lesser intelligence and say something I can understand."

Jake laughed and closed the door on the whole matter. "What do you say we go swimming in that big deserted pool?"

"We're not finished with this," Joanna said with authority.

"Oh, yes, we are," Jake countered. He grabbed her around the waist, pulled her off the bench, slung her over his shoulder and raced toward the pool in a swarm of girlish screams. When they hit the water, the conversation was over. The uproar drew angry shouts from awakened residents glaring down at them from overhead balconies. From the third floor came a voice that broke through it all.

"Wait for me!"

Moments later, Eli lumbered out of the building, and in a great, drooping swath of lime green swim trunks, cannonballed into the deep end.

Periwinkles. Driving hard toward Central Florida, Joanna tried to remember Jake's analogy, but the pool scene kept getting in the way. Her memory swept over the conversation by the bay that night, sucking up bits of dialogue that might point in some direction: "Periwinkles. . .gods. . .they've got me so confused."

After sifting through all the fragments of their conversation, only one word remained to pursue.

They.

CHAPTER 13

After driving north all night, Jake's captors pulled off the road early Monday morning and woke him. They forced him to eat an egg and bacon biscuit from a fast-food restaurant on the highway and changed the bandage on his arm. They had stopped at a convenience store for gauze, hydrogen peroxide, and antibacterial ointment. But the wound continued to seep blood.

Jake squirmed against the straps holding him to his seat in the old van and tried to see where he was. But mini-blinds covered all but the front side windows. In the light of day, he studied the three men who had attacked him. He didn't recognize any of them from Dominick's cult, and their mountain accents made him think they were local contacts Dominick had hired for the job.

"Where are you taking me?" he asked them but got no reply.

"What did Dominick tell you to do with me?" he tried again but still no response. The men spoke only occasionally to each other and completely ignored everything about their victim but his wound.

He could only see through the front windshield and watched for road signs that would tell him where he was. Soon he saw a sign that read "Baltimore—68 miles."

His arm was throbbing, and his body ached for more sleep, but he needed to be alert for anything they said to each other, anything that would reveal what Dominick's plans were. Steve's letter had said that Langston was no longer the target, but who was? Jake needed to know. He also needed to plan some kind of strategy for dealing with Dominick.

Jake finally decided that to escape, he would have to win Dominick's trust, to convince him that he had experienced a change of heart and was about to return to the family when these three jerks grabbed him. He would begin his charade now.

"I can't believe Dominick sent you to get me. All he had to do was ask, and I would have come on my own." He waited for a response, but his kidnappers continued to ignore him.

"I mean, Dominick and I are buddies. Did he ever tell you about our trip to New York?" Jake was quite certain these were not personal friends of Dominick's and doubted they had any spiritual leanings one way or another. But it was clear they were becoming irritated with him.

He preached his steadfast belief in all Dominick's teachings, using every metaphysical reference he could think of. He knew they would report everything he'd said to Dominick.

"You know, Dominick taught me this wonderful oneness with the powers of the cosmos. I bet you have it, too, don't you?" The looks he was getting were becoming more severe.

"In fact," he continued, "I'd like to hear each of you share about your spiritual journeys. Come on now. Don't be shy."

That did it. He finally got a response.

"Shut up, you idiot!" The man in the front passenger seat, who appeared to be the leader, had apparently heard enough.

Jake gave a fine performance. The rangy zealot tied up in the backseat had finally worn down his captors. By the time the van reached Baltimore, they decided Jake was either sincere or insane. After all the efforts to haul him in, he seemed harmless to them, and tongues were loosed.

"You know where to leave 95?" the leader asked the driver.

"Yeah, I know," the driver responded. "You want to go by the house first or the river?"

"House. She'll be at work by now."

Jake didn't understand.

The van exited I-95 northeast of Baltimore. Jake asked where they were headed. No one answered. The blinds in the back of the van remained closed. While searching the road ahead for clues to their destination, he continued his tiring soliloquy on the joys of self-realization and astral exploration.

"Will you shut your mouth?" shouted the driver. "I've heard all I'm going to hear from you!"

Jake obeyed and continued to listen.

After thirty minutes of rural, two-lane roads, the van turned onto a country lane that sprouted from the paved highway and crooked its way into the woods.

"What's back here?" Jake asked.

"Don't you already know?" the leader asked in a sly tone.

"No, I don't."

"It's the Langston place."

Jake swallowed hard, trying not to react. The target hadn't changed, after all. Steve's informant was wrong. Now they had closed in on this man's home. Jake struggled to appear passive. But inside, he wrestled with guilt over not warning Greg Langston. In spite of Dominick's bitter railing against the man, Jake never believed he would harm anyone.

"There!" said the leader, pointing out the right window. "On the other side of that pond."

Jake spun in his seat but could see nothing through the blinds. He didn't see the tall, cedar-sided house with the glassy tower on top, remote and private. He didn't see the trails through the woods where, observed by Dominick's people, Roxanne Langston and her son walked each afternoon before Dr. Langston's return from the college.

The target of Dominick's aggression was little known to Jake until his return from the weekend at the Connecticut farm. Before leaving for spring break, he'd visited the university library and searched the files for Dr. Greg Langston. The references were plentiful. His work in family counseling and his books were admirable accomplishments. But it was Langston, the man, that had sparked Jake's interest.

As several articles reported, Langston shunned television and rarely granted interviews. He acknowledged his need for solitude, for the house in the woods he'd built for his family, for "time to walk privately with Christ." It wasn't the image Jake had drawn of the man whose name Dominick had shouted. He'd pictured a face framed by television cameras, powdered and poised for his audience's adoration. He'd envisioned a man readily accessible to the media, groomed to promote himself and God—a man whose thunderous voice would proclaim glory to God forever and ever, amen.

That wasn't this man. This was a quiet man whose fame had taken him by surprise. Did Dominick really know him? Jake wondered.

"There she is!" The driver spotted Roxanne Langston walking toward the road. "Thought you said she wouldn't be home."

"She's supposed to be at that school. Just don't panic. Drive on by like we belong here. Try not to make eye contact."

Jake could only see straight ahead through the front window, and that's exactly where Roxanne Langston was, by the edge of the road getting a newspaper from the box. As the van approached, she turned, and with a bright smile waved as if welcoming them all to her home. Her image froze in Jake's mind. Small frame, curly blond hair, nice features—smiling at the ones who would return and kidnap her and her son. As if sensing Jake's urge to scream a warning through the closed blinds, the third captor sprang to the back of the van, and clamped a hand over Jake's mouth. "Just in case you get any silly notions," he said with a smirk.

They were well past the Langston driveway before the hand left Jake's mouth. But the smiling face of Roxanne Langston wouldn't go away. It hung suspended before him, haunting the one who knew and said nothing. *But I didn't think he'd really do it,* he pleaded for the face to understand.

Afraid of blowing his guise as the reconverted Dominick loyal, Jake slumped in his seat and pretended to sleep. He actually did for nearly an hour until something woke him. A large map was unfolded and spread out over the dashboard. Low, monotone voices were engaged in a hushed conversation in the front of the van. Jake didn't stir. He listened. The two men in front were debating the shortest route to some destination in the area. Jake didn't want to chance stealing a glance at passing road signs. He must feign a deep sleep and continue listening.

Only a few phrases reached the back of the van: "Susquehanna River. . .houseboat. . .near 95 bridge."

Jake continued his sleep watch. Moments later, he heard something else: "To guarantee old Jake's cooperation, Dominick wants the grandfather."

Papa? Jake's whole body jerked. He masked the sudden movement with an exaggerated yawn and a mere shift in position. But inside him, a fire had been lit. He knew he had to escape now. *Have to warn Papa. And Langston.*

By late afternoon, the old van pulled into the yard of the farmhouse in Connecticut. Jake was surprised to see two stretch vans and an assortment of cars parked to one side. Inside, the house was full of young people. Many were followers he recognized, but others were new to him. He was taken to an upstairs bedroom and tied to a bed post.

Dominick arrived from Washington a few hours later. He hurried to see Jake apparently after hearing the three men's report on the kidnapping and trip from North Carolina.

"So, you're ready to declare a truce, is that it, Jake?"

Jake knew he had to convince Dominick he'd seen the light and was ready to comply with Dominick's wishes for there to be any hope of escape. "I thought I would be better off on my own, but I was wrong. I was ready to come back anyway, Dominick."

"Is that so?" Dominick studied Jake cautiously.

"You'll see, Dominick. Turn me loose, and I'll show you how useful I can be."

"Not so fast, young man. This will take time." Dominick reached for Jake's left arm. "Now, let me see this cut."

Dominick treated and closed the wound using sterile strips of tape and started Jake on antibiotics from his personal supply. "You'll heal quickly, Jake. Now, go to sleep. We'll talk more tomorrow."

Before closing the bedroom door, Dominick turned back to Jake and added, "Oh, by the way. I understand you caught a glimpse of Mrs. Langston today."

Jake nodded slightly.

"Lovely, isn't she?" Dominick beamed. "So sad."

CHAPTER 14

Joanna had never liked to drive at night, even to the store for milk. It made her feel strangely uprooted and lonely. She would pass homes where the lights were on, and those inside were safe with the ones they loved. This particular night she felt more alone than ever. Jake was gone. And it seemed the dark might swallow her up, too.

She'd been driving for ten hours, and the oncoming headlights were beginning to blur. *Why did I have to move so far away?* But she knew the answer very well. To escape.

Enrolling at the University of Miami after high school in Deer Creek had been her greatest triumph. Against a tide of objections from Eli, she had persisted and won. She would leave the confining lifestyle of her grandfather's home and church. She would shape her own life.

Now she remembered the conversation with her grandfather as she packed for the move to Florida so many years ago.

"Joanna, you've changed so much in the last few years. You've always been headstrong, but you've never been this rebellious."

"If I don't leave, I'll choke."

"What a thing to say."

"Papa, I've tried my best to make you understand, but you just won't. All you know is Deer Creek and that Bible.

"You change your tone of voice, young lady."

"I don't mean to be disrespectful, Papa, but you don't know what's out in the world, and I want desperately to find out. I'm afraid that Jesus Christ, and what everyone around here believes about Him is just

a. . .a regional thing. You know, the Bible Belt mentality."

"Joanna!"

"It's true, Papa. Not everyone believes like you do. I need to know what else is out there, that's all."

"Are you questioning your parents' faith?" he asked.

"They never said much about what they believed. They just took us to church on Sundays and made us say our prayers at night. I was never sure anyone but them was listening. And I'm not sure now, in spite of what Reverend Willingham says."

"It's not what Luke Willingham says, Joanna. It's what God says in His Word. And His Word is the Bible."

"Well, I'm not so sure of that," Joanna said. "If you think hard enough and sing loud enough about anything, you can make it come true in your mind. Then it's easy to believe."

"You and Jake. You're both looking for the same thing, and it's right here under your nose."

Eli's words returned to her as she sped through Georgia. *Under my nose, indeed,* Joanna thought. *Poor Papa. All he knows is what's under his nose.*

Just south of Atlanta, Joanna pulled into a Holiday Inn. It was almost one in the morning. Asking for a wake-up call at six, she fell asleep and dreamed of two little children on a beach riding the breakers on matching rafts, eating hot-dogs-on-a-stick with mustard oozing between their fingers, and chasing periwinkles in the sand.

Tuesday morning, north of Atlanta, Joanna noticed the highway ahead had arched its back and twisted itself into the folds of the foothills. Rounding a turn a little while later, she gasped at the first sight of soaring peaks. Something stirred inside, a wavering conflict of emotions she couldn't deny. As much as she'd distanced herself from them, at her core she was drawn to the quiet dignity of the mountains and the people who lived there.

Three more hours and she was gearing down through the steep passes of the Blue Ridge. Four miles from Deer Creek was the turnoff to Rosewood Memorial Gardens. Here, she left the highway and turned in through the arched gateway.

She parked beside a cluster of granite monuments surrounded by a low wrought-iron fence and got out. A chilled wind gripped her, and she shivered as she climbed over the fence and stood before the Gaddy name solemnly repeated throughout the small yard. She passed great-grandparents, aunts, uncles, and a cousin who'd drowned in the rapids of the Chattooga River. She paused before a handsome monument with a rose cut in relief against the smooth stone. It was her Grandma Abby, the shy, gentle, small-framed woman who'd nurtured Joanna through adolescence and into womanhood, then died swiftly of a marauding cancer just four years ago. She pictured her grandmother at the piano in the parlor, singing the hymns Joanna had only pretended to understand.

Joanna walked slowly to the end of another row and stopped. She stared into the grass blanketing her parents' remains, then knelt before the two graves.

"There was nothing I could do to help you," she whispered. "You were gone before I knew. But I'm going to bring Jake back." A cluster of leaves blew against her legs and clung with a gentle embrace. "I promise."

After a few minutes, Joanna rose and walked toward the Jeep, stopping once to look back in hopes of a fleeting vision, a silent nod from a long-ago face.

Leaving the cemetery, she tensed behind the wheel as she began her final approach to Deer Creek. She passed the new high school she'd never attended. It had been under construction when she graduated from the old Boulder County high school, but Jake completed all four years in the new school. He had shone in those years, pushing himself to perform. But unlike Joanna, whose drive to achieve was tethered to her need for independence and self-sufficiency, Jake needed only to silence the howling void inside him. By the time he had left for college, he was no closer to filling the void than he'd ever been.

Joanna pulled into the Exxon at the first traffic light in Deer Creek. Jim Hornsby came up behind her, noting the Dade County tag.

"Long way from home, ma'am. Can I help you?" He stared for a moment and before Joanna could reply, he blurted, "Joanna Gaddy! Is that you, girl? Well, bless Pat, it is."

"How are you doing, Mr. Hornsby?" she asked politely.

"Oh, honey, we're all so worried about your brother. Your poor grandfather is just beside himself."

"I know. That's why I'm here."

"What a drive for a young girl like you to make all by yourself. Does Eli know you're here?"

"He's expecting me."

"Well, you'll just have to come out to the house and see how Bradford's grown up. He'll be tickled to death to see you. Now let me pump some gas for you and check everything out. This is a right nice piece of machinery, Joanna."

Bradford Hornsby was the first boy Joanna had kissed, and she'd sworn it would be the last. He was a big, slobbery mama's boy, and she wasn't interested in an update, especially if he was thirty years old and still home with his mama.

"Your car's ready to kick, Joanna," Hornsby declared at last. "Now you call me and Bradford if there's anything we can do to help you. Anything at all, you hear?"

"Thanks so much, Mr. Hornsby. I'll do that."

As Joanna drove through town, she peered anxiously at the familiar homes, storefronts, and parks. She lowered the window, and the damp vapors of the Nantahala River engulfed her with dizzying recollections of times gone by—rafting parties, camping trips, and Saturday hikes along the river's banks with Jake.

Joanna only glanced at the aging, brick Baptist church on the town square, its rising steps and white columns drawn into deep shadows. How many times she had climbed to its doorway and disappeared into its reverent chambers. How many times she had fidgeted through the sermons, the singing, the confusion in her mind. Though she sensed a peculiar peace about the old place, she had no desire to return.

When she reached the apple orchards two miles out of Deer Creek, her spirits rose. Papa was near. The old homeplace she'd visited in the summers when her parents were alive, then returned to with a mournful permanence after they'd gone, was just ahead.

She had attached a personality to the old house. It had always welcomed her and Jake with huge, open rooms filled with old rugs loomed in local mills, with family photographs in antique frames, and with gracefully carved mahogany and oak furniture. The smell of coffee and homemade biscuits had always refreshed the air each morning with a reassurance that all was well. Looking out through the wavy glass windows at summer-green lawns bedded with roses, hydrangeas, and phlox, who would have questioned the inherent good in the world beyond?

And there it was, set back from the road at the base of a steep mountain. Joanna could see the house through the trees lining the road. As she turned into the drive, gravel crunched beneath her tires. She had just entered the open yard when the front screen door to the house flew open with a resounding screech, and Eli sprang from inside.

"You're here!" Eli cried as he cleared the front steps and loped toward her. "Lord in heaven, look who You've brought me."

She was just setting the parking brake when he flung open the door and gathered her up into his arms. He smelled like home. His voice choked as he told her how much he loved and needed her, and as she rested fully in his tight embrace, she could almost feel the break in his heart.

"Papa, I'm home now. We'll find him." Clinging to each other, they walked to the house. As Eli opened the screen door, Joanna cringed at the sound. "Papa, when are you going to put some oil on these poor hinges?"

"Darlin', this door's been talking to me for seventy-nine years. That's longer than your Grandma Abby squawked at me. That sound is part of what makes this place home, and I'm not about to shut it up. And don't let me catch you with an oil can in your hands, you hear?"

Soon after her arrival, Joanna placed a call to Deputy Bruce Hobbs for an update on his investigation. He was polite yet matter-of-fact. There was simply nothing new to report. No leads, no conclusive evidence, but he assured her he was doing everything he could and would keep in touch. Joanna wasn't satisfied with his answers, but she was too focused on launching her own investigation to fret over the failures of local authorities. She had long since relied on her own authority over anyone else's anyway. She turned her attention to Jake's room upstairs.

The bright room with its double windows overlooked the front lawn. Its plastered walls were strung like a Christmas tree with ornaments of accomplishment. "First Place" medallions dangling from colorful, striped ribbons solidly draped one wall. Framed certificates and awards from science fairs, math contests, and debates blocked in another wall. An oversized poster-portrait of Jake in full sprint toward the finish line of a state championship hung over a bureau.

It was overwhelming. But she knew why. It was Jake's tireless effort to prove his worth.

"Oh, Jake," she moaned aloud. "I should have been here. To see the shape you were taking, to see if there were any distortions. Then I would have known about the periwinkles."

Joanna flipped open a photo album of track team pictures, but they blurred in her teary gaze. Already, the room seemed like a tomb scattered with treasures of no use to anyone.

She examined every page of every book and notebook left over from his college days. She emptied pockets, opened shoe boxes, lifted the mattress, looked beneath the rug—all the things Eli and the deputies had already done—and found nothing to lead her to Jake. She did, however, find his old girlfriend's phone number on a scrap of paper in a dresser drawer. She put it in her pocket and kept searching.

As the sun dropped closer to the mountain, Joanna started up the path to the cabin.

"Now don't you stay up there too long, Joanna," Eli called to her as she disappeared beyond the trees. "It's getting dark."

The abandoned cabin sulked in the loneliness of the woods. Joanna took the key Eli had replaced in the dogwood and opened the door. Inside there were no shiny medallions, no framed laurels. This bare, unevenly constructed room of raw wood was the soul of Jake Gaddy. Dark and contemplative. A womb where his life struggled to take crucial form.

It was just as the sheriff's deputies left it Sunday night, except for the lantern which had been taken away for analysis. She glared at the stains on the floor. "It can't happen again," she whispered to herself. "I won't let it."

The bookcase had been stripped bare. The drawers that contained his poetry, essays, and music lay upside down on the floor, their contents gone. The whole room had been violated. Evil had visited, and its rancorous breath remained.

Joanna went to the framed photograph on the dresser for comfort but saw only pleading in the faces of her parents and brother. She couldn't take any more.

She left the cabin, locking it once again and replacing the key in the tree. Then she ran, never slowing until she reached the house.

Wednesday morning, she returned to the mountain, but not to the cabin. For most of the day, she searched every place she'd ever been with Jake, the high meadows and sunken streams, the bluffs and caves, every crevice where they had hidden from make-believe monsters in the woods. She found nothing but Jake's indelible presence at every turn.

The strain of the last two days forced Joanna to bed early that night. But before she turned out the light, Eli came to sit with her a moment.

"God will send help, Joanna," he said, patting her hand.

Joanna smiled weakly.

"A signal will come," he assured her. "Watch for it."

The Boulder County Sheriff's Department was an orange brick, flat-roofed cube of a building about two miles from the town square of Deer Creek. Joanna arrived there Thursday morning for her ten o'clock appointment with Deputy Hobbs.

Walking through the parking lot, she was glad for her leather jacket and thick jeans. Though it was late March, the temperature still hovered in the wintry zone of the mountains.

Inside, she walked briskly toward the front desk, announcing her appointment, and was asked to be seated until Deputy Hobbs was off the phone. At 10:15, she returned to the desk, asking if Hobbs could see her yet. The answer was the same. She squirmed through another twenty minutes, fitfully reading the newspaper until she could stand no more delay. She stood up abruptly and walked straight toward what she believed was Hobbs's office, fending off the objections of his secretary. "I've waited long enough for my ten o'clock appointment," she tossed over her shoulder at the woman.

Deputy Hobbs was stretched out in his reclining, overstuffed chair. With his back to the door, he didn't notice that Joanna had entered his office and was now listening to his animated retelling of a recent hunting adventure—until she closed the door behind her with a loud clap.

The officer twirled wildly in his chair to confront the intruder. Seeing the tall, handsome young woman with the steely glint in her eye, recognition dawned in his eyes. He quickly ended his conversation and assumed a professional air as he apologized for keeping her waiting and asked her to take yet another seat.

He was a balding, middle-aged man with a drooping moustache and what appeared to be a hearty appetite.

"Miss Gaddy, I'm so glad you came by. How may I help you?"

The question dumbfounded her. "How may you help me?" she repeated. "Is it not very obvious what help I need?"

"Well, of course, Miss Gaddy. And I wish that I had something to tell you about your brother's disappearance, but I'm afraid that in spite of what your grandfather thinks, we have done all we can to locate your brother."

Joanna listened attentively as the deputy explained.

"None of the fingerprints we lifted from the cabin match any on record, and we didn't find any at the house except those that belong there. As you already know, the blood on the floor is your brother's type. Unfortunately, we found none on the lantern."

He paused for a response, then seeing she was waiting for more information, he continued. "We've talked with loads of people in town about what they might have seen or heard, and we have nothing substantial to help us. We have sent a picture and description of your brother to departments in the surrounding counties. So far, we've received no responses."

Joanna listened patiently as he continued to assess the situation as he saw it. He seemed intent on clearing himself of any negligence in the case by recounting every conversation, lab result, and investigative measure taken by his department.

Then he added, "Frankly, Miss Gaddy, except for this odd reference to a dead girlfriend in his letter, and the thing about the knife he supposedly lost, there's not much that points to a kidnapping at all. There wasn't that much blood on the floor, and it probably got there just like your brother said it did."

He met Joanna's fixed stare and continued.

"You know, it's possible the boy just wanted to get away without confronting your grandfather. You know how these young guys are sometimes." Hobbs winked at Joanna. "He probably just wanted a high old time with his friends somewhere and knew Mr. Gaddy wouldn't approve. That sort of thing." Hobbs relaxed in his chair, obviously feeling he'd adequately sized up the case and brought it to an unofficial close.

Joanna looked long and hard at him.

"Are you married?" she asked abruptly.

Hobbs raised his eyebrows in surprise. "Well. . .yeah. Why?"

"Do you know your wife pretty well?" she continued.

"After twenty-three years? What do you think?"

"I think you'd be playing a whole different tune right now if you had come home and found your wife gone, blood on the kitchen floor, and a farewell note telling you to get some dead person to come cook for you until she gets back. That's what I think."

Color rose in Hobbs's cheeks. His jaw shifted from side to side. "Now, Miss Gaddy, I—"

"Now, Deputy Hobbs," Joanna cut in. "It seems that you have reached a premature conclusion on what happened to my brother based on what you think was in his mind at the time. Have you ever met my brother, Deputy Hobbs?"

"No, I have not, and I don't see what—"

"Then how could you know what's in his mind?" Joanna interrupted again. "Do you have any idea how devoted he is to my grandfather? That he wouldn't dream of treating him this way? Of tormenting him like this?"

"I know that Mrs. McGill and Mr. Leday and several others said he was always going off on weekends," Hobbs replied curtly, "and nobody seemed to know where."

"Well. That must be it, Deputy Hobbs." Joanna said sarcastically. "Because Jake never reported his weekend itinerary to Mrs. McGill and the rest of Deer Creek, he couldn't possibly be a victim of foul play. Remarkable logic, Deputy Hobbs. Boy, is my mind relieved."

Hobbs rose to his feet. "Miss Gaddy, I won't stand for your insolence."

"Then sit down. There's more. Unless you intend to become intimately familiar with every resident in your jurisdiction and capable of making character judgments of people you don't even know, you'd better respect the testimony of those who do know what they're talking about. No one in this world knows my brother better than my grandfather and I. Jake has been taken against his will. Kidnapped, Mr.

Hobbs. A victim, Mr. Hobbs. And it's your job to find him!"

Joanna paused to regain her composure, then stood up to leave squaring her shoulders before Hobbs, who was still standing behind his desk glowering at her.

"We expect further investigation and continuous updates on your findings," she told him. "And don't you ever call my grandfather 'that squirrelly old man' again. You didn't hold your hand quite tightly enough over the receiver when you took his call yesterday."

Joanna was trembling when she reached the Jeep. An enemy she couldn't identify was before her, and now she knew there would be no help from the authorities. *Authorities. What a misnomer,* she fumed.

She thought of Eli and knew he would be waiting to hear an encouraging report. What would she tell him? That the sheriff's office considered Jake an irresponsible runaway? That they were doing nothing further to track these imaginary abductors? She wouldn't lie to him. She'd assure him Jake would be found. Then she'd have to do it.

If I could just talk it through with someone, she thought as she left the parking lot.

Lucy!

CHAPTER 15

Joanna hurried back to town, suddenly anxious to see her closest childhood friend. Her friendship with Lucy had begun awkwardly, just like Joanna's new life in Deer Creek.

By the time Eli and Abigail Gaddy had returned from Miami with their young grandchildren, all of Deer Creek was pulsing with tales of the awful tragedy. The students at Ridgeway Elementary School had been instructed by parents and teachers to welcome the two Gaddy children with open arms and few questions.

Joanna had felt obliged to accept the first offerings of sympathy, but she had visibly recoiled from any lingering attempts to comfort her. Instead, she had plunged instantly into the business of creating a new life for herself, making friends a little too quickly, joining clubs at school with too much enthusiasm, all to demonstrate her victory over the appalling circumstances. She never spoke of her parents or the accident to anyone outside the Gaddy household.

There was a vitality about the young girl that baffled her grandparents. They would have preferred a more gradual emergence from grief. Yet her new schoolmates were charmed, all except Lucy Wetherington. From her first encounter with Joanna, Lucy could see something besides the cool-headed young girl everyone else saw. To Lucy, it seemed that Joanna held her head a bit too high. Cautiously, she chose to observe this newcomer for awhile before offering her own friendship.

Lucy watched as Joanna ran for class secretary the following fall and won. Then there were tryouts for the girls' softball team. Joanna excelled over a field of contenders and was selected the starting first baseman.

Still, Lucy was cautious until one Saturday afternoon eight months after Joanna's arrival in Deer Creek. Lucy's father was a family physician who'd tended the community's ills and injuries for over thirty years and still made housecalls. Dr. Tad Wetherington was called to the Gaddy home that Saturday when Eli cut his hand on an electric saw. Lucy asked to tag along.

"Eli, what you need more than about eight or nine stitches is some new glasses. It wasn't three months ago that you fell over a log by the river and cracked your elbow. Now, are you going blind or are you just terminally clumsy?" He chose not to acknowledge the diabetes as the cause of Eli's failing eyesight. Eli was touchy about the disease that had altered his life.

"Nice bedside manner you got, Tad," Eli replied with a grimace. "Real uplifting."

"Hold still, Eli. Just one more stitch and we're through—until next time. Lucy, hand me that gauze, honey."

Lucy didn't notice Joanna anywhere about the house, though Jake had sat in rapt attention through every tug and howl.

"Where's your sister, Jake?" Lucy finally asked.

"She went to Lace Whitmore's house down the road this morning. They were going to—"

"Papa!" Joanna suddenly burst through the front door. "Grandma Abby!"

"In the kitchen, Joanna," her grandmother called with a worried frown.

Joanna rushed breathlessly into the kitchen in time to see the first adhesive strip applied to the huge bandage on Eli's left hand and stared with eyes wide with fear. Her grandmother, afraid of what such a scene might trigger, hurried to her to assure her all was well.

"Mr. Whitmore said something must be wrong because he saw Dr. Wetherington's car in the yard," Joanna said gulping air. "I ran as hard as I could to get here and—"

"Okay, calm down now, honey," her grandmother soothed. "Papa just cut himself out in the tool shed this morning. Dr. Wetherington sewed him up real neatly."

Joanna kneeled in front of her grandfather, examining the bandaged hand and stroking his arm with unabashed affection. Tears clouded her eyes, then she noticed Lucy cleaning her father's instruments at the sink and stealing curious glances at her. Joanna quickly wiped her eyes dry.

"Hi, Joanna," Lucy greeted her shyly. "You've been at Lace's?"

"Uh, yeah," Joanna answered, feeling off balance and vulnerable. She'd never liked Lucy, only because the girl seemed not to like her.

Joanna rose to her feet and wrapped a strong arm about her grandfather's shoulders. "Papa, are you hurt bad?"

"Not me. Just thought an impressive bandage would add to my tough-guy image."

"Oh, Papa. Be serious."

"Well, all right. I'll be serious about lunch. Abby, have we got anything tasty to offer our guests?"

"How about chicken and dumplin's and coconut cake?"

"Sure glad I came," Lucy remarked from the sink.

Joanna studied the girl she knew only from homeroom and Sunday school class. She was much shorter than Joanna and almost plump. Her platinum blond hair was straight and cut short above her ears. She was baby-faced and funny, and everyone liked her. But she seemed to have no interest in being Joanna's friend.

She always looks at me oddly, Joanna thought.

"Darlin'," Eli said to Joanna, "why don't you and Lucy spend some time together this afternoon? I don't think you girls know each other very well yet. I'm just going to sit up there in the parlor and let your Grandma Abby wait on me hand and foot. Tad here can find his way back to town without Lucy."

"You could take the boat out on the lake if you like," Abigail suggested. "We were going to take you and Jake out for a picnic and some fishing this afternoon. But you girls could still go."

"Great idea, Abby," Tad agreed. "Lucy, I can pick you up later."

Lucy and Joanna recognized that their day had been planned for them. They smiled wanly at each other and reluctantly agreed to go.

"Jake, you want to go with us?" Joanna eagerly asked her little brother, hoping for someone to talk to besides Lucy.

"No way. I'd have to bait your hooks for you all day long."

Eli kept a sixteen-foot aluminum boat with a small outboard motor in Jesse Canton's boathouse on Lake Tawanee just a few miles down the road. That's where Tad Wetherington took the girls that afternoon. He helped them launch the boat and get the motor started, then instructed them to meet him back at the boathouse at four o'clock.

Since her parents' accident, Joanna had been obsessed with learning everything she could about boating, even in a small craft on a mountain lake. Sprawling Lake Tawanee fed a hydroelectric plant and legions of fish. Its waters arrived chilled by the snows of Blue Ridge winters and settled against the forested banks of the vast basin. Joanna knew every foot of shoreline.

"You handle this thing pretty good," Lucy called over the roar of the engine as Joanna cleared the end of the dock and accelerated over the smooth surface of the lake.

"I lived on the bay in Miami. All the kids in the neighborhood had some kind of boat. Do you ever come out here?"

"Once in a while with my uncle Frank. He has a house on the other side of the lake. He taught me how to ski."

"On a pair or slalom?" Joanna asked perfunctorily, just trying to keep the conversation on plane.

"Oh, I need all the skis I can put on. But someday I'll get the hang of the slalom. I can never decide which foot to put in front. Do you ski?"

"Sure. All the kids in my neighborhood did," Joanna answered dryly.

"Maybe Uncle Frank will take you out sometime."

Joanna's antennae detected incoming sympathy, the old let's-do-something-nice-for-the-poor-girl efforts that turned her cold. "That's all right, Lucy." She paused and dredged up another question. "Have you lived here all your life?"

"All of it. I'll probably die here, too."

Joanna cut a sharp glance at Lucy and immediately saw the girl's regret over that last remark.

Joanna was quiet. She slowed to a gentle cruising speed, then after awhile breezed into another topic. "Mrs. Smithson was sure cranky yesterday, wasn't she?"

"She's always knotted," Lucy declared, visibly relieved that her mention of death hadn't soured the conversation.

"Always what?" Joanna asked.

"You know, twisted up in a knot. Watch her face when Andy Swank raises his hand in class. You can just see the muscles screw up into big red lumps because she knows he's going to say something crude. She lives with her brother and his family. Never even dates."

"Do you have a boyfriend, Lucy?"

"I used to until he kissed me. Slobbered all over me."

Joanna suddenly giggled.

"Made me want to throw up," Lucy went on, encouraged by Joanna's response. "Old Bradford Hornsby. Watch out for him. Something's not right about that boy. Sniffs too much gas at his dad's station, I think."

As Joanna kept giggling, an odd sense of release spread through her as she steered toward the center of the lake.

"Want to see Thieves Nest?" Joanna asked brightly.

"What's that?"

"It's a little cove to hide in. I've been there a lot with Papa. It's his favorite fishing spot. I'll show you."

The two girls raced across the lake, past a cluster of weekend cabins, the Lake Tawanee Marina, and the high bluffs that curved with the lake.

Ten minutes later, Joanna announced, "We're here." She throttled back to a near drift as they approached the entrance to the cove. The narrow passage was marked by huge cedars stationed like sentries on either side. Rock walls soared straight up from the expansive pool of still, cobalt water, wrapping it in the crusty vestiges of ages gone by. Upper ledges were overhung with vines and roots from trees growing somewhere between soil and midair. Joanna turned off the engine and dropped the anchor.

"Whoa. This place is creepy," Lucy whispered.

"My parents were anchored near a place like this the night they were killed." Her own words stung her. The thing she had struggled so mightily to suppress had broken free and surfaced without warning. She turned to Lucy, desperate to hide her emotion.

"I'm so sorry," Lucy said nervously.

Joanna didn't respond.

Lucy gathered her courage and asked, "Joanna, do you ever talk about it with anyone?"

"There's no point," Joanna answered bluntly. "It won't change anything."

"Have you prayed for help?" Lucy risked asking, not knowing if the girl who came to church with her grandparents every Sunday came in spirit, as well.

"To who?" Joanna sniffed.

The quick retort caught Lucy by surprise. "To God, of course."

"Who is that? Someone who punishes you by killing your parents? What kind of God is that? I don't want any part of Him." Joanna's bright mood was completely gone. "I don't need Him or anybody."

"Well, you were awfully scared when you came running into your grandparents' house this morning thinking something had happened to them. You need them, don't you?"

"I love them. I don't need them."

"Joanna Gaddy, that's a lie!" Now Lucy was angry. "Everyone needs somebody, and you're no different."

Joanna looked away to hide her face from Lucy.

"Joanna, I'm sorry. I didn't mean to hurt you. You've been hurt enough. But I've been watching you for a long time. You can't pretend. It just won't work."

Joanna suddenly sprang to the bow of the boat and yanked at the anchor. She said nothing as she hauled it up, coiling its chain neatly on the deck. Swallowing hard, she evaded Lucy's eyes and returned to the wheel. She gave a jerk to the ignition key, and the small engine cranked with a thundering echo against the walls of Thieves Nest.

Lucy's eyes stung with tears as the boat bounced over the lake. She'd intruded where she hadn't been invited, and now she and Joanna would never be friends.

Tad Wetherington was waiting at the boathouse. "Have a good time?" he inquired, helping Joanna tie up.

"I took Lucy to Thieves Nest, Dr. Wetherington. What a place. Ever been there?" Joanna spoke in a singsong voice that wasn't real. She was back in form. Lucy marveled at the transformation.

On the drive home, Joanna continued to converse brightly with Dr. Wetherington but had little to say to Lucy.

"Thanks for the ride, Dr. Wetherington," Joanna said when they pulled into the Gaddy driveway. As she climbed from the backseat, she turned to Lucy and said, "Lucy, this was fun. See you in Sunday school tomorrow." Joanna flashed a bright smile to no one in particular and ran to the house.

"So you girls really hit it off, I see."

"We hit something, Dad. I'm not sure what."

After that day on the lake, Joanna was surprisingly drawn to the girl who dared to meddle with her private torment. Eventually, they were inseparable, until years later when Joanna left for college in Florida. Lucy attended a small business college in Asheville and returned home after graduation to manage her father's thriving practice. She dated occasionally and was content to wait for the right man to show up.

Joanna turned off the town square onto Lucy's street. Claremont Lane climbed a gentle rise behind the Methodist church. It was a tree-lined promenade of white-painted houses with dark shutters, soaring gables, lace curtains at the windows, and wicker furniture on the porches, where neighbors still visited each other on warm evenings.

The Jeep turned into number seventeen. The old Victorian was replete with the gingerbread trim that house painters hate, a swing on the wide wraparound porch, and fern stands on either side of the massive front door. Lucy's General Motors relic was parked near the back gate. The baby blue '57 Chevrolet classic had been a high school graduation gift from her parents.

Joanna hurried along the brick walkway to the garage apartment behind the Wetherington house. Lucy had renovated it for herself during college. The door at the top of the steps was ajar, and Joanna peeked inside. Lucy was high on a ladder hanging wallpaper. She whirled on one foot when Joanna pushed open the creaking door and nearly plunged to the floor.

"Joanna!" Lucy cried. Both girls squealed as they rushed to greet each other.

"I knew you were coming," Lucy said releasing Joanna from a vigorous hug. "But I wasn't sure when. Let me look at you." Joanna, in faded jeans, a plaid shirt, brown leather aviator jacket, and boots twirled for inspection.

"Do you wear that stuff in Miami?" Lucy asked.

"Found the boots and jacket in my closet at Papa's. Forgot I had them. But look at you. You're going to disappear before long. How much weight have you lost since I saw you. . .when did I see you last?"

"Two Christmases ago. You somehow missed this last one with us."

Joanna sighed loudly. "Yes, and I'll be reminded of that fact for years to come, I'm sure. But I'm here now. So, aren't you the lucky one."

"Only if you tell me how thin and gorgeous I am," Lucy giggled.

Lucy had finally lost the extra weight she'd carried since childhood. The blond hair she'd always worn in a short, pixie cut was now shoulder length and loosely permed, and for the first time she seemed to feel as pretty as she was.

"Well, if Bradford Hornsby doesn't get here quick, someone else will get you," Joanna teased. "By the way, why aren't you at the office?"

"Vacation time, and look how I'm spending it. But I've been anxious to redecorate this old place. Mom's been helping me."

"I'd like to see her."

"We'll run up to the house in a little while, but you've got to talk to me right now." Her tone grew somber. "Joanna, we'll do anything it takes to find Jake. But tell me what you know so far."

It took Joanna only a few minutes to do that. "How can you know the things you need to know about your brother from three states away? I wasn't around when he needed me."

"Now you can snatch that guilty look right off your face," Lucy scolded. "None of this is your fault, you hear?"

Joanna fought the urge to cry, and years of practice paid off as she deftly slid into another matter.

"Well," she said clearing her throat, "I'll tell you what the sheriff's department thinks of my brother. That he's slipped away for a good time, and that's that. I just came from a dead-end meeting with a deputy who fancies himself a psychologist. He thinks Jake just wanted to avoid a confrontation with Papa over leaving and sneaked away while Papa was gone." Joanna hung her head and stared at the floor. "They're doing nothing else to find him."

Lucy watched Joanna's face cloud with a dark fear.

"Joanna, God knows where Jake is!"

Joanna's head jerked up as if she'd been struck. Her eyes riveted into Lucy's.

"Ask Him!" Lucy persisted. "With a heart that's ready for some answers, not one that's locked shut."

Joanna stood up abruptly and walked to the window overlooking Mrs. Wetherington's freshly tilled vegetable garden. She gazed into the raw clumps of earth for a moment, then turned wearily from the window. "Lucy, I'm just not going to get into this with you. I've got work to do this afternoon. Now, do you want to help me or preach to me?"

"Both," was Lucy's quick response. "But I'll save your soul later. Let's tend to Jake now."

Joanna brightened with relief. "Good. We'll start with his old girlfriend from UVA. I found her number in a drawer." She talked as she rummaged through her purse. "It was on a shred of paper. He was never much on address books. I guess he was afraid he couldn't fill one up. Anyway, she's in premed there and. . .here it is. Carol Gramelli."

"I remember her. Jake brought her home one time, and I ran into them at Mitty's. I remember how playful they were with each other."

"Oh, Jake was crazy about her. They dated for a couple of years while he was working on his doctorate degree. They seemed to be in genuine love, then all of a sudden, he broke up with her. And he was determined not to tell anyone why. Not even me or Papa. Do you mind if I call her from here? I'll use my card."

"Go ahead. How old is the number?"

"No idea," Joanna said as she dialed. "Just a chance. Maybe she can tell us something about the friends he had at school. Papa told me that Martin saw—uh. . .Carol Gramelli, please."

"This is she," came the voice at the other end.

"Carol, this is Joanna Gaddy. I'm Jake Gaddy's sister."

There was silence. "Oh?" she finally said, her voice lifting. "How is Jake?"

"Well, that's why I'm calling." Joanna heard a slight intake of breath on Carol's end. "He's disappeared, and I thought—"

"Disappeared?!"

Joanna was surprised by the emotion in Carol's voice and was sorry she'd jumped into the news so quickly. "We believe he's been kidnapped. We thought you might tell us about the people he hung out with at UVA. Any groups or organizations he was involved in?"

"Jake's been kidnapped?!" Carol asked incredulously.

"We believe so, though we're having a tough time convincing the local sheriff's department. They think he just ran off with friends, in spite of. . .well. . .some evidence we have." Joanna briefly told the story, describing the letter and cabin scene, but omitting the blood on the floor.

"Are you in Miami?" Carol asked.

"No, Deer Creek. I'd be grateful for any information you can give me."

After a long pause, Carol began, "Jake didn't associate with many people. Just a few from that fellowship group off campus."

"Fellowship?"

"Yeah, it was kind of a mystical group led by—"

"Hold on a minute. Are you saying that Jake was involved with a religious group?"

"I'm not sure 'religious' is the word," Carol replied. "Jake said they weren't any particular denomination, just a group of people whose ideas fascinated him. You know, Jake struggled with a lot of things, especially what happened to your parents."

"I know," Joanna said softly.

"He seemed to be lost," Carol said, then paused.

"Please go on. You were going to tell me who led this group."

"A guy named Father Dominick."

"A priest?"

"He thought he was, but not in the traditional sense. He started his own cult."

"Cult?" Joanna shot an I-don't-believe-this glance at Lucy, who was trying hard to piece together a story from half of the conversation.

"I'd call it that," Carol said. "But let me start from the beginning. Is that okay?"

"I want to hear it all, please." Joanna eased down on Lucy's sofa and braced herself.

"It was all so subtle," Carol continued. "Even the way they approached Jake. Another grad student, an old track teammate of Jake's, casually invited him to a barbecue at this lake house. He told Jake it belonged to a friend, an older man who just liked to have young people around. He said Dominick liked to take them water skiing and cook for them, even invited them to spend the weekend sometimes. Jake turned the invitation down the first time. But the guy kept asking, so Jake finally went.

"He told me how beautiful the place was and how nice everyone had been to him. Jake thought it was just a social group. They invited him back the next weekend, and he asked if I could come, too. Although he said it was all right with them, once I got there I felt like I wasn't really welcome. Later, I found out why.

"Joanna, I know I'm rambling, but all this has been a very disturbing thing to me. . .the way Jake and I drifted apart, I mean."

"Ramble all you want, Carol, please." Joanna shifted nervously on the sofa.

"That day at the lake, there were things in the house that were odd. There was an altar in the middle of the living room, books on transcendental meditation and reincarnation, and pyramids of all kinds sitting around. All that stuff fascinated Jake. Didn't he ever tell you or your grandfather about any of this?"

"Never. Go on." Joanna tensed. A foreboding crept through her.

"Well, this Father Dominick later invited Jake, not me, to come back for what he called 'gatherings.' Jake wouldn't tell me much about the first few gatherings he attended, but I could tell they'd had an effect on him. He started talking about the gods people could become and about designing your own destiny.

Joanna suddenly remembered the conversation with Jake that night behind her condo. "Wait a minute. Jake recently said something to me about 'gods' and something that confused him, something 'they' said."

"So he told you about them?"

"No. He never identified who 'they' were."

"Well, he also started carrying these crystals around with him, saying they would help him channel energy. I told him it sounded like a cult he'd joined and to watch himself. We argued about that for weeks. I pleaded with him to stop going to these gatherings, but he wouldn't. Then he started taking trips with them."

"Do you know where he went?"

"I know he was in New York one weekend, but other times he wouldn't tell me where he was going. Except, I do know he went to Connecticut earlier this month. I thought about calling your grandfather. You know, Jake took me home with him one weekend, and Mr. Gaddy and I got along so well. But I was afraid he'd think I was meddling where I didn't belong. And if Jake found out. . .well. . .things were bad enough between us as it was."

"I understand," Joanna said, but she really understood none of it.

"The more Jake got involved with them, the colder our relationship became. He saw me as an obstacle to some peace he was searching for. He thought they, not me, would lead him to it."

Joanna let out a long breath. "Carol, just before Jake disappeared, he mentioned something to Papa about some friends who were about to do something he didn't like, and he was trying to figure a way to stop them. Do you have any idea what he was talking about?"

Carol thought a moment. "I really don't."

"Well, last year a friend of Papa's saw Jake in a car with some people at an intersection in Asheville. Papa's friend waved and called to Jake, but Jake ignored him. Could that be the cult?"

"Asheville?"

"That's right."

"Do you remember when I said I didn't feel welcome at the lake house, and I found out why?"

"Yes."

"Well, after I discovered the nature of this fellowship group, I really put the pressure on Jake to pull out. One night he got angry and said, 'You've just been brainwashed by your sanctimonious uncle.' Joanna, I had never mentioned my uncle to Jake and asked how he knew of him. He told me Dominick knew all about him and that he called my uncle the witch hunter."

"Your uncle?"

"Yes. He's Father Mike Gramelli, a Catholic priest. A few years ago he exposed the activities of an occult group operating in his area. They had been meeting in a barn outside town, which was their right to do. But religious artifacts started disappearing from Uncle Mike's church and a few others in town. One night he received an anonymous phone call telling him that the stolen things were in that barn.

"Uncle Mike took a couple of police officers, friends of his, with him. They found the barn. Nobody was around, but all the missing artifacts were inside. Then they watched the place for awhile from the woods, thinking someone might show up. And sure enough, they did. Three men. The police took them in for questioning, and they confessed to robbing the churches."

"Forgive me, Carol, but how is all this relevant to Jake?"

"Uncle Mike's church is in Asheville."

Joanna squeezed her eyes shut. Her mind was a tangle. "Was it Dominick's cult?" she finally asked.

"We think he started it. One of the men arrested that night mentioned his name but testified that Dominick had moved away and had nothing to do with their group anymore. Uncle Mike believes otherwise."

"Where is Dominick now?"

"I don't know. But I'll make some calls right away and get back to you. Maybe tonight."

"Please do." Joanna's voice was strained as she gave Carol both her grandfather's and Lucy's phone numbers. "And don't tell anyone about this conversation. If Jake's involved in a crime, I've got to find him before the police do. They won't understand. I'm not sure I do."

Joanna thanked Carol and hung up, staring in disbelief at the phone.

"Tell it to me slowly, Joanna," Lucy gently coaxed.

After relating the whole story, Joanna almost whispered, "I wish Jake was a runaway. I could deal with that. But not some cult from the outer fringes."

"Joanna, we've got to track this Dominick guy down right now."

"We?"

"We'll go to Virginia, to this guy's house," Lucy insisted.

Joanna looked drained. Then remembering Eli, she jumped up and started for the door. "Right now, I have to get home to Papa. What am I going to tell him?"

CHAPTER 16

Three days had passed since Jake's arrival at the Connecticut farm-house, where the gathering storm of Dominick Swain's militant spiritualism had sucked in a wave of followers from around the country. During that time, Jake had continued his charade of fidelity to Dominick's cause and had succeeded in winning his trust once more.

Dominick was happy to see that his protégé was back, and by Thursday, Dominick was comfortable enough with his repentant follower to release him from the upstairs bedroom and take him into New York for two days of preparations for the mission. He seemed anxious to test the mettle of Jake's professed allegiance.

Besides Dominick and Jake, there were three "associates," as Dominick called them, all unknown to Jake. An attractive girl with short red hair and an English accent drove the gray van. A muscular young man with a blond ponytail sat on the bench seat behind Jake. Next to Jake, a fortyish man with a crew cut and enormous hands fiddled with an assortment of weapons he kept only partially concealed inside a canvas bag. They weren't along for their spiritual compatibility, Jake decided.

They drove to the Brooklyn house near the Verrazano Bridge, where the soldier watched Jake's every move. After lunch, Dominick announced his plans for the afternoon.

"Jake, you'll accompany me in a little while to the management office of the Hotel Internationale near Rockefeller Center. You will tell whoever greets you there that you and your father must have a word with your brother. One of our associates is now a waiter at the hotel.

We secured the job for him in order to deliver a very timely message to Dr. Greg Langston on Monday morning. If the good man cares a whit for his family, he will deliver not the propaganda of his choice that morning but an admission of guilt, as the note will instruct.

Jake's face remained passive. His heart was pounding.

"Now, when this young man is sent to us, he will escort 'his family' into a private corridor where we can talk confidentially. What he's really going to do is show us the quickest passage from the grand ballroom—where the breakfast will be held—to the alleyway behind the hotel. Are you prepared to join us in this excursion, Jake?"

"You can count on me, Dominick," Jake lied with stoic conviction. *The hotel,* he thought to himself. *My chance to run.*

"I'm pleased, Jake," Dominick said earnestly.

In the early afternoon, they all climbed back into the van, taking the same seats as before, and eased into the bustling streets of Brooklyn's Bay Ridge community. Jake watched people hurry along the crowded sidewalks of neighborhoods, which were so unlike the mountain hamlets he preferred. He wondered where everyone was going in such a hurry, so immersed in their own pursuits, so unaware of the peril the young man in the passing van faced.

Gas stations were jammed with cars puffing white plumes of warm exhaust into the late winter chill. He longed to be safe inside one of them, hidden away with a phone in his hand. *I've got to warn Papa.*

"Need gas, Dominick," said the girl. "I'm pulling in over there." Before the van stopped, the soldier sitting next to Jake took hold of his arm.

"You don't need to do that," Jake snapped.

"You must prove we don't," the man replied, strengthening his grip.

The girl got out to pump gas. Dominick announced he was going inside for more maps of the city. They would be distributed to the rest of the followers with escape routes clearly marked.

Jake looked across the street at the entrance to an open alley running the length of the block behind an assortment of storefronts. There was a hardware store, butcher shop, insurance office, pawn shop, and a discount bridal store. Down the street was a small park with a fountain in the center surrounded by benches. *Get to a phone.*

The side door next to Jake opened. Dominick stood outside with a handful of maps. He reached in to give them to the soldier, who relaxed his grip on Jake to take them. At that instant, a brisk wind whipped inside and seemed to howl, "Now!"

Jake lunged through the open door, knocking Dominick to the ground, and raced for the park. It had been too long since he had exercised his trophy-winning legs. They were tight and began cramping almost immediately. Halfway through the park, Jake knew he couldn't outrun the soldier already gaining ground on him and the blond bodybuilder, who was rapidly closing in behind the soldier. Another day, and he would have sprinted easily beyond the reach of his pursuers. But not this day.

Jake turned quickly from the park and headed for the alley he'd spotted earlier. Looking back would slow his stride, but he knew they were there. Horns blew and people shouted as he darted across the street. He saw the van lurch from the gas station.

In the alley a man carrying long white dresses was just disappearing through the back door of a store. Jake reached the door just before it closed and held it ajar long enough to watch the man carry his load to the front of the store. He slipped inside and locked the door just seconds before the two chasing him entered the alley.

Jake found himself in a stockroom packed with wedding gowns sheathed in plastic. Searching the room, he noticed a portable rack of gowns partially obscuring a doorway of some kind. Quietly Jake parted the gowns and stepped through them into a small office with a desk, chair, bookcase—and phone.

He dialed quickly. Eli answered. Jake was so relieved to hear his grandfather's voice, he almost forgot the urgency of the moment. In quick, hushed tones he began, "Papa. It's Jake. Papa. Papa. Don't talk. Just listen. You have to get out of Deer Creek immediately. Papa, please just listen. There's no time to ask questions. You're in danger. The same people who took me are coming for you. They could be there any moment. Leave now and don't tell anyone where you're going." Jake heard footsteps approaching the stockroom.

"Who's in there?!" the shopkeeper loudly demanded.

Jake ignored him. "Papa, please stop talking and listen. I'm all right, but you've got to leave Deer Creek now. And Papa listen carefully—"

"I've got a gun! Come out of there!" the shopkeeper yelled.

"Call Greg Langs—"

The barrel of a shotgun split the curtain of dresses in two as the shopkeeper charged Jake's hiding place. The receiver fell from Jake's hand, squawking with the transmitted shrieks of an old man left dangling in terrible confusion.

Jake pleaded with the man to understand that he was being chased, that his life was in danger from two men in the alley. At that moment, furious knocking sounded at the back door. The man looked desperately at Jake, not knowing whether to shoot him or help him.

Jake couldn't wait for him to decide. Ignoring the gun, he pushed past the man and ran to the front of the store. Flinging open the door he dashed onto the sidewalk and into the stranglehold of the bodybuilder and Dominick. The van rushed to a halt at the curb, the side door swung open, and as quickly as he'd sprung from it just minutes before, he was hurled back into the van, landing hard on the floor.

The shopkeeper burst through the front door as the van turned the corner, stopped for the soldier running from the alley and sped away.

Jake was tied up and strapped to his seat. No one would see him through the dark windows.

"No harm done, Jake," Dominick said with restraint, not turning in his seat to face Jake. He was unaware of the phone call to Deer Creek.

"That merchant waving his gun wasn't in the mood to help you, was he?" Dominick teased. "Pity."

Suddenly Dominick turned and slapped Jake hard in the face. "You'll not live to regret this," he seethed.

CHAPTER 17

Scolding herself for not calling Eli, Joanna backed quickly out of Lucy's driveway and pressed hard against the accelerator. It was already two o'clock, and Eli would be pacing by now, wondering where she was and what had happened with Deputy Hobbs.

She was still reeling from the conversation with Carol. Images of Eastern gurus and voodoo whirled into view as she drove. Haitian refugees had brought animal sacrifices and spells to Miami. Now her own brother carried crystals.

"Jake! What are you doing?" she cried into the windshield.

Dust billowed as her tires hit the Gaddy driveway. What would she tell Eli about his grandson? Down the curving lane, she was searching for words when suddenly Eli appeared through the trees running toward her. He was waving his arms and calling to her. She stopped the car and ran to him.

"Papa! What's the matter?" She reached for him.

"It was Jake! It was Jake!"

"What was Jake, Papa?"

"On the phone! Jake just called!"

Words wouldn't come to her. She could only stare at Eli in disbelief.

"Someone had a gun on him and was yelling at him. He called to warn me, Joanna." Eli spit the words in rapid succession, his lungs heaving.

Joanna grabbed both his arms. "Papa. You're going to have a stroke. Calm down."

Eli ignored her. "Joanna, Jake told me to leave Deer Creek right now and not tell anyone where I was going. That some people were coming after me. But I'm not going. I'll wait for them and tear them to pieces. Deputy Hobbs will send help.

It was no use trying to calm him down. "Papa, did Jake say anything else?"

"He said to call someone named Grayless. I didn't understand, then he must have dropped the phone, and all I could hear was it banging around."

"Grayless? Do you know that name?"

"No. But you've got to get out of here, Joanna. I don't want you here if there's going to be trouble."

Eli pulled Joanna to him and wiped frantic tears from his eyes. He looked toward the sky. "Lord, you can see my boy right now. Deliver him from this evil. Stay with him. In Christ's name, help us."

Joanna clung to Eli in a daze, not knowing what to do. Then a sudden strength overtook her, and her senses fell solidly into place. "Papa, come with me into the house." She pulled the old man swiftly by the hand, up the steps, through the screeching door and into the kitchen. "We're going to call Martin to come get you. You can stay at—"

"I'm not going anywhere. I'm staying right here, and I'm going to catch these fools."

"Papa, you can't stay here. It's too dangerous."

"I'll call that Hobbs fella. He'll come."

Joanna's jaw tightened. "Papa, I haven't had a chance to tell you about my conversation with Hobbs this morning. He's all but closed the case on Jake. He thinks he's a runaway, and that we should just wait for him to come home."

"You mean they're not even trying to find him?"

"Not anymore."

"But what if we tell him about the phone call? He'd know Jake was in trouble then."

"That's just it, Papa. Jake might be in. . .in trouble with the police. There's a lot I have to tell you."

"Jake's not a criminal!" Eli shouted. "What are you saying, Joanna?"

"Sit down, Papa."

Joanna threw off her jacket and got to work. While hastily gathering food and supplies into grocery bags, she told Eli about her call to Carol, the cult, Dominick, and Asheville. She finished by announcing her intention to leave immediately to search for Dominick.

"Joanna, you can't go hauling off after someone like that. You're just a young woman."

That hit her button. "Papa, I'm thirty. And capable of taking care of myself. I'm going to find this man."

"You can't go by yourself, Joanna," Eli pleaded.

"I'm not. Lucy's going with me."

"Lucy!" Eli shrieked. "The girl who still sleeps with a stuffed monkey?" Eli turned his face to the ceiling. "Abigail, are you hearing all this?"

Joanna was suddenly amused. "Papa, don't worry about us females. If things get rough, we'll just faint. Now, you go upstairs and pack a bunch of clothes and everything you need from the bathroom. Don't forget your medicine. You and Martin can stay at Frank Wetherington's place at the lake. You know Lucy's uncle. I'll call her to arrange it. And you'd better follow Martin out there in your car. If they don't see any vehicles around here, maybe they'll leave the place alone."

Joanna knew Eli wanted to be her strong protector, to go after Jake in her place. But he'd finally accepted the condition of his health and no longer riled against those who tried to subdue him.

"It's not right, Joanna," he called over his shoulder as he climbed the stairs. "You're just a child in search of wolves. It's not right."

While Eli packed, Joanna phoned Lucy and told her about Jake's call, asking if Eli and Martin could stay at her uncle's lake house. "I'll leave as soon as Papa does," she told Lucy. "I'll spend the night at your place, and, if you still want to come, we'll leave for Virginia in the morning with or without word from Carol."

Joanna called Martin next and retold as much as she had time to, promising that Eli would fill in the gaps later.

"Tell the old man I'm on my way," Martin said.

She ran to her own room and repacked what she'd unpacked just two days before. She whisked her luggage out the back door to the Jeep, locked it in the back, shoved the key deep in the pocket of her jeans, then hurried around to the passenger's seat. Underneath, strapped into a leather holster, was the .357 magnum pistol she'd bought for herself after a rash of break-ins at her condominium building.

Joanna also carried the gun on board *The Abbey* every time it left the marina. Drug runners continued to prevail on the open sea and would slip into Biscayne Bay at will. She visited the firing range often enough to capably wield the powerful handgun if her life was threatened. Her grandfather knew nothing about it. She preferred it that way.

She was locking the car door when Eli opened the back door to the house and called to her. "Joanna, come here, honey. There's something I want to give you." She followed him into the storage room behind the kitchen. From a gray metal box on the shelf, Eli pulled a .22 caliber pistol and handed it to her. "Even little David had a weapon against Goliath," he said. "So shall you. Come outside, and I'll show you how to use it."

"Uh, Papa, come out to the Jeep with me a minute."

Joanna opened the passenger door, withdrew the weapon from under the seat, and showed it to Eli.

"Where did you get this thing?!" he shouted.

"In Miami, Papa. There's been some burglaries where I live, and. . . a murder in the building next door."

Eli looked into Joanna's face as if seeing her for the first time. He touched her cheek gently with his rough hand. "What has the world done to you, my child? Alone with your gun. And your hurts." Joanna looked away.

"Can you shoot it?" he finally asked.

"Yes, Papa."

"Well, it'll make a good noise. I pray that's all you'll need." He was shaking.

"Where in blue blazes is everybody?" The voice came from inside the house. Eli and Joanna grinned at each other. They locked her gun in the car and hurried toward the back door. Martin was gathering groceries and luggage in the front hall, while fussing about no one being there.

"Well, if it's not Laurel coming for Hardy," Joanna greeted the burly old man who always wore a John Deere bill cap.

"There's my girl," he drawled, turning to bear-hug her like he'd done all her life. "If you're not the most fetching thing to come out of this family. So good to have you home, sweet thing. And aren't you glad to see me looking so fine myself?"

"Martin, you're just ravishing," Eli growled. "Now let's grab these suitcases and get out of here. Joanna, you follow us out to the lake."

"Papa, I'm not going with you."

He spun around to face her. "What do you mean? You can't stay here."

"I'm not, Papa. I'm going to Lucy's as soon as you leave. I'll call Carol from there, and then I'll call you, okay?"

"But I thought we'd discuss all this at the lake."

"Papa, I can't waste another minute. I have to leave now."

Eli excused himself from Martin and took Joanna by the hand. "Come with me, Honey." He led her into the parlor, which was full of her grandmother's handiwork. All about the room the essence of Abigail Gaddy was crocheted, tatted, and embroidered into a delicate composite of the woman who'd selflessly served others throughout a lifetime. Her old upright piano anchored the far wall, sheet music of Bach and Brahms still stacked on top. The three-legged spinning stool Joanna had ridden as a toddler was tucked beneath the keyboard. The towering, dark mahogany secretary with its beveled glass doors stood between the two front windows.

Eli pulled Joanna down beside him on the high-backed sofa covered in a faded chintz. "That gun of yours might scare a few people away, Joanna. Nothing but the hand of God will fully protect you, though. So, even though I know—and how sadly I know—that you don't accept Christ as your Lord, I'm going to ask you to pray with me anyway. And if there's a shred of belief somewhere in your heart, He will honor it. Now bow your head, darlin'." Joanna reluctantly obeyed.

"Lord Jesus, this is a simple prayer from a simple man who knows You're there. That's why we've come to You, my little girl and me. There's a boy out there who desperately needs You. You know Jake, though he doesn't know You. And this child here beside me, You know her, too, Lord. Speak to her. Show her how real You are and how much You love her. Show her the truth, just like You did for me all those years ago. Honor her love for her brother, lead her to him, and protect her and Lucy from all harm. Perhaps, Lord, you will bring my children into Your saving light on this journey. In the name of Christ, I pray. Amen."

Eli turned quickly to Joanna, gave her one more hug, kissed her cheek, and rose from the sofa. "Don't get up," he told her. "I want you to sit for just a moment in your grandmother's parlor. Her faith is all around you, Joanna. Let it touch you. Then leave quickly." He and Martin left through the back door.

In the wake of Eli's sudden departure, Joanna reeled from a surging solitude that pushed her deep into the still-life hush of the room. She felt like an actress alone on a stage, awaiting the moment when the curtain would rise, and the scene would spring to life.

Joanna gazed expectantly about the room. She saw her grandmother seated at the piano, at the secretary, on this very sofa, needles clicking as she worked the yarn, giggling softly at one of Eli's tales. Joanna ran her hand gently over the smooth fabric. Many times she and Jake had nestled deep into this sofa on either side of their grandmother, wide-eyed with visions from a storybook read to them in the waning moments of day. Jake would bring pictures he'd colored and stuff them behind the seat cushion when he thought no one was looking. Later, when Grandma Abby tucked him into bed, he'd whisper to her the secret of his hiding place. He would instruct her to go back when no one was there and find the treasures he'd left just for her.

Deep behind the cushion. The hiding place.

Prompted by the memory, Joanna slid her hand behind the seat cushion, deeper and deeper—until she suddenly touched something. Startled by the unexpected discovery, she sprang from the sofa and stared back at it.

This is silly, she scolded herself. It's probably an old picture of Jake's that Grandma Abby never found.

Again, Joanna reached behind the cushions, this time pulling her find to the light. It was not a child's colored picture. It was a letter. To Jake. Postmarked in New York just a week ago. No return address. The letter Eli had told her about. The envelope was slit open, and Joanna removed a single sheet of crumpled notebook paper and read:

Jake,
I tried to call you, but your grandfather said you were at the cabin for a few days. I couldn't tell him this. I didn't know how he'd react. We've got trouble, buddy. That nonsense Dominick was talking about at the farm is going to happen. I got word from the girl from Denver, who's now on the run. She says they're seriously

planning this thing, only the target has changed. A different vic-
tim. She didn't know who. Anyway, they're throwing out a net for
all who knew about it. You and I and the girl are the only ones
who've left them. She told me they'd be looking for me, and I
should lose myself in the city. They'll be coming for you, too, Jake.

Watch yourself.

I've moved. I can't tell you where in this letter. I don't know
who else might read it. But if you need me, contact my friend at
the museum, and I'll get the message. If she tells you she can't find
me, they've probably got me, and I'll need you bad. They closed
up Asheville and Virginia and moved everything to Connecticut.
You know the place.

Cut out of there, Jake. This is rotten stuff.

Steve

Audible minutes ticked by on the grandfather clock near the piano as Joanna held the letter before her. She fingered the paper, shaken by its surfacing at that moment. Suddenly her head jerked toward the door. Was someone there? She listened as her heart lunged.

Let it touch you. Joanna remembered Eli's words.

The old clock seemed to be ticking more loudly, more swiftly, reminding her of the hour. She glanced at its gilded face. Its filigreed hands motioned her on.

She reread the letter. He must be a friend of Jake's from UVA. But what museum? Where? Who at the museum?

She ran from the room, up the stairs to Jake's bedroom. She'd searched it twice already. Was there something she'd missed? Something about a museum? She threw open the drawers, the closet, the shoe boxes under the bed. She pored through the books and papers all over again. Nothing.

Joanna searched the kitchen, Eli's room, then her own. Still nothing. She returned to the parlor. She removed all the cushions from the sofa and every chair and searched the drawers of the end tables. Then she turned to the secretary. The glass doors locked with a key that remained in the latch. She opened the case and hurriedly flipped through family scrapbooks, photo albums, and volumes of poetry and classic fiction.

She picked up what looked like a leather-bound edition of *Treasure Island* and opened it. Inside, to her surprise, was a hollowed-out compartment full of papers. Then she remembered this unusual keep-safe Eli had given her grandmother for Mother's Day one year. The yellowed newspaper clippings folded neatly inside reported the deaths of a young Miami couple in a boating accident. Obituary notices, condolence cards, and a lock of hair were also placed inside.

Joanna fingered the hair she knew was her father's. Tears welled in her eyes. *Will the pain ever go away?*

Joanna put the book away, then closed the glass doors on the musty chronicles of her family's life. As she turned to leave, she remembered something. Her grandfather had purchased two of the unusual books. He'd given the second one to Jake on his twelfth birthday. Jake loved the strange gift and filled it with an assortment of things. *Where is it now? Nowhere in the house. I've searched everywhere.*

The cabin!

Joanna glanced out the window. The sun had dropped to the treetops, silhouetting them against brilliant corals and lavenders. *Are they coming for me, too, Jake?* she wondered. *Are they almost here?*

She was beginning to panic, but she couldn't leave without the key to the letter. She hurriedly switched off all the lights in the house, grabbed her coat from the kitchen table, shoved a flashlight into a pocket and dashed outside.

She stopped long enough at the Jeep to grab the gun under the seat and lock the doors.

The light grew dimmer as she raced for the cabin. Fit and pumped with urgency, Joanna closed the distance quickly. Just before reaching the clearing Jake had chosen for his retreat, she stopped. She listened for sounds of any kind, from any direction. They'd taken Jake from this spot. They would not take her.

With the stealth of an Indian brave, Joanna eased through the trees, the pistol firmly in her grasp. Nothing stirred. Once again, she retrieved the key from the dogwood and opened the cabin door.

Deputy Hobbs had said, "See, if he'd been kidnapped, he wouldn't have taken all his belongings with him." But his captors would if they thought any of it would incriminate them, Joanna reasoned. But did they leave anything behind? Anything that would help make sense of the letter she'd just found?

Joanna searched the cabin again but found nothing. How could she track Jake through some person at a museum in a city that might or might not be New York? She felt the sickening spread of helplessness. She sank to the bare, wood plank floor, her legs tucked beneath her, and her head in her hands. *What if Carol comes up with nothing on Dominick? What if she knows nothing of this Steve or a museum? What then?*

The hour grew dark. She couldn't stay, yet where would she go for help? No place. No help. With the heels of her hands, she pressed hard against her temples.

Eli's words came again. *Let it touch you.*

The sound came from deep inside, some place Joanna had closed off from the rest of her. It rumbled louder and louder on its way to the surface until she lifted her head and wailed, "Help me, God! If You're there, help me find Jake!"

Her words filtered through the musty air and disappeared. Her quivering breath hung like a mist in the chilled air, and she waited. For what, she didn't know. She stared blankly at the floor. *If He's there at all,* she thought, *why should He listen to me now? It's been too long.*

Ants scurried in front of her carrying scraps of food many times their weight. Burdens almost too heavy to bear. Like her own. She watched the tiny workers trail across the floor, then disappear through a crack under the desk. She kept watching. She found herself moving along with the ants toward the crack. Was she going mad? She pushed the chair aside and crawled beneath the desk. The ants were dropping one by one into a clean-sawn break in the flooring. Just a foot or so to the left, the wood plank had been sawn through again. She pushed against the section between the breaks, and it gave. A loose piece of flooring dead center under Jake's desk. A chill shot through her.

Joanna searched for something to pry up the board. She found a long fencing nail and went to work. In seconds, she removed the board and found a layer of plywood sub-flooring beneath. It, too, was cut in the same dimensions as the surface piece. Joanna worked furiously and finally removed the second layer of flooring. Crammed into a hole dug in the dirt below was a black plastic bag. Her heart pounded as she reached for the bag and carefully lifted it through the layers of flooring.

Tearing through the knot at the top, she looked inside then slumped against a leg of the desk.

"Did You do this?" she cried softly. "Is it You, God?"

Joanna withdrew the leather-bound book entitled *Treasure Island* and lifted the cover. Inside the hidden compartment was a wad of twenty-dollar bills, her father's college ring, pictures from their last vacation together as a family, a letter from Marian Farley, a scout watch, and a few trinkets he'd collected over the years. There was also a small leaflet with a picture of Egyptian pyramids on the front. She turned this last piece over. On the back in bold letters was written: The New Museum of Holography, 3801 East 51st Street, New York, New York. In the margin, in Jake's block letters, was the name Steve Michon.

Joanna's breath came rapidly, in and out until she grew dizzy. A numbing silence filled the cabin, just as it had the parlor moments earlier, and something inside her burst. The dam came down and the cleansing flood was sweet. She sobbed freely, rocking herself on the dirty floor.

The air stirred about her. A rush of hope swept through her and drew her to her feet. She pleaded into the dark, "Forgive me. And show me where Jake is. I. . .I need You, Lord." A sudden wind blew at the door, jerking Joanna from her thoughts. She shoved the museum leaflet into her jeans pocket and replaced the book in its bag beneath the loose boards. After locking the cabin door, she returned the key to the dogwood and bolted down the dark trail. Beams from her flashlight sped ahead. Her path was clear, and her head pounded with exhilaration. She ran hard and free, freer than she'd ever been before.

Joanna was about to clear the wood line behind the house when she saw it. A flash of light from inside the house, near the kitchen window. She instantly switched off her own light and threw herself back into the cover of the trees. *Just like Jake said,* she thought. Her hand closed over the cold metal of the gun in her coat pocket.

Another light in an upstairs bedroom. *How many are there? Are others searching the woods?* She stretched herself flat beneath a thicket of rhododendron.

Just then the back door opened, and two men emerged. Light beams swept the backyard and darted into the trees around her. The two moved slowly toward the Jeep, trying its doors and shining their lights inside. Their voices were muffled but grew more distinct as they approached the woods and the path to the cabin. They seemed to know exactly where they were going, heading quickly in Joanna's direction. She tucked her knees up under her and pulled the brown jacket over her head, creating as dark and undetectable a form as she could.

Their voices were clear now. "It's got to be the sister's car with that Dade County tag," said one. "Must have just gotten here. Hasn't even taken her luggage out."

"Yeah, she and the old man must be off somewhere in his car. We better check the cabin anyway. If no one's there, we'll come back and wait for them in the house." They passed within a few feet of Joanna and were gone. It would take them only twenty minutes to reach the cabin, find it empty, and start back. Joanna would wait until they were well up the path, then run for the Jeep.

After ten minutes, she scrambled from under the bushes. Running low to the ground she slowed only once to listen before reaching the car. In seconds the Jeep lunged to life, kicking dirt and gravel from the driveway as it sped alongside the house and into the front yard. She half expected someone to run at her or shoot. At the road, she turned sharply, tires squealing against the pavement. Only then did she flick on her headlights, catching a glimpse of something hidden in the high brush on the other side of the road. A truck or van, dark color. She watched the rearview mirror. Nothing moved behind her. Yet.

Joanna shot past the Deer Creek city limits sign, never slowing until she reached the town square, where she turned into Claremont Lane and again at number seventeen. The Jeep cleared the open gateway to the backyard and came to a lurching halt inside the garage.

Lucy and her parents ran from the house as Joanna pulled the overhead door shut. All three shouted at once. "What's happened?!"

"Shhhh! Get in the house, quick!" Joanna ordered, herding her alarmed friends through the yard while glancing toward the street in search of approaching headlights. None there. She'd made it.

The kitchen light burned well into Thursday night at the Wetherington house. Joanna called Eli at the lake house, reporting almost everything that had happened. Some things would have to wait. She wanted to watch his face when she told him the signal had finally come.

Joanna promised to call her grandfather every day, listened while he prayed aloud for her and Lucy, then said goodbye. Next, she called Carol Gramelli, who had uncovered no news of the cult. She'd found no trace of Father Dominick or any of his followers and never heard of Steve Michon. Her Uncle Mike had reported the Asheville cult gone from the area, concurring with information in Steve's letter.

By midnight, maps of the East Coast and New York City, gas credit cards, and various forms of currency were spread over the kitchen table. Tad and Virginia Wetherington had given up trying to persuade Joanna to call the authorities for help. Now that Joanna knew where to begin her hunt for Jake, there was no stopping her.

CHAPTER 18

In the shroud of night that now blanketed the Connecticut country-side, Jake was lifted from the van and carried to the basement of the farmhouse. Banished from the relative comfort of the upstairs bedroom that had been his holding cell since Monday, he was no longer being merely detained. He was being punished.

Dominick's rage over the attempted escape still stung against Jake's cheek. He tasted blood in his mouth, and one eye was nearly swollen shut, having caught the brunt of Dominick's ring finger.

The light of his captors' flashlights pierced the damp cement chamber, which seemed to inhale a current of cold air through the open door. Something hummed quietly in a far corner. It was a small, rusting space heater intended to just barely sustain life.

Jake was chained at the left ankle to a steel post in the middle of the room. Bowls of food and water were placed nearby on the concrete floor. He was left with his own jacket and gloves, a knit cap he'd never seen before, a tattered blanket, and a thick braided rug intended for bedding.

No words were exchanged as the heavy door was closed and secured from the outside. Jake was alone in a tomb.

He could imagine only the worst at Dominick's hands. He had seen the frenzy building since Monday. The cult leader was driving blind into the fury of the approaching hour. Driven by whatever spirits controlled him, he preached continually to his followers:

"There will soon be a revolt against the evangelical swindlers. The innocents who have been deceived will soon embrace their own deity.

They will have no need of a savior. They will see themselves as sinless and full of power. That hour, my young gods, is at hand."

Jake leaned against the pole, wrapped head to toe inside the filthy rug. He almost welcomed the numbing cold that spread with every vaporous breath. His mind churned with Dominick's words. At one time they were provocative words that challenged him to think beyond what he'd been taught at Deer Creek Baptist Church, to imagine his own destiny free of the God who'd hurt him so badly. But he didn't pay attention to the warnings that came with them. Asheville should have been warning enough.

Dominick had encouraged him to visit a small group of followers "like yourself" in Asheville one weekend. The words had settled uncomfortably in Jake's mind, and he wondered how Dominick knew what that self was, since Jake hadn't yet figured it out.

It didn't take long for Jake to see that whatever he was, he wasn't "like" the ones in Asheville. Their communal style of living, their random pairing of men and women behind closed doors, was uncomfortably different from the way Jake lived his life. But he told himself he would be broadminded. That's what this whole mind adventure he'd embarked on was all about.

There had been three men about Jake's age, two more in their thirties, several young girls, a woman who cooked all their meals, and others who had drifted in and out of the ill-kept bungalow they shared on the outskirts of town. They welcomed Jake with genuine warmth, and he appreciated their efforts. They insisted on touring him about the city and up onto the Blue Ridge Parkway, pointing out those places in the forest where they had left their bodies and merged with the trees.

Is this who Dominick thinks I am? he had wondered.

That weekend was when he saw Martin at an intersection in town. The others in the car were surprised when Jake told them to ignore the friendly old man in the truck. He'd felt shame and some inexplicable need to protect Martin from the people he was with.

Later, Jake discovered the Asheville group had been stealing Christian religious artifacts to desecrate, and some had gone to prison for it. *Dominick's not like that. I'm sure he's not,* Jake had told himself.

Jake dropped his head into the folds of the rug. He yearned for home. The heady forays into enlightenment were gone. The promise of spiritual peace had been vanquished by Dominick's embrace of the very thing he denied existed—evil.

During spring break, Jake had returned to the only source of peace he knew, the old house at the foot of the mountain, where love was unconditional and complete.

Where love was. That was the difference. There had been no mention of love in Dominick's impassioned deliveries. No show of it among his followers. Eli had always preached God's love, though Jake could never reconcile that with his parents' awful death. *How do the two fit?* he'd wondered. No one's answer was ever good enough. But he couldn't deny the love shown him and his sister when they arrived in Deer Creek. *It's been that way ever since,* he reminded himself. *It didn't matter if we didn't love all those people back. It didn't matter if we rejected their faith. They loved us anyway. There's no love in this house. Something has stolen it from the hearts of those upstairs. Is it gone from mine, too?*

He thought of Carol. She'd loved him, too. He'd been attracted to her from the moment they were introduced. She was smart, and Jake respected that. She was pretty with her long, raven hair combed like silk down her slender back. But more than anything, she was honest with him. There was no need to pretend he didn't hurt. She had gently persuaded him to admit his burdens. She was a salve, and he longed to be with her. But when she scorned his alliance with Dominick, her honesty hit too hard.

One evening, when he tried to support the validity of Dominick's teachings to her, she said, "You sound as if you're trying to convince yourself, Jake, not me."

Friday morning, Jake was jerked from a fitful sleep by the arrival of food. No words were spoken by the young woman who placed two plastic bowls before him, then left, securing the heavy wooden bar against the outside of the door. Jake gazed at the oatmeal and bread in one bowl, the milk in the other. He wanted neither. He was too physically and mentally spent to care if he ever ate again.

The dawn of that morning starkly lit the reality of his imprisonment. Narrow shafts of light pierced the concrete walls through two small glass windows at ceiling height. Each about the size of a license plate, the windows were set about twelve feet off the ground. Unreachable and impassable, Jake wearily observed. He turned inside his rug to scan the four walls that held him.

The basement was approximately eight by twelve feet. There was no direct access to it from the house, only from the outside. The single, wooden door was too small for the opening, leaving a half-inch slit along the hinged side and nearly an inch at the bottom. A frosty wind whistled though the cracks.

Except for the inadequate space heater and an antique chamber pot left for Jake's use, the room was almost bare. No light fixture. No tools. No ladder. No implements of escape whatsoever. Only a few open boxes shoved in a dark corner. Jake couldn't see their contents, if any. He sat staring at the boxes for a long time, the way one looks without seeing while the mind is far away. He'd succumbed to hopelessness and to the guilt over what he'd allowed to happen.

This kindling of remorse ignited some energy deep inside. Jake suddenly rose to his feet and shouted, "I won't let you do this!"

He threw off the rug and looked wildly toward the door. With all his strength, he lunged toward it, but the chain held, allowing only one long stride before snatching Jake's left foot from under him. He plunged to the cold floor, prostrate against its rough surface, his ankle throbbing against the steel cuff that bound him. His wounded arm stung with fresh pain.

Jake scraped his fingernails against the floor until they broke, and his fingers bled. His agony was complete. He moaned in utter defeat: "I don't know who You are. I don't know who I am. And I don't want to live anymore. It doesn't matter anymore. I looked for You, and You weren't there. And now I don't care."

Without moving from where he'd fallen, Jake laid his cheek against the cold floor and welcomed its punishment.

"I've hurt everyone," he moaned to himself. "I deserve to die."

Something tapped at one of the windows above him. A sharp, insistent rapping that pulled Jake's head from the floor. He squinted his eyes against the glare and saw the outline of a bird at the glass. It was fluttering its wings and pecking against the glass. Then it flew away. In a few seconds it returned, pecking even harder. Jake sat up, grimacing in pain from his fall. He watched the creature, not understanding its persistence to enter such a loathsome place.

"Go away!" Jake hollered. "There's nothing here for you!"

In a moment, the bird was gone. Jake moved toward the windows, as far as the chain would allow. A piece of blue sky filled each glass. He stood full in the beams of light that showered upon him. It was warm. He felt momentarily suspended from his sentence. He wondered if the bird would return.

Jake glanced about the room, noticing how much lighter it had become as the sun squeezed through wherever it could.

There again were the boxes, three of them in the far corner. He walked toward them until the chain jerked him to a stop. He lowered himself to the floor and stretched as far as he could. Though the boxes lay another two feet beyond his fingertips, he could now see what they held—his books and papers from the cabin! Though he'd seen the three men throw them into boxes, he'd forgotten about them. But why were they here? Jake wondered.

He gathered up the heavy rug and threw it like a net over the boxes, pulling slowly. Little by little they inched toward him until they were well within his grasp. He slid all three back into the light of the windows and dove into the familiar comfort of something from home.

There were volumes on Impressionism, physical conditioning, psychology, and Middle Eastern religions. There were his notebooks from classes in literature and philosophy. And there, near the bottom, its maroon, leather cover bent backwards from the rough handling, was the Bible his grandparents had given him on the first Christmas after his parents' deaths. Jake lifted it from the box and saw his name engraved in gold. He opened it to the inscription inside. "To our Jake, with prayers that you will let this book answer all your questions. Grandma Abby and Papa."

Flipping through the pages he noticed a yellowed piece of paper folded lengthwise and wedged deep against the binding. He unfolded it, and saw his grandmother's unmistakable, shaky scrawl. He was certain he'd never seen the paper before. On it was a list of verses. The first one was Psalm 46:10. Curious, Jake turned to the verse and read:

Be still, and know that I am God.

Something stirred inside him. He turned to the next verse, Lamentations 3:25-29:

The LORD is good unto them that wait for him, to the soul that seeketh him. . . . He sitteth alone and keepeth silence, because he hath borne it upon him. He putteth his mouth in the dust; if so be there may be hope.

Jake's full attention was now riveted to the messages unfolding before him. Next was John 8:31–32:

Then said Jesus to those Jews which believed on him, "If ye continue in my word. . .ye shall know the truth, and the truth shall make you free."

Jake was fixed on the last part of the verse. "Make me free? What truth?" He returned to the list and looked up John 1:1–14:

In the beginning was the Word, and the Word was with God, and the Word was God. . .all things were made by him. . . In him was life; and the life was the light of men. And the light shineth in darkness; and the darkness comprehended it not. . . He was in the world, and the world was made by him, and the world knew him not. He came unto his own. . . .

Jake stopped there. "His own? Who is his own?"

. . .and his own received him not. But as many as received him, to them gave he power to become the sons of God, even to them that believe on his name. . .and the Word was made flesh, and dwelt among us.

"God among us?" Jake turned to Colossians 1:21–22:

And you, that were sometime alienated and enemies in your mind by wicked works, yet now hath he reconciled in the body of his flesh through death, to present you holy and unblameable and unreproveable in his sight.

"He thinks I'm holy?" Then Acts 4:10–12:

The name of Jesus Christ of Nazareth, whom ye crucified, whom God raised from the dead. . .Neither is there salvation in any other: for there is none other name under heaven given among men, whereby we must be saved.

"No one else? There's no other truth?"
Then he read Colossians 2:8, then 2 Peter 2:1–3:

Beware lest any man spoil you through philosophy and vain deceit, after the tradition of men, after the rudiments of the world, and not after Christ.
. . .there shall be false teachers among you. . .

"Dominick!"

. . .Who privily shall bring in damnable heresies, even denying the Lord that bought them, and bring upon themselves swift destruction. . .and through covetousness shall they with feigned words make merchandise of you.

Jake paused and squeezed his eyes shut. He'd heard these verses before, but they'd meant nothing to him. "Why, now, do their words strike so deeply?" He wanted more.

He read John 14:27:

Peace I leave with you, my peace I give unto you: not as the world giveth, give I unto you. Let not your heart be troubled, neither let it be afraid.

"But I am afraid."
The last verse on the list was 2 Corinthians 6:18:

And will be a Father unto you, and ye shall be my sons.

Jake looked back at the creased paper with the familiar handwriting and ran his fingers along the inked words. Then he turned it over. There was one more message from his grandmother:

"When it's time, Jake, God will call to you through
His Word, and you will hear His voice. You will
know the truth at last."

Jake drew in a ragged breath as he remained fixed on the old woman's scribbled words. His pulse throbbed in his ears. Gentle rays from the sun showered him in light, and he lifted his hand to touch what he couldn't see.

CHAPTER 19

"Close your mouth, Lucy," Joanna chided. "You look like a tourist."

The bellhop at the Marriott Marquis at Times Square in New York had unloaded the girls' luggage from the Jeep and was now leading them to the registration desk in the hotel's towering atrium lobby. It was eight o'clock Friday night.

"Well, Dad," Lucy said, ignoring Joanna and rolling her head back to survey the lofty interiors, "you did us proud."

"I can't believe he set us up in this place," Joanna said, watching a glassed-in elevator rise grandly to its call.

They had been driving since dawn, were queasy from highway food, and the coffee they'd swilled all day was wearing off. Though they'd just arrived in the city that never sleeps, sleep was all they wanted —until the bellhop showed them into their room on the thirty-second floor and pulled back the drapes.

Lucy inhaled long and loudly, then let it all out in one gush, "Whoa! Look at that!"

Even Joanna gasped at the dazzling panorama of New York at night. "It's like someone strung lights all over the Grand Canyon."

"Watch it now," Lucy warned. "You're real close to looking like a tourist." She tipped the bellhop and flung open her suitcase. "Tell you what. Sleep or no sleep, I'm out of here. This town is going to see me tonight. And you're coming, too. We've got to eat anyway."

"Lucy, I'm dead tired. And after all we put away today, I can't stand to look at food."

"What we ate today wasn't food. And besides, you owe me. Fourteen hours on the road with a depressed woman is all the suffering I'm going to do in one day."

"I wasn't depressed. Just deep in thought."

"Look, Joanna. I haven't forgotten why we're here, but we can't get into the museum until tomorrow morning. We can, however, scout the place out tonight and get something to eat afterwards. What do you say?" Joanna's notion of sleeping disappeared during a taxi ride through midtown Manhattan.

"Please slow down," Lucy pleaded with the driver whose English was as broken as the springs in his back seat. "You're going to hit somebody!"

"No hit. No hit. Is okay. What museum you say?"

"The New Museum of Holography on East 51st Street," Joanna replied, grabbing for a handle over the door as the cab careened around a corner.

"Holy museum?" the driver asked.

"Ho-log-ra-phy," Joanna slowly enunciated. "It's three di-men-sion-al pho-tog-ra-phy. Do you un-der-stand?"

"Give the guy a break, Joanna," Lucy scolded. "He's probably earning his doctorate in nuclear engineering somewhere."

"Oh, hologram. I know this. Is there. See?" He pointed across the street as the cab stopped abruptly by the curb. "Is not open now. I take you back."

"No, no," Joanna cried, studying the gray stucco facade of the three-story building. "We get out. . .uh. . .we want to get out here, thank you." She handed the driver his fare, and the two girls jumped from the backseat. As the cab sped away, they suddenly felt abandoned.

"Maybe we should have told him to wait," Lucy said, glancing up and down the narrow street, which tunneled through a dark canyon of office and apartment buildings. People leaving restaurants and movie theaters hurried along the sidewalk.

"We'll be okay," Joanna said, feeling a surge of new energy. She led Lucy across the street to the front door of the museum. It was a sheet of heavy reflective glass framed handsomely in burnished brass. The museum's name was etched into shiny, black marble above the door. Except for a small sign detailing the schedule of tours and admission costs, there was nothing one could determine about the museum by standing in front of it.

"You'd think they would have a placard or something out front advertising the exhibits inside," Lucy remarked, scanning the narrow front of the building set between an upscale men's clothing boutique and an antique furniture store.

"Well, at least we know where it is and what the surrounding area is like. Who knows what might develop tomorrow when we start asking questions. What if we spook someone, and they send for help? What if we confront this Father Dominick, himself, and he sics his henchmen on us?"

"Joanna, is there any chance you've been watching too much bad television?"

"Be serious, Lucy. Jake's kidnappers are flesh and blood real. And we could stumble right into the middle of them tomorrow."

"Given that eventuality, I say let's fortify ourselves right away with some hot food served by a nonthreatening person who speaks good English." She slipped her arm through Joanna's and pulled her down the street.

"Here." Joanna stopped, pointing toward a doorway.

Lucy stared at her in astonishment. "We're standing in a cultural and culinary mecca, where people from across the globe flock for the pure dazzle of the place. . .and you want to eat at McDonald's?"

"It's familiar, Lucy. We already know the menu. Let's go in."

"Kicking and screaming, I will. Now, follow me. From the cab I saw a cafe down the street with one of those hooded canvas awnings and a brass nameplate by the door."

Two hours later, the girls were clinging to the seat of another lurching cab en route to the hotel.

"Well, for twelve bucks, that wasn't a bad tuna fish sandwich," Joanna declared with brittle sarcasm. "And for just another three dollars I could have had lettuce and tomato."

"It was a little pricey, I admit. Now get over it, and check out the guy and girl with purple hair on the corner. And that one. Joanna, she's wearing blue lipstick. Did you see her?"

But Joanna had grown still and reflective.

"What's wrong, Joanna?"

"I was wondering if Jake had anything to eat tonight."

"Oh, Joanna. I know you're hurting. But God's watching over him. I wish you could believe that."

Joanna looked intently at Lucy. "I do."

The reply took Lucy by surprise. "You do?"

"I found Him, Lucy. Or, rather, He found me."

"When?" Lucy stared expectantly at Joanna who told her about finding Jake's keepsake book under his desk.

"Ants led me to it, Lucy. Can you believe it? Ants!"

Joanna told Lucy about her final admission of helplessness, her discovery at the cabin, and the surrender of her will to God's.

"I knew it would happen," Lucy beamed, sorting through the story she'd just heard. "And that it happened at this time, Joanna, must mean that He's about to use you to help Jake."

At ten o'clock Saturday morning, Joanna and Lucy stood outside the museum waiting for it to open. A young man dressed in sharply pressed chinos and a navy blazer finally unlocked the heavy glass door and welcomed the girls. He took their entrance fee and asked if they wanted a guided tour.

Joanna affected a breezy, nonchalant manner in answering. "Actually, we're just trying to locate a friend of ours. We think his girlfriend works here, probably midtwenties, and since we're in town for a few days, we thought we'd look him up. We don't know this girl's name, but our friend's name is Steve Michon. Ever heard of him?"

Joanna searched the young man's face intently for any trace of reaction to the name. There was none.

"No. Don't know that name, but we do have a few young women on staff. I can ask them for you."

It was crucial that Joanna do the asking herself. To protect Steve, the girl, whoever she was, might lie about knowing him. Joanna had to be in a position to detect that lie.

"Well," Joanna drawled, "I don't want to put you to any trouble. Would you just show us where to find these girls?"

"Sure. That's fine. Well, let's see. Michelle Salini is in bookkeeping upstairs. Molly Januk is in the gift shop down that hallway, and Connie Toland is a tour guide who happens to be late for work."

"We'll start with the gift shop. Thanks for your help."

The girls had to pass through an exhibit room to reach the hallway to the gift shop. "What is a hologram, anyway?" Lucy asked.

"You know the woman's head you can walk around at Disney World? Looks like an apparition?" Lucy nodded. "That's a hologram. It's three-dimensional photography, only they don't use a camera. It's done with laser beams somehow."

The girls briefly inspected a shimmering three-dimensional light-house framed and hung near the entrance to the wide hallway, then hurried on to their mission.

The girl behind the counter offered a bright smile as Lucy and Joanna entered the small shop. Her long russet hair fell in waves about her face, entangling with an assortment of beaded necklaces. "Welcome to the museum," she called in a lilting voice as she arranged a display of silver jewelry boxes. "These are the hottest items in the shop right now. A different hologram on top of each little box. Aren't they stunning?"

"Sure are," Joanna replied with an ingratiating smile of her own. "Mind if we just look around?" Joanna didn't want to pounce. *Warm up to her,* she cautioned herself.

After browsing through most of the displays and engaging the girl in innocuous conversation about the museum, it was time to dig, but carefully. Joanna motioned for Lucy to remain in the back of the shop, while she strolled to the front, approaching a stack of boxed stationary near the sales girl. She picked up one of the boxes, and, with an inconspicuous eye on the girl, called to Lucy in a clear voice, "Lucy, these are the same note cards we saw in that bookstore at UVA."

The girl glanced up from the box she was unpacking.

"Oh, really?" Lucy replied in a too-loud voice, "are you sure they're the same ones we saw at the Uni-ver-sity of Vir-gin-ia?" Joanna cringed at Lucy's deliberate articulation.

But the sales girl didn't notice Lucy's extra effort. "Do you go to school at UVA?" the girl asked Joanna casually.

The door's open, Joanna thought. *I'm going in.*

"No, but my brother did, and now he teaches there. Do you know someone there?" Joanna held her breath, trying not to stare at the girl.

The girl studied Joanna, whose focus was now back on the cards. After a long pause, she answered, "Well, he's not there anymore."

It's her! Joanna told herself. *It's got to be her. Easy now. Don't scare her off. She's the critical link to Jake. Look. Her smile is gone. Her whole mood has changed. Steady now.*

"Oh, really?" Joanna said lightly. "It's a big school, but I knew most of my brother's buddies. What was your friend's name?" Joanna held her breath.

Another pause. "Uh, you wouldn't know him." The girl turned away from Joanna and busied herself with the display.

Don't stop the flow of communication, Joanna told herself. "Was he in engineering?" It was one too many questions.

The girl turned to face Joanna, and there it was. The first flicker of suspicion. Joanna watched helplessly as it grew into alarm. The girl grabbed a set of keys from a drawer and said curtly, "You'll have to excuse me. I need to close the shop while I go to the storeroom for more cards." The girl moved from behind the counter, keys in hand.

Joanna panicked. "Wait a minute!"

The girl flinched as if she'd been attacked.

Joanna could no longer subdue her desperation. "You've got to help me! You must be Steve Michon's friend, aren't you?"

The girl moved quickly toward the door.

"Don't be afraid. We're not part of the cult!" Lucy cried, rushing to Joanna's side.

At the door, the girl suddenly stopped and whirled toward them. "Who are you?!" she demanded.

"I'm Jake Gaddy's sister. Do you know him?"

The shock was visible. "Jake?"

Joanna clasped her hands together in victory.

"Jake was kidnapped last Sunday," Joanna told the girl. "I have a letter here from Steve warning him, mentioning a friend at the museum." Joanna pulled the letter from her coat pocket and offered it for the girl's inspection.

The girl took the letter from Joanna and read the familiar handwriting but couldn't be sure how Joanna came in possession of the letter.

"Please help us," Joanna pleaded. "Let us talk to Steve. He'll know where they're holding Jake. Will you do that?"

The girl fidgeted with the keys. "I have questions of my own," she responded.

"We'll tell you everything we can," Lucy said.

"We'll talk here until someone comes," the girl said. "First of all, what do you know about this group's plan?"

"All we know is what's in this letter," Joanna replied, "and some things Jake's old girlfriend told us about a Father Dominick and his followers."

The girl eyed Joanna nervously.

"Steve must have told you about Dominick," Lucy said.

The girl was still uncertain of Joanna and Lucy. "Do you have any identification with you?" she asked.

"Sure," Joanna said pulling her wallet out. "Here's my driver's license, voter registration, a Visa card, a—"

"May I see them, please?" the girl asked. She studied everything Joanna handed her, then glanced back at the open wallet. A picture was prominently displayed behind a clear plastic window. "Who's in the picture?"

The question caught Joanna off guard. She looked at the girl then down at the snapshot she'd always carried. "My family," she replied softly. "Jake and my parents. It was taken just before they died."

The girl searched Joanna's face and found what she was looking for. Truth. "I'm sorry," she told Joanna. "Jake told us about the accident. I'll do what I can to help you. My name is Molly Januk."

She got someone to take her place in the shop and led the girls to an unoccupied office where they sat around a desk.

"You should be warned about Dominick before you get any closer to him," Molly cautioned. "I'll tell you what I can, from the beginning."

Joanna and Lucy pulled their chairs closer.

"I met Steve last year. He and some friends came into the gourmet shop where I worked in Greenwich Village, and we started talking. We liked each other right away and started dating. After awhile, he told me about the cult, how it intrigued him at first, but then he started having doubts about the leader, Dominick. I was curious and wanted to meet the man, but Steve wouldn't let me.

"Just a couple of weeks ago, Steve dropped out of the group altogether. So did Jake. He came to visit Steve one weekend here in New York, and I was so impressed by him. He was bright and had such a gentle way about him."

Joanna nodded and bit her lip.

"It was obvious the two of them were upset about something they weren't going to tell me about. Said they didn't want to involve me."

"A few days later, this man came into the gourmet shop asking for me. It was Dominick. He asked to speak privately with me and told me he wanted Steve back in his family, as he called it. He asked if I would persuade him to come back. I agreed to talk to Steve, then quickly excused myself."

"What was he like?" Lucy asked.

"Older. About sixty. Blondish hair, kind of long. Very distinguished looking, in a European sort of way."

"How did he know where to find you?"

"That's what worried Steve," Molly replied. "Then a couple of days later, Dominick came back to the shop. He was determined that I was going to help him get Steve back. But that time I wasn't very polite. I told him that Steve wanted nothing more to do with the group and that he should leave us both alone. Steve insisted that I move to another job in a different part of the city. That's when I came here. I just started last week."

Joanna and Lucy hung quietly on every word.

"Then one morning, Steve found an envelope with a note inside taped to his apartment door. They'd finally found where he was living. I have it in my purse." Molly produced the note and read:

Steve,
Don't learn too late the error of your ways. It would be a difficult lesson to endure, for you and your lovely young lady. You know where to reach me.

> *Kindest regards,*
> *Dominick*

"What happened then?" Lucy asked nervously.

"Well, Steve was outraged over the threat to us. Then this girl called him from Denver. She'd left the cult, too, and warned Steve that Dominick was getting paranoid about those on the outside of the family who knew about some plan. Steve still won't tell me what it is."

"What did you and Steve do?" Lucy asked.

"We moved out of our apartments in the middle of the night and into my aunt and uncle's house in White Plains. That's when Steve wrote that letter to Jake."

"What is Steve doing now?" Lucy asked.

"He works in my uncle's dry cleaning business, but I insisted on keeping my job at the museum. He warned me to be alert for anyone asking personal questions." Molly cocked her head at Joanna.

"I'm sorry we frightened you," Joanna said. "But what do we do now?"

"Leave me a number where I can reach you. I'll talk to Steve and call you. That's all I can do."

Joanna and Lucy left the museum and returned to the hotel. They called Eli, Lucy's parents, and Carol Gramelli to report their findings so far, promising to call every couple of days.

An hour later, the phone rang. It was Molly with a question Steve wanted Joanna to answer. "Steve wants to know what your mother's address book looked like."

Joanna swallowed hard before answering, "It was covered in cloth. Yellow daisies."

Molly breathed deeply. "Steve will meet you at the side entrance of your hotel in the morning at seven o'clock. He'll be in a black Honda Civic wearing a denim jacket and a baseball cap. Be on time so he won't have to wait. I'm sorry I had to ask you about the book. Goodbye."

CHAPTER 20

A light rain was falling on the woods at the Langston home Saturday night. Wet leaves clung to Cort Peterson's boots as he moved silently toward the house. Dark waterproof paint covered his face. His clothes were black and clung tightly to his muscular frame.

The lights inside were ablaze. Even the glassy room high above the house was glowing amber. Peterson could see just the top of Greg Langston's head as he moved about inside. No floodlights lit the yard. Peterson was grateful for that.

He slipped through the dense undergrowth alert for the growl of a watchdog. His observers had reported seeing no dogs around the place, but it was better to be cautious. He had dog treats in one pocket and a tranquilizer gun in the other. Strapped to his leg was his handgun.

With the trees so close to the house, stealing close to the windows was easy. There was still no sound of a dog.

Through the back of the house, Peterson could see clearly into the great room with its soaring stone fireplace, rocking chairs, and over-stuffed sofas. The room was a huge square in the midsection of the house. The front and back doors opened into it, and he could see stairs rising from the front entryway. There was a deadbolt lock on the front door, but there was also a sidelight window next to the door that would be easy to cut.

A wide plate glass window to the left of the great room exposed the breakfast room and kitchen on the back of the house. That's where Roxanne and Jeremy Langston were at this moment. Seated at the kitchen table by the window, they were engrossed in what looked like homework. With the light so bright inside and the woods so dark outside, there was no way they could see him, though he was no more than thirty feet from their table. *Surprise!* he chuckled to himself.

Three smaller windows overlooked the back yard from the second story. They were all dark, but Peterson guessed one was the boy's. *I have to know which one.*

Moving to the side of the house opposite the kitchen, he was hurrying through the trees when he noticed the light in the high room had gone out. How long had it been off, he worried as he crouched to the ground. Moving cautiously, he turned the corner and saw light coming from two side windows that were heavily draped. He knew it was the master bedroom but needed to see inside. *Where's the bed?*

He hoped the front window of the room wasn't draped. He moved quickly in that direction. Since the front yard was clear of trees he had to follow the wood line along the drive until he was at an angle to see inside. The drapes were open, but the window was too high to see in. He would have to leave the cover of the trees and approach the window in the open.

He moved closer to the house along the tree line. When he got even with the front corner, he dropped to his hands and knees and crawled quickly into the open toward the shrubbery against the front wall. When he reached the front window, he listened for movement within the bedroom. Hearing nothing, he was slowly raising his head to peer inside when a form suddenly appeared at the window.

Peterson dropped to the ground brushing noisily against the bush behind him. He slipped from the hedge and ran straight into the trees beside the house. No doors opening and closing. No footsteps. No beams from a flashlight. Confident that no one was in pursuit, he returned to the woods behind the house and waited again, not wanting to leave until he knew which room was the boy's. *I won't have time to hunt for him.*

Just then a light came on upstairs, and Peterson could see a lamp shaped like a football helmet on top of a chest of drawers. The wall behind it was full of colorful pennants. Young Jeremy walked to the chest, pulled open a drawer and got out some clothing. *His jammies, I bet. Probably got little football players all over them.* Peterson tugged at his left ear and scowled. *How cozy. But not for long, kid.*

It was nine o'clock Saturday night, and Greg Langston was pacing his "navigation room," searching for direction in the acceptance speech he would deliver at the awards ceremony Monday morning.

Langston gazed at his image reflected in the expansive windows of the room. Rain pattered softly against the panes, streaking the mirrored view of himself. Tonight, the dark beyond his private study seemed invasive. An uneasiness washed over him.

They're hoping the nice religious fellow will just say "thank you" and sit down, he thought. *That's all they want. So, do I oblige them? Or do I seize the opportunity to say what's on my heart? Appeal to their moral sensitivities to get the smut off the television and newsstands, even the computers. Kids doing their homework at the family computer can pull up a digital sex orgy in color. Sanctioned by advanced technology. Aren't we proud?*

He paced. *Why can't I get the words right?*

He went to the window trying to see out, but the dark was forbidding.

"Greg," his wife called from the stairway, "do you need help packing?"

He turned from the window and walked to the steps that dropped steeply to the house below. "No, thanks, Rox. I'd rather you help Jeremy with his math. Better you than me."

"You might be right about that. Well, call if you need me."

Langston returned to the blank screen of his computer. *I've stared into this thing enough,* he decided. As he straightened his desk, he assured himself the words would come when he needed them. He turned out the lights and glanced through the back window. Then he looked again. Had something moved in the trees? There, beyond the garden. Langston tried to focus quickly to the darkness, but he could barely distinguish one tree from another in the dim glow from the downstairs windows.

He continued to watch, but nothing stirred. *I'm losing it. I'm looking for the bogeyman.*

In the bedroom downstairs, he hurriedly packed his clothes, thinking of the friends he would stay with the following night. Rod and Janis

Nettles would meet him at the airport about noon on Sunday and take him to their new condominium on the Park. He was anxious to see how they'd matured from the starry-eyed young graduate students at Highgate Christian to cosmopolitan New Yorkers.

He dropped his shaving kit and shoes into the suitcase and turned toward the sound of the rain. He moved to the window and heard the crackling of branches in the shrubs below and saw their leaves fluttering.

I don't understand this fear inside me.

CHAPTER 21

The first light of Sunday morning found Jake asleep, cocooned in the braided rug that barely shielded him from the chill of the basement. Supporting his head was a pile of books. Tucked inside the inner folds of the rug was the one book that had converted his prison to a cradle of hope.

Awakened by sharp beams of light advancing across the floor, Jake pressed the small Bible against his side. As he opened it to read more, he heard something rustle in the tall grass outside the door.

The heavy wooden bar fell with a thud on the ground, and the door opened. Dominick's ponderous form filled the doorway. Jake hadn't seen or heard from him since their return from the city Thursday night.

"Not a bad place to work through your penitence, eh, Jake?"

Jake didn't move or respond.

"Food. Water. Just uncomfortable enough to make you sorry for what you did. And—" Dominick spotted the boxes of books and frowned. "I don't recall reading materials being left for you. Did someone bring these to you?" he demanded.

"They were already here," Jake replied.

Dominick approached the boxes and stooped to examine each book. Jake had already slipped the Bible inside his jacket, not wishing to relinquish it.

"It seems I have more than one incompetent in my midst," Dominick complained. "You, of course, and whoever failed to clear this room. I should have seen to it myself. But no harm done. You've just been entertained more than I wished you to."

Jake said nothing.

"I'm not surprised that you have so little to say, Jake. What's the point, right? Our ties are now severed. You're useless to me and as lost as ever. I once counted on your sharp wits and what I thought was your loyalty. No matter. We will succeed without you."

"Don't count on it, Dominick," Jake said sharply.

"Oh, but I am. Then I'll be gone. . .for a short while. Until things cool down. I'll return, but you, Jake, are going nowhere. After we leave tomorrow morning, there'll be no water, no food, and no one to hear you scream for help. Nor will they hear the young Miss Patterson."

"In Denver?" Jake asked in alarm.

"You didn't know about her, did you?"

Jake feigned ignorance.

"She ran, too. But we have her now. As for Steve, well, he's still eluding us. But I'm not concerned. He's too weak-willed to interfere."

Jake studied the man standing over him, then asked, "What happened to you, Dominick? Who gouged away your soul?"

"You'll not play therapist with me. My motives are pure. My conscience free. And soul? My soul is of god. It is god."

"You're not a god of any kind, Dominick. I've just met the real God."

"Oh, you did? Did you find him under this dirty old rug?" Dominick teased.

"I found Him here," Jake said, producing the small Bible from beneath his jacket as he rose to his feet.

"Well, well. Look what Jake found in his toy box."

Dominick's composure suddenly turned. He snatched the book from Jake's hand, flipped it open and tore at its pages.

"Are you so threatened by that book?" Jake asked calmly.

Dominick's face twisted with rage. He threw the book to the ground, clenched his fists and came at Jake, then stopped short. In a moment, a cool, leering countenance spread slowly across his face. "Die in your glory hole, Jake!" He left quickly, slamming the wooden bar against the door.

But soon the door opened again. The young girl who'd brought most of Jake's meals during his confinement entered the basement. She placed the bowls of food and a thermos of coffee on the floor, then turned to leave.

"What is your name?" Jake asked her. "Why are you with these people?" He had questioned her many times before, but she would never reply, preferring to tuck her head and retreat quickly. She was a small person with fair skin and freckles across her nose. She wore her light brown hair in a short boyish cut, though her clothing was gauzy and feminine. There was the scent of vanilla about her. He had commented on the fragrance once when she brought his breakfast, and her face flushed. But still she said nothing and left.

This time, though, the girl gazed at him for a long moment, then answered, "Theresa." She ignored the second question.

Jake had broken through. "Theresa, you must help me," he pleaded.

"No!" she snapped and started for the door.

"Please wait! Don't you know that Dominick is about to kidnap a woman and her son?"

"Yes, I know." Her voice trailed off.

"We can't allow that to happen. Please help me escape so I can stop them. Go with me. Don't be there when these people are caught. And they will be caught."

She paused for a moment, then said with defiance, "Dominick knows what he's doing. I support him." She left quickly, shoving the door closed, and securing it once again.

Jake dropped his head in despair. Tension seized his weakened muscles, and he began to shake. His body groaned for release. He began to run in place, slowly, then furiously. He bore down hard on the concrete floor, imagining he was suddenly free.

Recovering the scattered pages Dominick had torn from the Bible, Jake was replacing them in the book when his eyes fell upon a rumpled page from Isaiah. One verse had been marked: *But they that wait upon the LORD shall renew their strength; they shall mount up with wings as eagles; they shall run, and not be weary.*

"Lord," Jake whispered, "let me run."

CHAPTER 22

At seven o'clock Sunday morning, Joanna and Lucy leaned against a planter near the side entrance of the Marquis, waiting for a black Honda Civic. When it finally came rushing up to them, they weren't sure what to do. A strange man they'd never met, on the run from an even stranger cult, was about to whisk them away. But remembering he was Jake's friend gave them the courage to approach the car.

The passenger window was lowered, and the exultant face of Steve Michon appeared. "Joanna Gaddy?"

"Yes."

"I can't tell you how happy I am to meet you. Jake sure loves to talk about you. I'm Steve. Come, get in."

Lucy stooped low for a wary look inside the car. "Where's your baseball cap? You're supposed to be wearing a baseball cap."

Turning nervously to Joanna, Lucy announced, "Joanna, he's not wearing a baseball cap."

"And this is Lucy," Joanna said to Steve with a half grin.

"Nice to meet you both," Steve said, producing the cap. "These Japanese cars don't give guys like me much headroom. I had to take it off. You see, the car belongs to Molly's short uncle." He opened the door for them. Joanna crawled in the back seat, pulling a reticent Lucy in behind her.

Steve twisted in his seat to face them, his easy smile curving to a frown. His features were nice and just missed being handsome. His long, slender nose ended just above a wide mouth, which at this moment was stretched in a thin somber line. "Joanna, we'll find Jake. I know where to look. You and Lucy stay at the hotel, and I'll go—"

"We're going, too," Joanna interrupted.

A slow smile spread across his face. "You're just like Jake said you were. But, Joanna, you don't understand these people. They're dangerous."

"I'm not losing Jake, Steve. I'm going after him, and I'm counting on you to lead the way. Will you?"

Steve looked resigned. "I knew it'd turn out this way. Okay, I'll pick you up right here at midnight tonight."

"Why can't we go now?" Lucy asked impatiently.

"We need the dark. We're going to a farmhouse in Connecticut, and approaching it in the daylight isn't a good idea. It's a headquarters for Dominick. Are you with me?"

"We'll be ready," Joanna assured him. "But first, you've got to tell us what this whole thing is about. What are these people trying to do?"

Steve took a deep breath. "Some pretty awful stuff. You won't believe it. You see, Dominick not only believes that Jesus Christ is a fraud whom Christian leaders lie about to gain power over the masses, but that those same leaders are behind the bombing of the Crown Prince casino."

Lucy's eyes grew wide.

"So what does he plan to do?" Joanna asked.

"He believes that if he can get a famous Christian figure to admit the Soldiers of the Cross are taking orders from Christians United, he'll be doing the country a big favor."

"Who's the Christian?" Joanna asked.

"I don't know now. Originally, it was Greg Langston, but I was told they've chosen someone else."

"How do they propose to get someone like Langston to admit such a thing?" Lucy asked. She was very familiar with Langston's books. Joanna knew the name, but not the man's work.

"By kidnapping his family."

"What?!" Joanna and Lucy shouted simultaneously.

"Shh. Keep it down. That bellhop's already giving us funny looks." The girls sat in stunned silence.

"I told you these people are dangerous."

"How was this man supposed to make such an announcement?" Lucy asked, recovering from the shock.

"There's some awards function, big thing, you know, going on at the Hotel Internationale here in New York on Monday. This guy's supposed to receive an award of some kind. It's even going to be televised. But that plan must have changed since Dominick chose someone else. I don't know anymore than that. But that was enough to send me and Jake packing."

"Incredible," Joanna whispered, then focused again on Jake. "Wherever we have to go, we'll be ready, Steve," Joanna assured him. "And I'll drive my Jeep."

Steve laughed. "Now, how did I know that?"

Joanna ignored the tease. "Now let me ask you something. How did you know about my Mom's address book?"

"Jake told me about you pulling him into your parents' bedroom and locking the door, and how you fumbled through her address book looking for your grandfather's number. The book stood out in Jake's mind."

"You got that close to my brother?" Joanna asked with a twinge of jealousy.

"We were just searching for the same things."

Seeing Joanna's dark frown, Steve added, "Don't judge him too harshly. What we got into was sort of a whimsy that went haywire. A little exploration that took us where we didn't want to go. But we'll pull him out of it. Now, I suggest you two get some rest today. This could be a long, difficult night coming up.

"Oh, and Lucy," he added, "you'd better tell me what you'll be wearing, so I'll know it's really you." He winked, and Lucy grumbled something under her breath as she climbed from the back seat.

Joanna turned back for one more question, "Did you ever find what you were looking for, Steve?"

"Not yet," he answered, then drove away.

Later that day, Joanna called Eli at the lake house and told him everything but her plan to go with Steve. "No need to worry him more than I have to," she told Lucy.

It was nearly one o'clock Monday morning before Steve guided Joanna up Highway 278 through Brooklyn, Queens, and into the Bronx where they picked up I-95 and the Hutchinson River Parkway north to Connecticut.

"What are we facing up here, Steve?" Lucy asked uneasily. "And do you have a plan?"

"A big old farmhouse on a lot of open land. No way to approach it by car without being seen. We'll go in on foot and hide in one of the outbuildings they never use, until we get a feel for how many are inside and where. Especially, where Jake is. He'll either be in the attic or the basement. Might even have him tied to a living room chair for closer supervision. I'll do the scouting, come back to you, then decide how to get him out."

"Why don't we go to the police once we're sure Jake is inside?" Lucy asked in a practical tone. "For that matter, why haven't you already reported any of this, Steve?"

Steve's face clouded. "Who'd believe me?" Then he quickly changed the subject. "To answer your other question, Lucy—they'd hide Jake as soon as they saw a car, especially a squad car coming up the road, and Dominick would paint us up to be the biggest acid heads on the face of the earth. I can hear him now. 'Officer, these young people have hallucinated so many times on drugs, they can't distinguish reality from a preposterous tale dredged from some LSD trip. I'm sorry you've been troubled.' "

"And the cops would believe him over us?" Lucy asked.

"Dominick is a popular guy around Milford, Connecticut. The people in that little community think he's the greatest. Gives big parties at the house, takes in all these young druggies trying to go straight, contributes to every fund the town council comes up with. He's got a phenomenal front for himself. The police would slap us with something like attempt to slander or some such thing, maybe find some reason to hold us, and we'd be farther away from Jake than ever. Sorry, Lucy, but we're on our own."

The night sky was a dingy wash of city lights filtering into ebony. Somewhere beyond the haze was a beacon-moon lying in wait.

CHAPTER 23

They severed the outside utility wires to the Langston house. Neatly and quietly, they cut a hole through the sidelight next to the front door, then entered the house just after two o'clock Monday morning.

While two men in ski masks moved slowly up the stairs to Jeremy Langston's bedroom, two others entered the master bedroom downstairs. The wide-planked floor creaked loudly, and Roxanne Langston rose suddenly from her pillow. Before she could speak, a hand slapped duct tape against her mouth. She swung her arms wildly clawing deep into the face of one intruder. Cort Peterson howled as he grabbed his cheek, then clamped an iron grip against her wrist and jerked both arms behind her. Another man tied them tightly together.

Just then Jeremy screamed for his mother, and she lunged off the bed. Hands grabbed at her ankles and tied them together. She was lifted from the floor, rolled up inside a blanket, then hauled quickly through the bedroom door.

Jeremy had been bound and wrapped just like his mother. When the kidnappers reached the bottom of the stairs with his wriggling body, they lost their grip on him and he fell against a lamp on the front hall table and rolled to the floor. They quickly removed him from the blanket to assess the damage. They saw no blood or obvious contusions, but the eyes of the small child pierced them with rage, and they covered him quickly.

Mother and son never saw each other through the ordeal. Not until they were carried aboard a swaying, stinking houseboat nearly an hour later and removed from the blankets could they look into each other's terrified faces.

CHAPTER 24

Sunday evening, someone besides Theresa delivered Jake's dinner. It was the soldier.

"So the whiz kid athlete tucked his tail and ran." He waited for a response but got none. "Eat your porridge, Goldie," the soldier ordered, pulling the door shut, "while the bears are away."

Jake watched the last remnant of day fade into twilight. He jerked repeatedly on the chain, as he had for days, hoping something would snap, a link or the lock on the ankle band.

An earthquake loosed Paul's chains once, Jake recalled from his recent reading. Into the night, he was alert for tremors, then finally succumbed to a heavy sleep. About three in the morning, he was roused by a blast of cold air from the open doorway. Someone was there. He clambered to free himself from the rug, to fight if he had to. He felt a hand reach for his right foot, then his left. He threw off the rug, preparing to lunge through the darkness, when he breathed in the first wisp of vanilla.

"Theresa?" he called.

"Be quiet," came the whispered command. "And hold still."

Jake felt a tug at the metal band around his left ankle. "What are you doing?"

"What I have to do," the girl replied. At once, the lock on the ankle band sprang open, and the heavy restraint fell into Theresa's hands.

Jake rose unsteadily to his feet and reached for the hand of his liberator. "Theresa, why are you doing this?" he asked.

"Something's different," she said, pulling him toward the door. "I don't know these people anymore. They've been blinded by this crazed passion to turn the whole world into one big cult. They don't care at all if that man's family gets hurt. I think they would like it, and it scares me."

Jake reached for her arm, but she pulled away.

"Go quickly, Jake," she urged.

"Go with me," he said.

"No. Cort already has the woman and child. He just called to tell Dominick. He's waiting for further instructions. He took three others to help him. I don't know what they'll do to those poor people. And I don't know where they are."

"I think I do. Something I overheard."

"Jake, just go," Theresa insisted.

"Why won't you come with me?"

"If I stay, I can keep them from coming down here and finding you gone. That will give you more time. I'll get away from them later. I promise."

"Will they suspect it was you who did this?"

"Not if I get back before someone misses me." She reached inside her coat pocket and handed him sausages and a biscuit wrapped in foil. "Fuel," she said, then ran from the basement to the side entrance of the house.

Jake watched as Theresa reentered the house. Only when he felt sure she was safe and her deed undetected did he sprint toward the open field and the most direct route to town. With a heavy cloud line concealing the moon, the field was dark, and no one would see the lone figure struggling for speed over the rough ground.

Muscles suddenly sprung from a long, cold bondage labored against the urgent demands of the runner. Jake lurched painfully over the ruts and rows of the fields behind the house. Desperately coaxing his body to reclaim its champion form, he ran the land he'd run many times during his last visit. It suddenly occurred to him that those daily runs just weeks ago had prepared him for this night, imprinting the lay of the land on his memory. Could it be that all his years of training were to groom him for this one solo run?

Knowing the land rolled unobstructed to a tree-lined stream just ahead, Jake maintained his darkened course, unable to see the land break, but knowing it was there.

His breathing began to slow. The tension in his legs eased, and the old power performance that set records in two schools gradually returned. He was soon floating almost free of the ground, like an eagle in flight. An eagle. Isaiah. He remembered: *"They shall mount up with wings as eagles; they shall run, and not be weary."*

There was ecstasy in the run, a surge he'd never felt before, as if a river had overflowed its banks and now plunged through all the canyons of his life, smoothing the jagged places that had hurt for so long. He was riding the crest of the flood, unburdened and free. Sure of his destination.

Jake's flight was soon slowed by taller grass, signaling his approach to water. In the dark, he could only guess at the location of the stream and the place he'd always crossed it to pick up the trail through the woods. In the light of morning, the passage was easy to find, but where was it now?

He'd come to a complete stop at the tree line, wondering which way to go, when suddenly, a brilliant light spread its beacon along the ground and into the trees. Jake threw back his head to see a round, purposeful moon sliding from its long wait behind the clouds. Appearing a moment sooner, the light would have revealed the fleeing figure to anyone watching from the house. But now, Jake was safe in the shadows flickering with moonlight, leaping stone to stone across the stream, with his sights on the old wagon path lit clearly before him.

Only now could he afford a glance behind him. No one coming. No lights in the house.

On the other side of the woods was the road to town, but it meandered from farm to farm, and was not the straightest route. Jake would cross it and cut through the fields beyond, across land that was unfamiliar to him. The journey would be long and perilous.

CHAPTER 25

"And that would be Milford," Steve announced as the Jeep topped a hill and slowed on its approach to the dimly lit town.

"Everything on the main drag is locked tight for the night," he observed, "but hook a right at the first corner, and let's check out the local sheriff's state of readiness. We might just bring in some business tonight."

Joanna eased around the corner. "Where, Steve?"

"There, on the other side of that yellow-painted funeral home, across from the church. Handy, huh? Book 'em, bag 'em, and bury 'em, all in one block."

"Steve, did you have a normal childhood?" Lucy asked, raising one eyebrow.

Before he could answer, Joanna stopped in front of the sheriff's office and lowered the window.

"What are you doing?" Steve scolded. "Keep going. We can't draw attention to ourselves."

"Well, there're not any cars around," Joanna said. "I was just listening for—"

"They park their cars in back, I think," Steve said. "Turn the next corner, and we'll look up the alley."

There was one car parked behind the office. "That'll have to do," Steve said. "Let's keep going."

They pulled slowly away from Milford and accelerated toward the open road.

"This is a long winding two-lane all the way to the turn-off to Dominick's place—about twelve miles. Better slow it down, Joanna. You don't want to hit a deer. They're all over the place."

Joanna was consumed by the hope of finding Jake. *Could it have been only a week since I dashed up the Florida Turnpike, wondering if I'd ever see him again. And if—no, when—I find him, what state will he be in? Has he been drugged? Beaten? Will he know me? Could they all be killed? Have I brought Lucy up here to die?*

"Joanna, slow down," Steve demanded. "You're zoning out on me, girl. Now pay attention."

"Sorry. I'm a little preoccupied. I still can't believe all this is happening."

"Just don't get rubbery on me here. We've got to keep every wit we've got about us if we're going to—"

"What was that?" Joanna interrupted, pointing ahead.

"What?" Steve asked.

"Something just ran across the road up there," said Joanna.

"I told you about the deer," Steve reminded.

"It didn't look like a deer," she said.

"What did it look like?" Lucy asked.

"I'm not sure, but it—there! Running up the bank by the road! See it?" She sped up.

"Yeah, I saw something," Steve said. "But I'm sure it's just a deer."

When Joanna reached the spot where she'd seen the figure disappear over the bank, she stopped. It was too high to see over from the road. She drove to the top of the hill then stopped again, turning the Jeep sideways in the road and switching on the high beams.

"Joanna, what are you doing?" asked Lucy, puzzled by her friend's untimely interest in deer.

"I have to see what that was," she said.

"There it is!" Steve pointed toward the open field.

A full moon suddenly emerged and cast the running figure in a hazy light. Joanna jumped from the car and climbed onto the hood, stretching as tall as she could. She saw a human form. And something familiar in its running.

"Jake!" she cried.

Joanna leaped to the ground and sprinted toward the bank. She reached the top and kept going. Lucy and Steve scrambled from inside and mounted the hood. They stared after the crazed young woman struggling to find her own stride, until they, too, could see that it was no deer in flight across the field. But what if it wasn't Jake?

"Let's go!" Steve blurted. He and Lucy jumped back inside the Jeep. Steve shifted into four-wheel drive and drove straight for the bank. As they lunged over the top, they could hear Joanna screaming for Jake. But the lone figure in the distance never slowed.

"Help me, God," she pleaded. "Make him stop."

She kept running even after she heard the Jeep moving up fast behind her. Steve pulled up alongside and stopped long enough to throw open the passenger door. Joanna jumped in, and the Jeep tore across the rutted field, tossing its occupants in every direction.

"Are you sure it's Jake?" Lucy asked breathlessly.

"It's got to be!" Joanna shouted. "Hurry! He's heading for those woods!"

Moments later, the figure disappeared through the trees. The Jeep raced for the edge of the woods, training its headlights on the dense foliage, then slowed. Joanna jumped out before it stopped, running again and calling for Jake.

"Jake, it's Joanna!" She ran unafraid into the dark thicket. "Jake! It's Jo-ann-a!"

She saw a stream before her just in time to hurl herself across it, landing hard on the opposite bank. She'd just pulled herself from the mud when she heard something rushing through the trees. A shadowy figure came at her, and she screamed as arms reached for her.

Jake grabbed her before she could fight him off. Before she knew she'd found her brother.

"Joanna?!" he shouted.

She spun around in his arms and gasped as if inhaling her last breath. "Jake!" She threw her arms around his neck and shook with heaving sobs.

"God led you to me, didn't He?" Jake finally said, still holding her tight.

Joanna stopped crying. She pulled away just enough to look into his face so faintly illuminated by moonlight. "How did you know?"

He smiled down at her. "I know Him."

"Me, too, Jake. Can you believe that? Me, too. But what's happening? Are you all right?"

Jake was about to answer when he heard the sounds of two others thrashing through the bushes.

"Hold it, buddy!" Steve's voice commanded. "Let go of her, or I'll shoot you."

"What are you going to shoot me with, Steve, a rubber band?"

"Jake!" Lucy hollered, rushing out from behind a startled Steve and jumping the stream. It was her turn to hug and sob, and she did so freely. "We thought you were a deer," she cried with her face buried in his chest.

"Well, what do you know?" Steve said, wading toward Jake with a bear hug of his own. "We warriors came to spring you, and you're already sprung. How'd you do that?"

"I didn't. God used a little angel named Theresa. I'll tell you all about it, but we've got to move now. What time is it, Steve?"

"About four-thirty."

"We've got to get to New York by nine at the latest. But we have to stop in town first. Let's go." Jake helped Joanna and Lucy back across the stream.

Like a race horse primed and ready for the getaway, the red Jeep, its engine left humming and lights blazing, was all but pawing at the ground when the four emerged from the woods at a full run.

"I'll take the wheel," Joanna shouted. Steve and Lucy hopped in back, and Jake slid in beside his sister.

Joanna kept stealing a glance at her brother as she guided the Jeep back to the road. "I just can't look at you enough," Joanna said, her voice breaking. "I wasn't sure I'd ever get to again." Jake reached around her shoulders and patted her arm.

At once, the questions started flying.

"What's going on at the house, Jake?" Steve asked.

"How in the world did you find Steve?" Jake asked Joanna.

"What did they do to you at the cabin?" Joanna asked Jake. "We found blood."

"Who are they going to kidnap?" Lucy asked Jake.

To the last question, Jake replied, "Greg Langston's family. And they already have."

"No way!" Steve exclaimed. "It wasn't supposed to be him."

"But it is. Your friend was wrong. And all this time we had to warn him. It makes me sick. I make me sick."

"Jake, you're not to blame," said Joanna. "If you had called the man, he would have thought you were a kook and ignored you."

"Greg Langston." Joanna repeated the name, then said, "Greg Langs. Grayless! That's the name you were trying to tell Papa on the phone, isn't it? I'd forgotten about it. You see, if I'd remembered, I could have asked Steve, he would have figured out who it was, and warned the man himself. You're no more to blame than I am, Jake." Joanna was prepared to protect her brother from anything, even guilt.

By the time they reached Milford, only a few stories had been told. The rest would have to wait. Joanna parked in front of the sheriff's department, which still appeared lifeless. They all went to the door, which was locked.

Jake knocked a long time. Finally, a uniformed deputy opened the door, but hesitated before letting the four strangers come inside. Before him was a muddy girl picking briars from her jacket, two guys, one who hadn't seen a comb or razor in some time, and another girl who looked normal enough, but something wasn't right.

"Officer, we need your help," Jake began. "We've got a long story and very little time."

CHAPTER 26

Senator Ramsdale couldn't sleep. He rose about four o'clock Monday morning and went downstairs to make coffee. By seven he would have to be fresh and inspiring for an early meeting with his staff. Later, he would drive to Newark for the mega-media dedication of a new BMW plant. But now, he was trembling and soaked with sweat.

Plagued with visions of maimed bodies and a woman screaming after her abducted son, he had fought the dark nights as long as he could. Now, he was desperate to call Dominick off his mission. *I can defeat Wellon all by myself. I don't need any commando tactics to make me win. I don't need Dominick and his fanatical obsessions.*

Ramsdale called the farmhouse and got no answer. He tried the van mobile and got no answer. There was nowhere else, no one else to call. All he could do was wait for the news from New York.

He took a cup of coffee into the family room of his Georgetown home and sank into a wingback chair. He sat in the dark room gazing at the streetlights beyond the window and thought of Angela. It soothed him to remember their love and carefree days together. Life at the communes had been simple and pleasurable. They were often high on weed together, exploring each other with uninhibited eagerness. They were in love, but his family had threatened to cut him off if he pursued her.

He recalled their chance encounter that day in London over twenty years ago. He was already married with three children and a seat in the Nevada legislature. But seeing her that day, her red hair flowing and her face still young and beautiful, he would have tossed it all aside just to live the rest of his life with her.

His had been a marriage of convenience. Voters preferred solid, family men to run their government. So he had proposed to the first girl who had come along after Angela. But it wasn't the same. He knew it would never be the same again.

He and Angela had returned to her flat that day in London and conceived a son.

It was Cort who had discovered she'd had the child and told Ramsdale where to find them. The senator had returned to London to see his two-year-old son, but such liaisons were too dangerous for a rising young politician, and he never visited again. All ties were then severed as if Angela and the boy had never existed.

But he yearned for her still. *I'll see her again,* he promised himself. *I'll find her and love her again, secretly.*

CHAPTER 27

Deputy Warren McIntyre of the Lawrence County Sheriff's Department in Milford, Connecticut, listened sternly as Jake unfolded an abbreviated version of his kidnapping, the abduction of Roxanne and Jeremy Langston, and the possible assault on Dr. Greg Langston in just a matter of hours.

"That's the wildest tale I ever heard," McIntyre finally declared with unveiled contempt. "Dominick Swain is one of the most generous, respected members of this community. And you expect me to fall for some harebrained concoction as I just heard."

"Now, wait just a minute!" Joanna blurted, rising quickly to her feet. But Jake caught her hand and pulled her gently back onto the chair before she could continue.

"Let me," he said softly to her.

"Deputy McIntyre," Jake began calmly. "It looks like it's going to take more time than we have to convince you we're telling the truth. So, if you'll allow us to just use your phone, we'll make a call and be on our way. I'll use my sister's long distance card."

The deputy studied Jake for a long time, then asked, "Where are you from?"

"Deer Creek, North Carolina, sir."

"I think you'd better start heading back that way, son."

"Sir, this is an emergency. I'm not sure my sister's mobile unit will connect from here. Are you really going to deny us the use of your phone?"

McIntyre slapped both hands on his desk and stood up. "Go on over there and make your call," he ordered angrily, pointing to a desk in the corner, "then get on out of here. And by the way, I'll be listening to every word."

The four moved quickly to the corner desk. Jake dialed long distance information. "Manhattan. The number, please, for the Federal Bureau of Investigation."

McIntyre moved closer to the table. "What do you think you're doing?" he asked Jake, who ignored him as he dialed again, and waited.

"Hello? I need to report a kidnapping that took place a few hours ago." His call was quickly transferred.

Deputy McIntyre glared at Jake. He moved to interrupt the call when Jake spoke again.

"My name is Jake Gaddy, sir," he responded to the agent who took the call, "and it is urgent that someone listen very closely to me without asking a lot of questions. I don't have much time." He paused for a response, then proceeded.

"A famous author named Dr. Greg Langston is due to appear at an awards ceremony at the Hotel Internationale in Manhattan sometime around nine o'clock this morning. He—

"Now, sir, let me finish before you start your questions. I have to be at the same hotel before then, and I'm about two hours away. Please just listen." Deputy McIntyre stood over him like a hawk ready to dive. Joanna watched her brother closely, admiring the way he was handling the call, fielding what must have been a barrage of questions from the other end.

"The man's wife and son were kidnapped from their home in Rockledge, Maryland, around midnight by members of a spiritual. . . well, I guess you could call it a cult that's headquartered in a farmhouse near Milford, Connecticut. I'm at the sheriff's office in that town right now. The leader of the cult is named Dominick Swain, and he and his followers are probably en route to the Hotel Internationale this moment.

"Please let me finish, ma'am." Joanna grinned at the change in Jake's tone, suspecting that he was now on speaker phone before a growing number of FBI personnel. Her pride in her brother grew.

"Dominick's purpose in kidnapping Dr. Langston's family is to force him to acknowledge before the world—this thing is also being televised—that Christians United is responsible for the bombing of the Las Vegas casino."

Several voices spoke at once in New York.

"I realize how bizarre this is," Jake said, glancing at Steve, who twitched nervously in his chair. "Yes, I realize the penalty for perpetrating a hoax on your department, but, sir, this thing is really happening."

There was a pause while Jake listened. Joanna shook her head slowly as she stared into space over Jake's head.

"Yes, sir," Jake answered. "It's actually Dr. Jake Gaddy. I'm an associate professor of engineering at the University of Virginia, and they'll be happy to verify that for you."

McIntyre squinted at Jake in disbelief.

"That's right," Jake continued, "in Charlottesville. Yes, unfortunately, I became involved with this, uh, group about a year and a half ago. But I dropped out when this plan was first proposed." Jake paused and seemed uncomfortable. "No, sir, I didn't report it because I never believed they would do such a thing. I thought it was just a lot of nonsense." Jake and Steve exchanged painful expressions, and Jake continued.

"Then they kidnapped me. That's right. . .from my grandfather's home in Deer Creek, North Carolina. That's Eli Gaddy. Now let me explain. When they decided to really carry this scheme out, they wanted anyone who'd heard of it in their control. There were three of us who'd dropped out by that time. I'll tell you about the others later."

Steve squeezed his eyes shut and dropped his head. Lucy reached out and patted his knee.

"They've been holding me in the basement of the farmhouse until I escaped a few hours ago. I'm here with Deputy McIntyre in Milford—who, I might add, has been so kind and eager to help us." Four sets of eyes turned on the deputy now fidgeting with his badge. "Yes, sir, I'll put him on in a minute." McIntyre's face blanched.

"I think they're being held—well, no, sir, I'm not sure, but I overheard them talking about a houseboat on the Susquehanna River just north of the I-95 bridge. You'll have to hunt for it. No, I'm sure they said houseboat, not boathouse."

Another pause. "Dominick? Yes, sir, I can describe him. He's early sixties. Close to six feet, very heavy, longish gray-blond hair. He may not make himself visible, though, or he might be in disguise."

Just then, another voice entered the conversation. Then another, each asking questions in turn. One of them said he was very familiar with Dr. Greg Langston. He introduced himself as Agent David Hutto.

"Jake," said Hutto, "if this guy finds out you've escaped, what do you think he'll do?"

"His people are already holding the wife and son. I think he'll proceed with his plan, trusting that I can't do him much harm. He's probably thinking that by the time I reach the police and convince them I'm not a lunatic—" Jake peered sideways at McIntyre "—the deed will be done."

"Are you certain the family has already been abducted?"

"I was told by a member of the cult, the young woman who freed me, that the kidnappers had called to say they had succeeded. So, yes, I'm quite certain. By the way, the man who actually kidnapped Mrs. Langston and the boy is Cort Peterson." Jake described Peterson and the brief encounter he'd had with the man. He knew nothing else about him.

"The Susquehanna, close to the I-95 bridge, in a houseboat?" asked Hutto. "That's all you know?"

"I'm sorry," said Jake. "That's all I heard about the location."

"When do they plan to tell him about his family?" another voice asked.

"One of their group is on staff at the hotel. A waiter. I don't know who. He's supposed to slip a note to Langston before it's his turn to speak this morning."

"Is Langston staying at the hotel?"

"I have no idea."

"Put Deputy McIntyre on the phone, Jake."

McIntyre took the phone Jake handed him. He cleared his throat before speaking. "This is Deputy Warren McIntyre in Milford. What's that? My badge number? 109. Yes, I've heard everything this young man has been saying. Yes, I know Dominick Swain. No, I never suspected him of any such activity. We've never so much as given him a speeding ticket around here. Yes, he does house a number of young people out there from time to time. He also takes in a few druggies, I hear, to help them. What do I think of Jake Gaddy?" McIntyre looked at the mud and grime on Jake's torn clothing and the dark stubble on his face. "Well, he's not too clean right now. I could believe he's been somewhere he shouldn't have been. And one of the girls looks like she's been drug through some mud. Yeah, there's three more of them here. Two girls and a guy. No, he didn't mention that, did he? Yeah, I can wait a few minutes."

While verification was being run on McIntyre's identification, Hutto asked to speak to Jake again.

"Who's with you, Jake?"

"My sister, Joanna, a friend of ours from Deer Creek named Lucy Wetherington, and another friend, Steve Michon, who quit the cult when I did. No, the girls never had anything to do with it.

"Well, sir, you'll have to get my sister to tell you how they wound up here. It's a long story we don't have time for. We've got to get to the hotel. My friend Steve and I are the only ones who can identify Dominick for you. If you start asking questions and looking for him yourself, he'll know. It'll spook him. And I don't know what he'll do. He could order the Langstons moved before you can find them. Now, sir, I really have to go."

"Yes, you do, Dr. Gaddy. UVA just confirmed the existence of such a person, and it had better be you," Hutto said firmly. "We'll have a chopper there in thirty minutes. Let me talk to McIntyre again."

"A helicopter?" Jake was stunned. "You're sending a helicopter up here?"

McIntyre dropped his jaw again.

"Jake, get McIntyre." There was now urgency in Agent Hutto's voice.

McIntyre took the phone again. "Good. I'm glad I'm still on record. Where? Well, let's see. I guess you won't have any trouble seeing old man Winkler's huge red barn down from the water tower on the southeast edge of town. Set it down behind that barn. It's level there, and there aren't any trees. I'll tell him you're coming. He'll want to move his cows, you know. Yeah, I'll have them down there in a few minutes for you. What's that? Yeah, they look scared. Too scared to be lying, I guess. I never heard such a tale. Goodbye."

"Jake, we have to call Papa," Joanna said as soon as McIntyre hung up. "He's got to know you're safe."

"I can't talk to him just yet, Joanna. I've done too much to hurt him. You call him. Tell him not to worry."

There was no answer at the lake house. Nor the Gaddy house. Joanna couldn't understand where they would be at that hour of the night. She finally got an answer at the Wetherington house.

"Honey, your grandfather and Martin flew to New York last night," Tad Wetherington announced.

"What?"

"Joanna, what's wrong?" Jake demanded.

"Papa and Martin are in New York!"

"I tried to stop them," Wetherington continued, "but Eli insisted on going to help you. It was no easy task getting those two in the air, believe me. I tried to reach you at the hotel, but you weren't in."

"What time were they supposed to arrive?" Joanna asked.

"About eleven o'clock. Probably got to your hotel about midnight. I made the reservations for them. You haven't seen them?" There was alarm in his voice.

"We left the hotel about that time. Must have just missed them."

"Well, what's happening?" Wetherington asked impatiently.

"We have Jake."

"Oh, thank God!" Wetherington exclaimed.

"He's a little ragged, but he's fine. Would you please try to reach Papa at the hotel for me? Tell him about Jake, and to stay put until we get there. And thanks for everything, Dr. Wetherington."

Joanna gave the phone to Lucy, who told her dad all she could about the cult and their plans for that morning before McIntyre signaled it was time to go.

CHAPTER 28

It was no ordinary Monday morning for Amos Winkler. An early call from Warren McIntyre—Mac to everyone in Milford— started it. He asked Amos to move his cows out of the pasture behind his barn so the FBI's helicopter could land about six-thirty. Then he asked if this girl from North Carolina could leave her Jeep inside Amos's barn for a few days.

It was getting stranger still, Amos observed from his fence-top perch near the barn. There was that girl, her three friends, and Mac huddled over there on the ground talking in excited tones about how the guys would need to disguise themselves.

Amos didn't understand why Mac couldn't tell him what it was all about, but if the FBI was whirlybirding in all the way from New York City to get these young folks, he thought they were probably in a heap of trouble. Best to stay clear of them, he decided. But then here came two of them walking right up to him.

"Mr. Winkler," Joanna said, "we want to thank you again for helping us. You've gone to a lot of trouble for us, and we're indebted to you."

"We sure are, sir," Steve agreed. "You must think all this is pretty strange."

"Doesn't happen every day around here. But you young folks seem real well-behaved, and I'm sure whatever you've done, they'll let you off easy."

Steve and Joanna exchanged amused glances with each other.

"Oh, no, sir," Joanna said, "we're not being arrested. We're just trying to stop some people from getting hurt."

"It's a very long story, sir," Steve added. "Get Deputy McIntyre to fill you in later. I think he's pretty uptight about the whole thing right now."

"Mac does a good job for us. You just got to know him."

"I guess you do," said Joanna with a tight grin. "But about my car, I'll be happy to pay for the parking space."

"Naw," Amos replied shaking his head, "just bring me back some souvenir from the big city. The wife and I haven't been there in twenty years or more."

"You got it," Joanna said. "Now here's an extra set of keys to the Jeep just in case you need to move it. And thanks again."

Amos was watching the four young friends and Mac continue their animated discussion when a dull roar crept into the early morning stillness. "Listen!" he called to the others.

In seconds, the sound magnified to the unmistakable pulsating currents of a helicopter, the one now swooping in fast on its intended cargo. Six people alone in the tender warmth of the early morning sun waved to the mechanical beast alighting in that gentle pasture. As the rotation of the blades slowed, the door opened and a man emerged. He walked hunchbacked away from the aircraft toward the anxious party at the barn.

Deputy McIntyre was the first to approach him, shouting his name and some semblance of a greeting. Jake followed.

"Are you Jake Gaddy?" asked the handsome man in suit pants and a leather flight jacket.

"Yes, sir."

Displaying his badge in one hand and extending the other hand toward Jake, the man said, "I'm Agent David Hutto." He was early thirties, medium height, lean, and deeply tanned.

I hope that's from running or fishing, Jake thought, *and not some tanning bed. I can't trust a primp.*

"Are you ready to go?" Hutto asked quickly.

"We're all ready," Jake replied. "My sister and friends are coming, too, aren't they?"

"That's why we brought the big bird. Tell them to hurry."

Hasty introductions were made all around. Then Hutto took

McIntyre aside for a quick word on searching the farmhouse and providing information on Dominick and his group.

McIntyre bade the young people a fonder farewell than the greeting he'd extended them earlier. He'd come around, they observed, and seemed genuinely concerned about their welfare.

Before boarding, they all turned and waved to Amos who hadn't budged from the fence. He waved back as the helicopter lifted off and banked toward the south, gaining speed and altitude. As it disappeared over the treetops, Amos waved again.

"Godspeed," he whispered.

CHAPTER 29

Dawn broke with calamity that Monday morning on the river. From the bed Roxanne Langston was tied to, she had watched vigilantly through the night for anyone entering the small bedroom where she and her son were kept. About four o'clock in the morning, though, she had finally succumbed to the gentle rocking of the houseboat, and now she and Jeremy slept side by side on the bare, rotting mattress.

A sudden movement near the bed woke her. She opened her eyes and through the tape still covering her mouth, let out a shrill, piercing squeal. Seconds later the same sound erupted from Jeremy's taped mouth. Dangling above their heads was the thick, convulsing body of a snake. The man holding it laughed down at them from behind his dark ski mask.

Suddenly the door burst open and Cort Peterson, also in a mask, shoved a gun to the side of the man's head. "Get it out of here! Now!"

The man shuffled slowly from the room, carrying the snake and still laughing.

Peterson lingered long enough to see that the bindings on both mother and son were still secure as they lay flat on their backs, then left.

A radio suddenly blared from the living room of the houseboat, and Roxanne guessed it was to cover the men's voices. Still shaking, she turned the only part of her she could move, her head, to Jeremy. Tears streaked his cheeks, and his eyes were wide with terror.

Roxanne started to hum "Jesus Loves Me" to him, pleading with her eyes for him to seek the same comforter. In a few minutes he joined her, and as his small voice hummed the song, she saw hope and trust finally spring to his eyes.

A fight erupted in the living room. Peterson withdrew a knife from his pocket, hacked the snake's head off and flung it at the man he'd just held a gun to. "I'll kill you if you go near them again!" he snarled.

"I was just playing with them, Cort."

"I don't pay you to play! And if you want to see a dime of the money, you'd better straighten up."

"Okay. Okay. Back off, man."

The other two men didn't say a word. They were afraid of Peterson. They'd seen him in action and knew he'd kill with little provocation.

At 7 A.M., Peterson announced he was going to survey the area. "Just want to make sure we're still alone down here. Don't want any surprise visitors. Be back in about thirty minutes. Check on those two every ten minutes. And don't forget to cover your faces before you go in—and never, never take off your gloves. Your prints would set off sirens in the FBI lab. Do you understand everything I'm saying?"

All three nodded their heads.

"Keep their door closed and the music loud," he added, then hopped through the open door onto the dock that ran along the side of the houseboat. Dominick had found the abandoned houseboat in a remote crook of the river and had it watched for weeks before the abduction. No one ever showed up, and the condition of it suggested no one was tending it at all.

Later, Roxanne heard the dock outside the window creaking. Then she heard voices. The music in the other room was still blaring, but the voices outside were clear. She caught Jeremy's attention and darted her eyes toward the window for him to listen. They both strained to hear every word.

"That guy's about to push me too far, Ron."

"You know he's crazy, Jack. Why do you pull stupid stuff like that? He's always ready to blow."

"Speaking of blowing. Do you know about the hospitals he's going to bomb?"

Roxanne's eyes flashed.

"You're out of your mind."

"Nope. He doesn't know that I heard him and Dominick talking at the farm. I was in the attic working on the wiring. They were in the bedroom below. Heard everything they said. It ought to bring me a nice bit of cash someday."

"What hospitals?"

"Didn't hear that. Some kind of abortion places. Clinics, you know. Going to blow them after they take care of Greg Langston."

Jeremy's face twisted as he turned toward his mom, alarm in his eyes. Roxanne's heart raced, but she lay still and silent, trying to hear all she could.

"Then they're going to say it was some Christian group that did it. Christians United or something like that."

"I think you'd better keep your mouth shut, Jack. You could wind up like that snake."

"Hey, you two." It was the third guy coming down the dock. "What do you think you're doing? Get inside. You want someone to see you?"

"There's nobody around here. I'm going to hunt me another snake."

"Get in here, fool!" the third man commanded.

"Who made you God?" Ron demanded.

Just then Roxanne heard a truck coming through the woods, then three sets of feet racing down the dock and jumping onto the houseboat, making it rock and crack like wood splintering. She choked back the sobs rising in her throat.

Father, help us!

CHAPTER 30

Three dark gray sedans streaked through Monday morning's rush-hour traffic in Manhattan. The airlift into the city, as thrilling a ride as that, paled against the lightning maneuvers of the agent at the wheel of the lead car, the one in which Jake and Steve rode with Agent David Hutto. Joanna, Lucy, and six more agents followed. It was nearly eight o'clock.

Hutto hadn't located Greg Langston, who, according to the event's sponsors, had canceled his reservations at the Hotel Internationale months ago, but was still scheduled to appear at the awards ceremony.

Two agents were standing by in the office of the hotel's general manager, Nick Sasha, who'd been roused from sleep by Hutto. The director of security, Jon Friedman, was also present. Hutto had arranged for the agents to enter Sasha's office, announcing themselves to his staff as representatives from a local television station scheduled to air portions of the nine o'clock breakfast and awards ceremony. The event was being held in the hotel's grand State Room, a cavernous, elaborately appointed ballroom on the main floor. Not knowing where Dominick, his plant on the hotel staff, or any other cult members might be stationed in the hotel, Hutto strictly forbade any mention of the FBI.

Within seconds after Jake's call, Hutto had dispatched the Baltimore agents to the Langston's woodlands home. They found no one there, a hole cut into the front window, a broken lamp on the floor of the entry hall, and two cars parked in front of the house. The utility wires to the house had been cut. Hutto immediately ordered a massive sweep of the Susquehanna River near the I-95 bridge.

He felt certain that, by now, Dominick knew Jake had escaped from the farmhouse. He knew the cult leader and his friends would be looking for Jake and any police support he might bring along. That's why Jake and Steve were dressed as they were. Jake was sporting a full beard beneath the bill of his baseball cap. Steve was already scratching at a long-haired wig held in place by a bandana. He also wore a pair of dark-tinted eyeglasses and a bushy moustache. The boys would pose as broadcast technicians, carrying a convincing cache of video equipment, especially coils of cable that could be draped about the shoulders and raised to face level at any moment. Sasha had informed Hutto there would be several news crews milling about the hotel. Each would think Jake and Steve belonged to another.

Most of the FBI agents were attired in an assortment of disguises from security guards to bellhops to waiters. Hutto and two other agents, all dressed in business suits, would mingle with those attending the breakfast affair. Everyone, including Jake and Steve, were wired inconspicuously for communication with each other.

In the backseat of the speeding sedan, Steve glanced at Jake with an incredulous frown. "Can you believe this?" he asked, his voice rising to a squeak. "Headed for a stake-out with the FBI, looking like Charles Manson."

"Ah, I think the bandana's a nice touch, Steve," Jake teased. "Maybe they'll let you keep it."

Hutto turned away and smiled. Just then a call came in on the mobile. It was Baltimore. No sign of a houseboat yet. They were still searching.

"I just thought of something," Jake blurted. "We don't know what Langston looks like."

"I do," Hutto said calmly.

"How?" Jake asked.

"He spoke at a conference I went to not long ago," Hutto replied.

"What kind of conference?"

"On the separation of church and state. It was part of a class I took at NYU."

"What did you think of him?" Jake asked.

"He definitely touched some nerves. Says what he thinks. I admire him."

"Do you believe what he believes?" Jake asked bluntly.

Hutto shifted nervously in his seat. "Maybe. Not sure."

"Do you, Jake?" Steve asked.

"Yeah, I do."

Before Steve could reply, Hutto announced, "This is it. Gather up your gear."

The three cars passed the front of the hotel, turned the corner, and continued down the side street behind the hotel's service alley. Jake had informed Hutto of Dominick's plan to escape through the back entrance to the kitchen. Agents were already stationed there in various service trucks parked near the door.

The cars were parked out of sight of the hotel. The occupants unloaded and scattered, approaching the hotel from different directions. Joanna and Lucy weren't allowed to walk with Jake and Steve, who had assumed their roles as stragglers hurrying to catch up with their news crew. After putting up fierce resistance to remaining behind at FBI headquarters, the girls were allowed to accompany everyone to the hotel. But once inside, Hutto ordered, they were to stay clear of all operations. Joanna and Lucy agreed.

The sidewalks were full. Blending with the crowd was easy. Jake and Steve studied every face. They approached the hotel just in front of Hutto and two other agents. If either of them saw a subject, as Hutto called the cult members, he was to quietly alert the agents through the tiny mike beneath each boy's lapel.

Turning the corner toward the hotel's front entrance, the boys were grateful to see a tangle of humanity in which to lose themselves. Site trucks from three television stations were parked in the circular drive. The crews were unloading equipment and hauling it inside. Pedestrian traffic along the street was heavy.

Jake and Steve tucked their heads and approached the massive glass and brass front doors to the hotel. They were virtually ignored as they took up their designated station just inside the doorway. They were to scan both inside and outside that area for ten minutes, then move to another station closer to the State Room entrance. They were to rotate stations every ten minutes looking for Dominick and the others. They were being watched constantly by agents who, upon the alert, would relay the identification of a subject to Hutto. Other agents would then begin surveillance. Hutto had ordered his men to arrest Dominick, once identified, on the spot, but not any of his people—not until they had Dominick.

The first ten-minute watch ended with no signal sent. Jake and Steve moved hurriedly along to the next station, just as anyone setting up for live coverage in less than an hour would do, yet continuing their search for familiar faces, even disguised ones.

Hutto, meanwhile, determined that Langston had not arrived at the hotel, and there was no message for or from the man. Sasha was unable to identify Langston, but indicated that a desk clerk named Ronnie had struck up a friendship with the author during one of his previous visits to the hotel. Ronnie, currently on duty, had been instructed by Sasha to watch for Langston and notify him the minute he entered the hotel.

Jake had just reached to balance the cable hanging from his shoulder when his eyes locked on the soldier. The man was sitting on a sofa in the lobby, toying with a small video game while surveying the crowd about him. Jake uttered a soft alert into his mike. The agent watching Jake moved closer to the soldier, signaling another agent to take his place monitoring Jake and Steve.

Jake had turned to move toward his next station when he all but collided with the girl driver who whisked him away after his capture outside the bridal shop. She glanced up at him, but through the beard and all the cable draped across him, she noticed nothing and kept walking through the lobby. Jake gave the signal again, and the girl was soon under watch.

The boys had stumbled upon the nest. Steve caught the swagger of the bodybuilder approaching from a hallway running alongside the State Room. Steve had seen him once before at the lake house near UVA and instantly recognized him with his blond ponytail. He was dressed handsomely in a dark suit and tie, as though he intended to be included in the audience that morning. With a quick yank on Jake's sleeve, Steve managed to whirl them both around to avoid making eye contact. Another signal. Another tail. That was three. But no Dominick.

Just then Jake saw Hutto and another man emerge from an office behind the front desk. The two men quickly made their way across the lobby toward a sandy-haired gentleman in a light gray trench coat who had just arrived at the hotel.

"Keep watching, Steve," Jake said. "I'll be back."

Jake moved close enough to hear Sasha say in a conspicuously clear voice, "Dr. Langston, I've been watching for you. I'm Nick Sasha, general manager of the hotel." Motioning toward Hutto, Sasha added, "And this is Tom Harrell, a friend of mine from the *Boston Globe*." Hutto and Langston exchanged polite greetings. "Tom has asked me to introduce him to you in hopes you might grant him a quick interview regarding your latest book, before you join the others in the State Room. I've told him that if you agree, the two of you may use my office since the lobby is so busy right now."

Sasha was nervous, and his words tumbled rapidly. Langston was reluctant.

Hutto knew the little scene was being carefully observed. He could feel it. They were here, listening to every word. They must not suspect anything, not until Dominick was in cuffs, especially since Langston's family had not been located.

"Dr. Langston," Hutto addressed the man warmly and with deliberate calm. "I've read your latest book and was thoroughly intrigued. My editors would be deeply grateful if you would allow me just a moment of your time to discuss its message." *Please say "yes,"* Hutto silently implored. *If he resists, how will I insist without arousing suspicion in those who are watching?*

"Well, just for a moment," Langston agreed.

Hutto exhaled with relief and escorted the man to the office. Sasha followed them inside.

Hutto closed the door behind them and immediately turned to Langston, who was removing his coat and settling into an armchair by Sasha's desk. Hutto saw the same expressive face and congenial manner he'd seen behind the podium at NYU that night at the conference, the same confident man whose powerfully compelling words had plucked a sensitive chord deep inside him. Langston had challenged his audience that night to look beyond the futile trappings of this world and into the face of their creator for a vision of what life was meant to be.

Looking at Langston now, Hutto wondered why the world turned so savagely upon the good.

Hutto pulled a chair directly in front of Langston, sat down, and leaned forward, searching the unsuspecting face. He'd been dreading this for hours.

"Dr. Langston," Hutto began slowly, reaching for his identification, "my name isn't Tom Harrell, and I'm not from the *Boston Globe*. I'm Agent David Hutto with the FBI."

Langston frowned and started to speak, but Hutto cut in.

"Sir, I apologize. But listen very carefully to me. I'm going to trust that you're as strong a man as I think you are in order for us to get through a situation that's just come to our attention."

Langston was now focused intently on the man before him.

"There is a cult led by a man named Father Dominick, or just Dominick. Is that name at all familiar to you?"

Langston thought for a moment. "No, it isn't."

"The man's last name is Swain. Is that familiar?"

"No. Why?"

"According to an informant who contacted us just hours ago, it is this man's intention to force you to get up to the podium this morning and admit publicly that Christians United is responsible for the recent casino bombing in Las Vegas, and that the Soldiers of the Cross, who I'm sure you've heard of, is an arm of Christians United."

Langston looked at Hutto as if the agent had gone mad. "What in the world are you saying?"

"You've got to believe that everything I'm telling you is the truth, sir," Hutto said. "We have very little time left. Please listen to me. Once you're inside the ballroom, someone—we think it will be a waiter—is going to slip a note to you. We're not sure what it will say, but we have reason to believe it will inform you that—" Hutto paused for a breath. "—that your wife and son are being held by members of this cult."

Langston's response was instant. He reached for Hutto's arms and gripped them hard. "Roxanne and Jeremy?" Langston cried. "What's happened to them?!"

Hutto was jarred by the sudden reaction, but remained calm. "We believe they have been kidnapped, sir. We've already been to your home." Hutto told him what the agents had found, making no move to loosen Langston's grip on him.

"Your son's school reported him absent this morning and also indicated that your wife, who's a librarian at the school, I believe, never arrived either. They said that today, especially, she should have reported to work since there was a grand opening of some new library. They hadn't heard from her." Hutto paused a moment. "Sir, we believe this is real."

Langston released Hutto and sprang to his feet.

Hutto continued, "We think they're being held in a houseboat on the Susquehanna River near the I-95 bridge. We're searching for it this moment. I expect word of their rescue soon. Until then—"

"Who told you about this cult?" Langston demanded.

Hutto wanted to console the stricken man, but didn't know how. "A young man escaped from them earlier this morning to alert us. He says the note they'll slip to you will also instruct you to acknowledge that Christian leaders are perpetuating a lie for their own gain. That the gospel is a fraud."

Langston searched Hutto's face as if appraising his level of sanity.

Hutto continued. "Our informant believes Dominick will release your family if you cooperate."

"And if I don't?"

Hutto chose his answer carefully. "Sir, that would be unwise. We've already spotted several members of the cult in the lobby—"

"Then arrest them!"

"We can detain them at any moment and interrogate them, but if we do that before we find Dominick—who we also believe to be in the building—we run the risk of scaring him away. He could contact his people and tell them to move the hostages, and right now—"

"Roxanne and Jeremy are. . .hostages?" Langston was still reeling from the blow.

"We need time, sir. Until we have either Dominick or your family in custody, we shouldn't do anything to disturb their plan."

Langston was strangely quiet. He was staring into the carpet. His lips moved almost imperceptibly. Hutto realized the man was praying and paused before speaking again.

"We have some instructions of our own for you, sir." Langston turned slowly and stared at Hutto, who proceeded to brief him.

"You will need to signal a designated agent in the room as soon as the note is passed to you. We need to know who delivered it. I will tell you how to do that in a moment." Langston locked on every word Hutto spoke.

"It is imperative that you remain in the room. If for any reason you should leave, before or after the note is passed, Dominick might panic. You must give no indication whatsoever that you have been warned or that you are unwilling to cooperate with Dominick's demands.

Langston squeezed his eyes shut and stroked his brow with trembling fingers.

"They will be watching your every move, your every expression. You are to enter the room full of glad tidings and pleasure over the whole affair. When you receive the note, you are to react as if it has taken you by complete surprise. Though your impulse might naturally be to rush for help, be comforted that someone named Jake Gaddy has already done that.

The grave expression on Langston's face grieved Hutto, who admired the man for the strength of his convictions, but pitied him in the worst way at this moment.

"And now, Dr. Langston," Hutto continued, "if we locate Dominick or your family before you have to speak, we will clearly notify you, and you can either proceed as planned or excuse yourself. If we've accomplished neither by that time, I suggest you comply with their demands. We need time to search. You can retract your statements later when this whole sordid affair comes to light and your family is returned. People will understand why you said what you did."

After a long silence, Langston rose steadily to his feet. Hutto and Sasha stood, also. Langston studied their faces, then placed a hand on each man's shoulder and closed his eyes. "Father," he prayed softly, "thank You for these good men. Grant us wisdom and courage to do what we each must do. Hold my family in Your mighty hand and deliver them safely back to me, if that is Your will. Speak through me this day. In the name of Jesus Christ, who sustains me, I pray. Amen."

Hutto saw peace in the man he'd pitied. It was genuine. And he wanted it. *But how,* he wondered. *I'm so far away.*

Langston took his coat and moved toward the door. Hutto walked with him, prompting him into his role. "They're out there, sir. Watching you as you leave. This was just a chat with an eager newspaperman, remember?"

At the door, Hutto gave final instructions to Langston on signaling that the note had been delivered, then watched him walk slowly toward the lobby.

CHAPTER 31

Greg Langston paused near the front desk before reentering the sprawling hotel lobby with its dazzling chandeliers, shiny chintz sofas, and lofty potted palms. He watched people hurry past him, dropping into quick conversation with others arriving for the ceremonies. How light and convivial the mood in that magnificent room. *How deceiving,* Langston thought. *Look at them. Do they not know what lurks among them?*

The crowd began to drift toward the State Room. He was supposed to follow along. To take his reserved seat, make small talk about printings and promotions, and wait patiently for his turn to accept an award for highest volume of sales in the category of religious books. But what did that matter? He didn't want any award. He never even wanted to come. And now, he wanted to tear out of the building and race for the river, calling the names of his wife and child again and again.

Lord! he cried out in his heart. *Take hold of my senses before I shame You. Grip my hand and lead me through this. Protect my wife and child and forgive me for my fear.*

His mind was still racing down the river when his eyes suddenly beheld a curious face. A young man, looking straight at him. Langston panicked. *One of them! I've stood here too long. They must know something's wrong.*

He remembered Hutto's warnings and struggled to compose himself. Instantly, he turned and called cheerfully to Ronnie, the desk clerk.

"Ronnie, I've been standing here trying to remember the name of that restaurant you told me about last time I was here."

"Oh, the Beefeater's Banquet, sir. You'll love it."

Langston prayed the ruse worked, that the man watching him would not suspect he'd been warned. But the man was gone. Not far, though, Langston suspected.

Moving slowly into the lobby, he passed a soaring wall of glass and peered outside the building. Across the street he could see people queuing up for hot pretzels, doughnuts, and coffee from the street vendors. Just a normal day. Full of demons and indifference.

And there, just ahead was the media, poised to chronicle the events of the day. What would they be? As Langston waded into the crowd, he withdrew into the quiet garden of his thoughts, unreachable by those around him. His name was called several times by some who recognized him, but he didn't hear.

Langston had just turned the corner near the entrance to the State Room when Hutto caught his eye, jerking him back to the immediacy of the situation. The agent was standing with a couple of long-haired, bearded young men, obviously with one of the television stations, for all the gear they carried. One of them stared in his direction for a long time, as if he knew him, though Langston didn't recall ever seeing the boy before.

As he passed, Langston nodded professionally to Hutto as was natural for one who'd just granted an interview with the so-called reporter. Role playing. He'd done it a thousand times in his classes. Surely he could summon his skills in this critical hour.

Hutto's expression urged Langston into his performance. The author smiled pleasantly as he entered the great hall, registered with the hostesses, and was escorted to one of four tables near the dais reserved for honored guests.

Every five years, the nation's leading publishers and broadcasters turn an investigative eye on themselves to determine what made the charts and ratings rise or fall since the last time they met. For two days, media representatives from around the country plunge into think tanks rippling with new ideas for peddling the news and entertainment and inspiring the masses to read more books. They track shifts in social mores, education levels of the viewer/reader, regional demographic patterns, and anything else that might indicate it's time to modulate their voices. That's the academic side.

Marketing panelists, however, sharpen the focus. *What's the prediction on horoscopes?* they ask. *Do they have a future? Is the six o'clock news too early? Why is it that everyone who's good at holding a microphone has his or her own talk show? What's the trend in book jacket art?*

In recent years, the conference had become a news event in itself. Organizers decided that the brightest stars in each industry's constellation—celebrity journalists, authors, performers, screenwriters, producers, and others who'd attracted the public eye—should be honored during a high-profile breakfast ceremony.

Greg Langston had been asked to address the issue of the conservative Christian right and its movement into politics and entertainment at one of the conference's workshops. This topic assigned by the event's organizers had amused him. He remembered the conversation with Roxanne after receiving the invitation to speak. . . .

"Somebody's nervous, Rox. They're seeing the Christian right as a growing power to reckon with, like an offshore, atmospheric disturbance that's moving toward land. They want me to track the hurricane for them, don't they?"

"They're just curious, Greg," Roxanne replied.

"More like unduly concerned. If they're worried about the Christian community at large massing themselves in a frontal assault on the status quo, then they haven't seen what I've seen."

Roxanne had heard the familiar despair in his voice.

"They haven't seen people openly worship God on Sunday mornings," he continued, "then hardly mention His name the rest of the week. Wouldn't want anyone to think they were a fanatic. No, Rox, there's no revival hurricane out there to track. A gust every now and then, maybe. Nothing threatening, I'm sorry to report."

"I think you're wrong, Greg. I think the few God has deployed to the Christian front are making an impact that will, in time, motivate others to speak up. You're too impatient, sweetheart. Just do what you were called to do and never stop. Never question why or what for."

Roxanne's words refrained in his head. *What I'm called to do. What is that? At this moment, what is that?*

Langston fidgeted with his napkin as two *Newsweek* editors chatted with each other on the other side of the table. The remaining seats were empty. The commotion in the lobby had moved inside and magnified. People stood in scattered groups, assessing each other's professional accomplishments, golf games, and families. A small chamber orchestra played reverently in one corner.

Langston kept watching for a sign from Hutto, who now stood alone near the main door. A slight turn of the head from one side to the other indicated there was still no word of a rescue, or that Swain had been located.

The two young men Hutto had been talking to earlier were now roaming separately about the room. Langston watched them. It appeared to him they were looking for someone. Then it struck him. The one who escaped from the cult! The one who'd stared at him? It had to be him. They were searching for Swain.

It occurred to Langston that he was too obviously withdrawn from the rest. He stood up and looked for someone to talk to, about anything. Then he noticed one of his editors standing with a group near a hospitality table set up on one side of the room and headed in that direction.

Halfway there he saw the young bearded boy who'd made eye contact with him weaving his way slowly through the throng. Langston was careful not to look directly at him, but could tell the boy was moving closer to him. At the moment they passed each other, both surrounded by the buzz of conversation, Jake leaned slightly toward Langston, never once looking at him, and in a hushed but clear voice said, "Be still, and know that He is God." Jake never stopped walking. Langston slowed, then moved on. He'd heard every word.

"Greg!" called an editor who'd noticed him approaching. "Come over here, and let me introduce you to some futuristic cable folks."

Langston smiled brightly as he shook hands and launched into light-hearted banter. Only then did he look after the young man who'd delivered a message of hope. But he was gone. So was Hutto. As he listened to the discussion on the international role of American cable news, his imagination rumbled through the possibilities of what was happening that moment. His prayer had always been that God's will, not his own, be done. Could it be His will to take Roxanne and Jeremy home before him? Was that happening? Were they suffering?

A voice from the podium microphone asked everyone to quickly take their seats. When the two gentlemen from cable news excused themselves, Langston's editor turned to him and asked, "Greg, is anything wrong?"

"No, why?" Recover quickly, Langston warned himself.

"You were awfully distracted, and now you're positively ashen."

"Not enough sleep, I guess. Maybe a bug coming on. Sorry."

"No problem. We have to take care of you, you know. Especially after today."

"What do you mean?" Langston asked abruptly, before catching himself. Of course, this man didn't know what was happening.

"Well, Greg," the editor began, surprised by Langston's sharp retort, "look around at the people you're about to address. They're the ones who decide what news we hear or don't hear, which politico to expose and which one to protect. It's up to them how the movie's going to end and what the message is. They'll disseminate whatever information they choose, editorialize all they want. It's power, Greg. And on prime time news tonight, that same power will replay the remarks you make this morning. That is, if they don't edit you out." He chuckled good-naturedly, patted Langston on the back and left to find his seat.

Langston felt himself sinking, his strength ebbing. Then he realized he'd taken too long to return to his table at the front of the room. Most everyone else was already seated as he maneuvered through the aisles. He could feel their eyes following him. *Which ones are Dominick Swain's?*

CHAPTER 32

The young woman on Langston's right introduced herself as a screen-writer for a hit television sitcom he had to admit never watching. On his left was a woman whose reporting on the final days of Romania's brutal dictator, Nicolae Ceausescu, had won the acclaim of her peers. He attempted to chat casually with the two women, making polite inquiries into their backgrounds and feigning interest in their answers, while masking his torment.

Breakfast was being served as the president of a major television network welcomed everyone to New York. It was his corporation's turn to host the conference this year, and he was joined on the dais by his fellow directors, whom he introduced to great applause.

Langston glanced toward the door. Hutto still wasn't there. Nor was anyone else giving him a signal of any kind. He couldn't find the boy in the crowd either. Was anyone there? The possibility that this had all been an outrageous hoax began to creep into view. Could he not just phone his wife immediately and see for himself? If he got no answer, he could call for Jeremy at the school. That's what he must do, he con-cluded. He must get to a phone at once, he told himself, tossing aside all Hutto's warnings.

He was waiting for a lull in the opening announcements when food arrived at his table. While one waiter poured coffee, another served hot Belgian waffles, scrambled eggs, bacon, and fruit com-potes. Then Langston remembered Hutto's words: "We think it will be a waiter. . . ." He remained in his seat.

He was next to be served. A plate was lowered before him. He waited anxiously. Nothing. The waiter moved on around the table, then left. Mechanically, Langston cut into a waffle and began to eat. His mouth was dry, and it was hard to swallow. He lifted his water glass, half expecting something to drop from it. Still no message.

It must be a horrible trick. He must get to a phone. He was about to rise from the table when a young woman appeared with a coffee pot in her hand. "More coffee, sir?" she asked sweetly.

"Uh, I suppose," he answered absentmindedly. He was already scanning for an exit. He wouldn't leave through the main door. Hutto, or whoever he was, might be nearby. Spotting a side exit, he reached for the linen napkin in his lap to place it back on the table, when another napkin fell on top of his hand. He instantly looked up to see the young waitress with her coffee pot hurrying away from the table.

The napkin that was dropped into his lap was identical to the one already there, except the one just delivered was folded and taped together. There was no need to pretend. Langston's surprise was genuine, since he'd already convinced himself there would be no note.

He could feel the eyes boring through him as he carefully removed the tape from the napkin. A plain piece of white stationery was folded inside. Hands trembling, sweat trickling through his scalp, he was unfolding the paper when he remembered the signal. He grabbed the handkerchief from his coat pocket, flipped it open, took off his glasses, and wiped the lenses quickly while looking in the direction of the waitress just disappearing through a kitchen door. He replaced the handkerchief in his pocket and with a staged expression of mere curiosity, continued to unfold the paper.

The color drained from his face. His wife's wedding ring was taped to the page, just above a typed message. Langston read it carefully. When he finished, his hand crushed the paper into a wad and his head jerked up in a frantic attempt to see the girl who'd delivered it. Anger flared all over again. *How dare they?* He glared about the room, wishing to catch a knowing eye. He was searching for Dominick. Though he didn't know what he looked like, Langston would see the treachery in his eyes and know. He would pounce. He would kill to save his family. He was at once consumed by hate, twitching in his seat, ready to lunge.

Suddenly, the young screenwriter, without turning her head,

reached for Langston's hand beneath the table. She gripped it hard and shoved something inside it. Startled by her move, he stared at her in open confusion. She turned slightly in his direction, eyes still on the speaker at the podium and barely moving her smiling lips, commanded quietly, "Don't look at me. Read the note."

In his hand was paper folded to the size of a postage stamp. He quickly opened it and read:

> I'm FBI. You must trust us. REMAIN IN YOUR SEAT. We need time to find your family.

Langston didn't move. His head remained down. The white paper reflected light from the overhead chandeliers. He gazed long and hard into that light. *You speak and I don't listen,* he prayed inside. *I let the world's hate flood my heart and carry me away from You. Forgive me. Give me the courage of that young man, the compassion and control of the woman beside me.*

Slowly he refolded both notes and tucked them inside his coat pocket. He placed his wife's wedding ring on his little finger and looked to the doorway. There was Hutto. A side-to-side turn of his head, though, signaled no success.

Langston had lost all track of activities at the podium. He could see from his program that three honorees had already received their awards, and he couldn't remember a thing any of them had said. The woman reporter on his left was being summoned as the next recipient.

In her acceptance speech, the woman spoke of Ceausescu's cruel manipulation of the Romanian people, of how he'd isolated them from certain truths in order to control them. As she spoke, Langston was drawn to her words and their curious relevance to the hour. Was that not what Dominick Swain was attempting to do? To gain power by defiling the truths of God?

When the woman returned to the table, Langston heard his own name announced. His stomach convulsed. One last time he looked for a signal. Hutto gave it clearly: no news.

Langston rose slowly to his feet as the audience politely applauded. He looked down into the eyes of the agent beside him and saw reassurance. It was enough.

The applause continued until he reached the dais and stood next to the conference chairman. He was introduced as one of the foremost authors of Christian books in the country. His publisher and sales figures were acknowledged. A brief biographical sketch was read. A large plaque was presented, and he was left alone at the podium before a crowd already growing weary of the steady stream of acceptance speeches.

Langston studied his audience. They were restless, preoccupied with getting another cup of coffee, checking their watches, flipping through the program. He reached inside his coat pocket and brought out a folded piece of paper. He glanced up and read the faces before him clearly: Oh, no, the guy's got a prepared speech.

From his elevated perch, he could see Hutto's cautioning expression. But it didn't matter. Langston was now in command.

At an even, measured pace he began, "Ladies and gentlemen, about ten minutes ago, this note was slipped to me by a young woman pouring coffee. I would like to read it to you."

Hutto swept into the room, glaring incredulously at Langston and moving toward Jake's position in the bank of cameras.

Langston observed Hutto's quick movements and ignored them. In a clear, steady voice, he continued. "The note says:

> *Dr. Langston,*
>   *Yes, it is your wife's wedding ring. We are holding her and your son, Jeremy, far from your home. DO NOT GET UP! DO NOT SPEAK TO ANYONE! WE ARE WATCHING EVERY MOVE YOU MAKE! Your family is safe and well, but their continued welfare depends on your strict obedience to our instructions. . . .*

A hush fell over the room. People looked up from their plates and programs in confusion. The conference chairman made an awkward move toward Langston, who waved him away as he continued to read from the crumpled note:

> *. . .Announce to this audience that Christians United and the Soldiers of the Cross are one in the same. That Christians United ordered the destruction of the Crown Prince casino in Las Vegas and that the bombings will continue. Tell them,*

and your family will be saved.

Langston looked up to confront a silent sea of contorted faces. Some frowned contemptuously at him as though he'd shamed them all with such a preposterous performance. Others were quizzical at what they thought was just a bizarre opening. Still, others looked into the countenance of the man with horrifying comprehension.

"The note isn't signed," Langston said. "But I know who wrote it."

Immediately, FBI agents bolted into action. No more surreptitious surveillance. Langston had called Dominick's hand, and the agents were now forced to counter any attack the cult leader might have planned for unexpected developments.

By showing themselves, the FBI now risked scaring Dominick away in order to protect Langston. Agents moved swiftly to surround the dais. All exits from the ballroom and the entire hotel were blocked. The six cultists under surveillance were instantly apprehended. They would be interrogated for information on where the hostages were being held. Jake and Steve now openly roamed the aisles searching for Dominick, while cameramen jockeyed for position, frantic to record something they didn't understand.

A turbulence of alarm spread throughout the room, yet Langston persisted in his steady delivery. "This is my wife's engraved wedding ring," he announced, holding the wide, yellow gold band up for all to see. "The last time I saw her, she was wearing it. Now it is in my hand, and I've been told that she and my son have been kidnapped."

In a doorway to the kitchen, the large figure of a man leaned forward, gripping the door frame. In a dark wig and waiter's coat, Dominick gaped at Langston in utter disbelief.

Unable to contain himself any longer, Langston snatched up the note, held it high, and boomed into the microphone, "What are you afraid of, Dominick? You must be desperately afraid of something to threaten an innocent woman and child. To force such a preposterous lie. Christians United abhors the violence in Las Vegas."

Langston's eyes swept over the room searching for his target, but no one stirred.

He continued. "Is it the bombers you fear, Dominick? Or is it God Himself?"

"You're mad!" Dominick shrieked as he stepped into the room. The audience lurched in unison toward the sound of his voice.

"It's Dominick," Jake called to Hutto. Five agents dashed in the cult leader's direction.

"Stop!" Langston ordered them. "We will finish this."

The agents looked to Hutto. He signaled them to stand by, then called his marksmen to take their positions. Dominick would not escape.

"Your God doesn't frighten me!" Dominick declared as he strode confidently toward the dais.

That voice, Langston thought. *I know it.* He tried hard to place it.

Dominick kept coming, his arms flailing. "You and your holy brotherhood have deceived the masses but not me. Your God is a fake!"

Then Langston knew. The debate at Ellis-Dohn. It was the voice that had challenged him so aggressively from the back of the auditorium. As the man grew closer, Langston noted the obvious wig, then something else familiar. The face. It was Herbert Long! The strange visitor to his classroom.

At once, Langston remembered what Roxanne had told him the same day as Herbert Long's visit: "There were men in the woods today," she'd said. And with that, the pieces of an obscure puzzle fell into place. He and his family had been stalked. For how long?

"You have watched my wife and child from the woods," Langston accused. "You have followed me across three states. You have invaded my classroom and ravaged my home. Why?"

"Because you must be stopped. Because your precious gospel is a lie."

Nearby, a woman dropped a coffee cup onto its saucer, splitting the tense silence with a sudden clank. Dominick whirled viciously in her direction and she gasped in fear. Quickly, he spun to survey the room, fixing a steely glare on those agents with deadly aim upon him.

"Dominick! Turn to me!" Langston commanded.

Dominick glanced back at him, defiance leering in his face.

Langston gripped the podium, his sights on no other but Dominick. "I'll answer your challenge with a question: Would you sacrifice yourself for a lie?"

"I'll not play your game. Answer your own questions!"

"If anyone knew the gospel story was a lie, it would be those who were present during the life and death of Jesus. It would be the disciples. Yet many of them were executed for proclaiming what they had seen. Would they walk straight into death for what they knew to be a lie?"

Dominick sneered at Langston, his body rocking back and forth. "It is a lie. And you'll pay for it."

"Will you pay for what you've done to my family?"

Dominick didn't respond.

"In His disgust with us, God levied a penalty on us all. It's death."

"I'm prepared to leave this life," Dominick declared. "I'll come again in another." He swept his hand before him in a triumphant gesture.

"On whose authority?!"

Dominick dropped his hand and clenched his fist. "You won't entrap me. It's you who creates your own authority."

"And what have you created? A crime. And after the court determines the penalty for your crime, will there be anyone who steps forward and announces that he will pay that penalty for you? That you are free to go? Will anyone do that for you, Dominick?"

"You're just a street preacher looking for an offering, Langston."

"Answer me! Will anyone serve your sentence for you?!"

There was no reply. Dominick's body continued to rock.

"That's exactly what God did. He sacrificed Himself on the cross to pay the very penalty He imposed on us. Which of your gods would do that for you?"

Dominick suddenly stiffened. He seethed with visible hatred. He started to move again, slowly toward the podium. Agents moved closer.

Stopping directly in front of the podium, Dominick raised his fist above his head and screamed, "You're a liar!"

Just then Langston saw something in the man's eyes. He'd seen it before and prayed for help as he backed away from the podium but not in retreat. He turned and walked behind those seated in hushed panic on the dais, stepped off the platform, and advanced cautiously toward Dominick, fending off the agents' attempts to block his path.

The frustrated agents kept looking to Hutto for the signal to seize Dominick, but Hutto refused to give it.

Dominick stepped back as Langston approached him. "Get away from me!" he shouted, his body rigid, his eyes flashing a warning.

Langston appealed urgently: "Release the one who holds you, Dominick. Don't listen to him."

Dominick's eyes flared, and his voice proclaimed, "Your God is weak, and we are strong. This world feeds on the pleasures of our kingdom, not His. You're a fool."

"If I'm a fool, why are you afraid of what I teach?"

A jeering laugh erupted from deep within Dominick's throat, and his face twisted in contempt.

Langston didn't wait for an answer. "It's because I teach the Word of God, and the power of that Word will crush the one who holds you."

Dominick's hand quivered as it rose from his side, and his voice bellowed, "Get away!" His body began to shudder violently. He shrieked through clenched teeth, then suddenly pitched forward as Langston and David Hutto lunged to catch him.

His unconscious body drenched in sweat, Dominick rested in Langston's arms on the floor. Quickly, though, he came to and opened his eyes, struggling to focus on the one who held him. When recognition dawned, he jerked to get away, but Langston gripped him tightly. Hutto had already cuffed his hands and feet and was kneeling nearby.

"Where are they, Dominick?" Hutto demanded. "Mrs. Langston and the boy—where are they?"

With all the strength he had, Dominick wrenched himself free of Langston only to find himself in the iron grip of three agents. They lifted him to his feet as Langston also rose from the floor.

"You'll never find your wife and kid, street preacher." Dominick spat the words.

Just then Jake broke through the ring of agents. Dominick's startled expression froze on his face, then melted slowly into full comprehension.

"So, it was you," Dominick hissed. "Got away, did you? We'll find you again."

Before Jake could respond, Hutto grabbed Dominick's arm and flung him around. "You see this?" He held up the revolver he'd just taken from Dominick's hip pocket. "If Dr. Langston hadn't gotten hold of you and whatever spell you were under, you probably would have tried to use this thing. And if you had, we would have shot you dead. He saved your sorry life, Dominick. And now you can spend the rest of it in prison, and Jake won't ever have to see your ugly face again.

So, choke on your cheap threats."

Hutto turned quickly to his agents. "Get him away from here. And get Baltimore on the line now.

"I've got a real bad feeling about this."

CHAPTER 33

Cort Peterson leaned against the open doorway of the houseboat, stroking the scratches Roxanne Langston had left on his cheek the night before. It had amused him to see her fight so hard.

He glanced at his watch and frowned. *What is happening in New York?* he wondered. He touched the flip-phone in his pocket, anxious for it to ring.

Inside, the other three men played poker and listened to the radio.

"Hey, Cort, how much longer?" asked one.

"Yeah, shouldn't we have heard from Dominick by now?" asked another.

"Any time now," Peterson replied irritably. "Just play your little game and be quiet." But privately he was worried. It was almost eleven o'clock. *Something's wrong. He should have called by now.*

He pulled on his mask and went to check on the hostages, returning a few minutes later.

"They okay?" one man asked.

"Just great," said Peterson with a smirk. "Back there humming to each other. You'd think they were glad to be here."

He walked outside and stretched. "I'm going up to the truck a minute. Be right back."

He was checking provisions for his getaway when one of the men called to him.

"Cort! They got Dominick! It's on the radio!"

Peterson shot through the doorway in time to hear: ". . .but we can't be sure at this time. All we know is that the alleged kidnapper, Dominick Swain, and members of his cult are now in custody and being questioned regarding the whereabouts of Dr. Langston's family."

Peterson stared at the radio with unblinking eyes, then sprang to action. He jerked on his mask and rushed to the hostages, flinging open the door. Roxanne Langston met his eye. He stared coldly at her. Young Jeremy squirmed, his pleading cries lost in the thick folds of the gag. Assuring himself they were still tightly bound, Peterson hurried from the room, refusing to look at them again.

Seconds later, the old truck lunged to life, kicking up dirt as it raced through the woods, the four men inside never looking back at the listing houseboat.

FBI agents apprehended nine cultists besides Dominick—six inside the hotel and three more in vans that arrived at the back entrance. Hutto had immediately begun questioning each one individually in a small conference room at the hotel. So far, he was no closer to learning the location or condition of the hostages.

Greg Langston had been taken to FBI headquarters to await further developments. Jake and Joanna were huddled with Steve and Lucy in a corner of the empty ballroom waiting for directions from Hutto. Three agents guarded the only unlocked door to the ballroom. Hutto was taking no chances of reprisal from some unidentified cult commando still loose on the premises. Media crews surrounded the hotel, clamoring for coverage of the bizarre news story.

In the ballroom, Jake and Steve, gratefully free of their disguises, had finally gotten around to explaining to the girls how they'd gotten involved with Dominick when they heard a voice so familiar, but so out of place. . .

"Is anybody named Gaddy in this room?" Eli and Martin, dressed in their Sunday finest, craned their necks to see past the knot of agents stationed at the door. "Now, son, if you don't get out of my way I'm going to get real upset with you," Eli was heard saying. "And I'm not nice when I'm upset."

"Papa!" Joanna flew to them. Convincing the agents the two old men were harmless, she pulled them into the room and nearly leaped at her grandfather, so grateful for the touch of home. She smothered his crinkled old face with kisses and clung to his stooped frame, knowing then that she would never again leave his side.

"What are you two doing here?" She giggled with unabashed joy as she turned to hug Martin.

"I couldn't hold him back, Joanna," Martin said. "Not after Tad Wetherington told us what was happening up here."

"Aw, what do you mean?" Eli scolded. "You were packed and out the door before I could get off the phone." But his voice softened when he asked Joanna, "Where's Jake?"

Joanna just pointed.

Jake had watched the whole scene from across the vast room. His heart wrenched. He'd caused his grandfather so much agony, and now the ailing old man had traveled all the way from Deer Creek to find the boy who'd disappointed him. Shame and remorse wouldn't let him move.

Eli read it all in Jake's face. As swiftly as he could, he closed the distance between them, then opened his arms wide to embrace his grandson. They clung to each other for a long time. Finally Jake broke the silence.

"Papa, I—"

"Don't say a word," Eli comforted, still hugging him tight. "I've never been more proud of you than I am right now. I heard what I needed to from those news people outside."

Eli pulled away and looked into his grandson's solemn face. "You found the One you were looking for, didn't you?"

Jake looked puzzled. "How did you know?"

"Just did."

"You were right all along, Papa. Something had to knock the blinders off me. Anyway, I'll tell you all about it later."

Eli suddenly remembered something. "Where are you hurt, son? Blood was all over the cabin floor."

Jake pushed up the sleeves of his shirt and jacket to show Eli the healing wound on his left forearm. The sterile strips of tape Dominick had used to close the gash from the kidnapper's knife were still in place.

"What happened?" Eli asked gravely, gently pulling the injured arm to him for closer inspection.

"Well, you see, there was this grizzly bear outside the cabin, and—"

"A straight answer is all I want, but I can wait for it. In the meantime, I know you've been through something awful. And my goodness, son, you smell like it, too. You need a long bath and a sharp razor."

"That bad, huh? I'll clean up soon, Papa. But Mr. Hutto—he's the FBI agent who ran this whole thing—he told me to wait for him here. He needed to talk to—well, here he comes now."

"Jake," Hutto called, walking briskly toward them, "we need to get going."

"Mr. Hutto," Jake said, "this is my grandfather, Eli Gaddy, from Deer Creek."

Hutto's expression was clear: *What are you doing here?*

Eli caught the look. Accepting Hutto's offered hand, he said, "Got here as quick as I could. I don't know what a cultist is, but I knew I didn't want one messing with my boy. Pleased to meet you, Mr. Hutto, and thanks for taking care of things for me."

Hutto smiled graciously. "You're very welcome, Mr. Gaddy. I hope you'll excuse me, sir, but I've got some hostages to find."

The agent turned to Jake. "I'll need you and Steve at headquarters right away. Maybe you can persuade these people to cooperate. They won't tell me anything."

"Want me to talk to them?" Eli offered. "I've got a few things to say."

Hutto blinked rapidly. "Uh, no, sir. That won't be necessary. But I would appreciate you loaning Jake to us for awhile."

"Just make sure I get him back, you hear?"

"Yes, sir. And it was nice meeting you." He turned to Jake. "Let's go."

Before leaving the ballroom, Hutto excused himself from Jake, stopping briefly to talk with Joanna. "Your Jeep is on the way," he told her.

She looked surprised.

"That farmer, Mr. Winkler, is driving it into the city for you."

"What a nice thing to do," she said.

"Yeah, well, he says he and his wife were due for a little visit with the great, green lady. I sure hope he means the Statue of Liberty."

Joanna laughed. "Is there more than one green lady around here?"

"New York's got them in every color." He smiled warmly at her.

She laughed again. Then she touched his arm lightly to keep him a minute longer. "I know you're in a hurry, but I want to thank you for helping Jake. For believing his wild story."

"I've heard wilder. But you're welcome. Now, I do have to go."

He turned to leave, then stopped and looked back at her. "Maybe I'll see you again before you leave New York."

"I won't leave until Jake does."

Nick Sasha had just rushed up to Jake when Hutto joined them. "Mr. Gaddy, we would be honored to have you, your family and friends stay with us. I shudder to think what might have happened in my hotel this morning had you not warned us. Please accept our appreciation."

"Thank you," Jake said, glancing at Hutto, who nodded his approval.

"Just register anytime you're ready. And, I realize you've just been released from, uh, accommodations of a very different sort. So, we've taken the liberty of providing some things you might need—toiletries, clothing, and so forth. I hope you enjoy your stay, Mr. Gaddy."

Jake asked Joanna to check everyone into the hotel. "I don't know how long Steve and I will be needed."

"Take as long as you have to, Jake. Mrs. Langston needs your help more than we do."

Minutes later, Jake and Steve were about to climb into an FBI van with Hutto when another agent ran toward them.

"David! They got 'em! They found the Langstons!"

Hutto whirled around. "Condition?" he asked immediately.

"Bruised and weak, but they seem to be okay. It was a houseboat, just like this guy said. But barely afloat. Another couple of days and they would have drowned."

"Where was it?"

"Way up the river from the bridge, moored down a creek. But David, there's more."

Jake and Steve listened intently.

The agent looked at the boys and hesitated.

"It's okay," Hutto said. "They can hear. What is it?"

"Mrs. Langston overheard them talking about blowing up abortion clinics."

"What?!" Jake shouted.

"What exactly did she hear?" Hutto demanded.

"That they were going to do it right after this thing with Dr. Langston. And that they were going to say that Christians United was responsible."

"Who is 'they'?" Hutto asked.

"Mrs. Langston heard a couple of guys talking outside her window. Ron and Jack were the only names she heard. She said they seemed like underling types, not really in on decisions. One of them said it was Dominick and another kidnapper who planned the bombings. She never heard the other guy's name."

"Did she see any of them?"

The agent shook his head. "They wore masks."

"Where is she now?" Hutto asked.

"En route to a hospital with the boy."

"I want to talk to her. Call Dr. Langston with the news. Make arrangements to get him to his family as soon as possible."

"I never heard anything about blowing up hospitals!" Jake nervously insisted.

"Me either," Steve added. "But the other guy she's talking about has to be Cort Peterson."

"We've already run a check on him. We know all about him. Did they ever mention any clinics or hospitals? Any names?"

"I don't recall anything," Jake said.

"No, I don't either," Steve agreed, but he seemed troubled, and Hutto noticed his distraction.

"Steve, do you—" Hutto began, but was interrupted.

"Sir, I have to make a phone call," Steve said abruptly. "I need to, uh, call someone and tell her where I'll be."

"You can use the mobile," Hutto said, looking hard into Steve's face.

"Uh, it's kind of private," Steve said, quickly breaking away. He turned and walked toward the hotel, calling over his shoulder, "I'll just be a minute." Then he broke into a full run.

Jake looked after him curiously. So did Hutto.

"Jake, how well do you know Steve?"

Jake was surprised by the question. "Good enough to know he's got nothing whatsoever to do with this, sir." He glanced toward the hotel as Steve disappeared inside and added, "I'll go after him."

"Both of you get back here on the double."

Jake found Steve at a pay phone off the lobby and overheard the last part of his conversation: ". . .I'll meet you in front of the Apple Theater down the street. Hurry!"

"Steve, who are you talking to?"

Steve jumped at the sound of Jake's voice. There was a grave expression on his face. "Jake, there's something I've got to do, and I can't talk about it now. Tell Hutto I had a family emergency, and I'll call him later today."

Jake looked scornfully at him. "Was that Molly?"

"Yeah."

"Well, this is no time to be running off to play, Steve."

"It is an emergency, Jake. If this bombing is real, there's someone who could stop it. Someone you don't know about. Cover for me, please. And above all, trust me." He brushed past Jake and ran out the side door of the hotel.

Hutto was waiting in the van at the back door when Jake returned.

"Steve will meet us later, sir."

"Where is he?" Hutto snapped.

"He's gone. Said he had a family emergency and would call you later."

Hutto glared at Jake. "Does he know something about these bombings that he's not telling?"

Jake struggled with an answer.

"Jake! Does he?"

"He just said he might know someone who does."

Hutto slapped the dash in anger. "Your friend is in very serious trouble," he said as he jumped from the car and ran into the hotel looking for Steve.

Half an hour later, he returned. "He's gone, all right," he announced, then ordered the driver to go.

Their van turned the corner and passed the front of the hotel. Jake searched for a theater marquee.

It was lunchtime, and the streets and sidewalks were crowded. He scanned the signs along one side of the street ahead, then the other. And he saw it. The Apple Theater. Should he tell Hutto?

Jake was agonizing over what to do when he suddenly saw Molly standing at the curb next to an old blue Grand Prix. Then he saw Steve jump quickly into the driver's seat of the car and speed away.

Trust me. Jake remembered Steve's words and said nothing to Hutto.

Senator Linc Ramsdale was bathed in light as he stepped from his limousine that Monday morning to the thunderous applause of admirers in Newark, New Jersey. In the parking lot of the new BMW plant outside Newark, colorful, grand-opening banners fluttered in the stiff, March breeze as the senator worked the crowd along the route to the platform. His silver hair sparkled, and his smiling face crinkled with pleasure at the rousing reception. He would deliver a patriotic address, praising American resourcefulness in recruiting international industry to the home shores of the great state of New Jersey.

He had not yet announced his plans to seek the Oval Office, but newspaper columnists across the country had unofficially declared him a front-runner candidate in the election just a year and half away.

As he mounted the steps to the podium, he surveyed the exuberant throng gathered at his feet, and a surge of power lifted him almost beyond his mortal body. He paused to bask in the ecstasy of it all. *I will be president,* he told himself. *I will.*

He raised both arms in triumph as a local high school band played and balloons were released to the atmosphere. As he beamed in appreciation, he wondered what words Langston was using to disgrace President Raymond Wellon's political machine. There had been no news from the hotel yet.

I didn't need Dominick's magic tricks to win this election, he brooded behind the flashing smile. *Why did I let him do it? The guru just wanted his own spiritual opponent destroyed.*

As the speaker began his lengthy introduction of the honored senator, Ramsdale was still troubled by the uncertain events unfolding in
New York. *Even if it doesn't work,* Ramsdale concluded, *I'm still going to
take the election.*

His name was called, and the band and crowd reached fever pitch
before his lone voice broke through and he began his rather lengthy
address.

Twenty minutes later, Ramsdale relinquished the podium to cor-
porate executives eager to indulge in America's love affair with foreign
cars. An hour later, it was all over. Ramsdale, recognized one last time,
waved farewell from the platform and began the tedious trek back
through the clamoring audience. He shook hands and chatted with as
many as he could on the way to the limo. His cheeks ached from the
perpetual smile, and he was terribly anxious to turn on the news. But
as long as there were voters to impress, he was "on."

A woman shoved a two year old in his face for a kiss while her husband stood by with the camera. A man in a wheelchair, waving a small
American flag, raised a hand, and Ramsdale grabbed it. He was a
Vietnam vet and Ramsdale, alert to a media opportunity, lingered in an
emotional moment with the man, assuring him that never again would
our soldiers be sent into senseless combat. The man wept, and Ramsdale even wiped a tear from his own eye, then proceeded down the line
of extended hands.

The elderly and the young, those in suits and those in overalls, they
were all pressing for their moment with the senator when a young man
stepped forward and said one thing that stopped Ramsdale cold.

"They arrested Dominick."

The words struck like a bullet. Seeing Ramsdale instantly recoil, his
bodyguards immediately grabbed the young man and searched him.
But Ramsdale objected.

"Let him go and bring him to me!" he ordered as he broke from
the alarmed crowd and hurried to the limo.

Those closest to the scene were stunned and pushed back against
the crowd behind. Seeing Ramsdale flee to the car, they began to scat-
ter, thinking an assassination attempt was underway. Realizing this,
Ramsdale turned suddenly, and through a tight grin, assured everyone
that all was well. He made a joke about his overprotective bodyguards

and got into the car, motioning for the young man to follow.

Ramsdale didn't recognize him but assumed he was one of Dominick's people sent to warn him. Ramsdale's shirt soaked rapidly with sweat.

The young man crawled slowly into the back seat of the limo. He was large-framed with a receding hairline and wire-rimmed glasses, and he stared intently at Ramsdale.

Ramsdale closed off the window from his aides in the front of the car. The bodyguards hovered outside.

"Who are you?" Ramsdale anxiously demanded.

Steve Michon studied the bare fright in the senator's face, then smiled contemptuously as he answered.

"Your son."

CHAPTER 36

In a long-haired blond wig pulled back over his mangled ear and tied off in a ponytail, Cort Peterson hurried through the Baltimore airport Monday afternoon with a small duffel bag slung over his shoulder. Inside was a change of clothes, shoes, maps, and a few toiletries. In his hip pocket was a counterfeit passport and driver's license, a set of car keys, and an envelope full of cash.

How could you let this happen, Dominick? What went wrong? He was seething inside as he swept through the gate at the last call and boarded the plane. He was reeling from the shock of news bulletins broadcasting Dominick's name across the nation. *Will I hear my own name next?* He jerked his seat belt on and stared out the window.

It was so simple. Just take the family. Slip the note. Watch the guy make a fool of himself. Embarrass good Christian Wellon. Then call a radio station and tell them where the woman and kid are. No problem. So what happened?!

After takeoff, he asked for a blanket. Then he reclined his seat and drew the blanket up over his face. He knew there was no chance of anyone recognizing him. He just felt better in the dark. He always did.

He tried to sleep, but his thoughts churned. Dominick would never talk, he assured himself. But what about the rest of them? That little family of his. *It'll take just one of them to trade me for a lighter sentence. And that Gaddy kid. . .*

He drew the blanket up higher on his head. The kid couldn't know about Bimini.

The night of the accident came back to him. Racing into the cove. The shock of seeing the other boat anchored in front of him. Leaping into the water just seconds before impact. The projectiles of sharp metal that shaved his ear from his head. The devastating failure of his first drug run.

He could still see the lifeless face of his friend Paco who hadn't jumped far enough from the doomed vessels. Peterson guessed the boy was still buried deep in the palm grove where he left him. No dead body, no questions, no leads to follow. And Peterson wasn't about to arouse suspicion now. No need to. He knew all he needed to know. A check on old records at the library confirmed that Jake and Joanna Gaddy were the children of accident victims Travis and Paula Gaddy. After a casual inquiry, Dominick told Peterson that Jake had a sister named Joanna.

Poor, stupid Dominick. He never suspected why I wanted that bit of information. It doesn't matter anyway. The boy will never know.

Peterson's thoughts turned back to Dominick, and he almost felt sorry for him. His dreams of sharing power with the president of the United States were now shattered. *But what about Linc?* he thought. *No one will ever suspect he had anything to do with the kidnapping. He's safe. He can still be president. He could even pardon Dominick.* Peterson almost laughed aloud at that scenario.

Linc will also do anything for me that I ask him to. How can he deny me anything? One word from me and his throne would topple, now wouldn't it?

Peterson shifted to a more comfortable position and began to relax. All the more reason to help old Linc get himself up on that throne.

Soothed by the prospect of a liaison with the most powerful man in the world, Peterson drifted to sleep, only to be awakened suddenly by a message from the captain boomed through an overhead speaker:

"This is Captain Bob Stiles. We have begun our descent into the Atlanta area and should arrive on time at 5:20 P.M. at Hartsfield International. The temperature is 58 degrees on the ground, with gusting winds and rain moving quickly in from the west. It's been a pleasure—"

Peterson ignored the rest of the captain's message. His attention was now on the rain outside his window.

It would stop, he was certain. *Everyone will see the place burn good and long after the explosion. Then I'll make Dominick's little phone call for him. He'd like that.*

CHAPTER 37

"Angela O'Shea was my mother," Steve declared proudly.

Ramsdale couldn't speak. He'd been struck twice in several minutes. By the news of Dominick's arrest and the sudden appearance of this boy who claimed to be his son. But he struggled to respond.

"Stephen?"

"Steve."

Ramsdale studied the boy's face. . .the long, slender nose and wide, expressive eyes—brown like his own.

"How do you. . .why are you. . .here, now?" Ramsdale's hands shook as he reached for a handkerchief in his breast pocket. He mopped his face and neck never taking his eyes off Steve.

A guard tapped against the dark-tinted window. Ramsdale lowered it and assured him he was fine, then raised the window and turned quickly back to Steve, desperate for answers.

"I know you're involved in this," Steve accused coldly. "I've been watching you for a long time. I even joined Dominick's cult to keep an eye on the two of you. I've followed you to the cabin on the river. I've watched your family in Georgetown, your other sons." Steve's severe expression didn't betray the years of hurtful rejection by his own father.

"I saw you once at Dominick's lake house when you thought no one else was around," Steve said. "I listened at the window."

"Why?"

"Because I wanted to know what kind of man you were. Mom

painted you up pretty good to me, making excuses for why you ignored us. She wanted me to be proud of you like she was."

Ramsdale swallowed hard. "How is she?" he asked timidly.

"Dead," Steve said bluntly, almost happy to deliver yet another blow to the proud senator.

Ramsdale gasped. His pain was real and pitiful.

"How? When?" It was all he could say.

"Colon cancer. She died four years ago in California."

"California?! You mean she was. . ."

Steve looked at him with disgust. "Yeah, she was here. She followed you to the States when I was five. Had yourself another family right around the corner and didn't know it, did you? She never got over you, even when she married that jerk Michon. She knew she was sick and wanted someone to take care of her wild teenage son after she was gone. Even insisted I take his name. I wound up cleaning up after his drunken binges. Then he died, too."

Ramsdale looked suspiciously at Steve. "How do I know you're telling the truth?"

Steve was ready for this. He pulled an envelope from his coat pocket and handed it to Ramsdale.

"What is this?" Ramsdale snapped.

"Open it. You'll find pictures of me and Mom together and a letter from her to you."

Ramsdale took the envelope and quickly tore it open. The first thing he saw was a close-up picture of Angela and Steve at the beach in Santa Cruz. He stared at the two people in the shallow surf, at the young woman he'd loved so desperately in another time. Ramsdale delicately fingered the snapshot as if it would shred in his hands. Then he picked up another picture, and his eyes widened in shock. "Her hair," he gasped.

"Chemo," came the dull reply.

Ramsdale pored through other pictures of Steve at various stages in his life, and it became increasingly clear that the boy in the pictures was the young man beside him.

He picked up one more photograph, and his eyes glazed. With a scarf wrapped tightly about her head, a middle-aged woman was seated on a bright yellow sofa with her frail arm around a grown-up Steve. She was holding a small homemade sign that said simply: "Linc, this is your son."

"I didn't want her to do that," Steve said. "I didn't care if you ever knew."

Ramsdale sagged deep into his seat. The senator's grief was visible. But Steve couldn't bring himself to feel sorry for the man who'd caused others so much more torment, even if he was his father.

Ramsdale suddenly jerked himself back to the present. "How do you know about Dominick?"

"I saw the whole thing. A friend of mine escaped from him and warned the FBI. They were ready and waiting for the great Dominick Swain. They also knew where to look for the hostages."

"They're okay?" Ramsdale was eager to know.

"Like you care," Steve sneered.

"I didn't want him to do it. It wasn't even necessary."

"What did Dominick think would happen when the nation found out the man lied to save his family?"

"By then the damage would already be done. All the rumors about the Soldiers of the Cross taking orders from Christians United would be grounded, no matter how much Langston later denied it." Ramsdale suddenly grew restless.

Another tap came at the window. Ramsdale hesitated before lowering it. "Give us a few more minutes."

"Sir, people are staring at the car, and the police keep asking what's wrong. I think we need to go."

Ramsdale considered this, then asked Steve, "Will you come with me? We'll talk while we ride."

"Sure, I've got plenty to say to you."

Ramsdale gave instructions to his driver to cruise slowly back to his hotel in New York. He'd arrived just yesterday from Washington for the plant opening in Newark and a guest spot on the *Today* show at NBC. Steve knew about both appearances. He always knew what the senator was doing.

"You'd better cancel NBC," he told Ramsdale. "You've got more important things to tend to."

"You mean Dominick?"

"I mean the bombing of women's clinics, and don't pretend you're innocent of that, too."

"Bombing clinics? What are you talking about?"

"I told you not to pretend," Steve snapped.

"Look, I knew about Langston and about the casino, but—"

"The casino? The Crown Prince?!" Steve was livid. "You did that?!"

Ramsdale suddenly seemed defeated. He turned to look out the window as if watching something beautiful fade away.

"Answer me!" Steve couldn't contain his fury. There was a tap on the front window from still anxious security personnel.

"Ignore it," Langston ordered his guard. To no one in particular, he half whispered, "It doesn't matter anymore. It's all dead."

Steve's mind raced to piece together this latest development. He jostled faces and motives and sequences of events until a plan more inconceivable than the Langston kidnapping came into view. He opened his mouth to speak, but the words caught in his throat. He swallowed hard and started again. "Are Dominick and Peterson the Soldiers of the Cross?"

Ramsdale nodded silently, his head still turned toward the window.

"And. . .all this time. . ." Steve struggled to understand even as he spoke, ". . .Dominick was pretending to be outraged over their attacks. . .when it was really. . .him?" Steve squinted his eyes as if to focus on a possible motive.

Ramsdale turned and stared into Steve's strained face. Something in the senator's eyes told Steve what he wanted to know.

"To destroy Wellon," Steve declared with finality.

Ramsdale's face expressed nothing at all.

"All those security guards died so that you might defeat the president. . .and take home all his toys."

It was Steve's turn to stare out the window. After a long silence, he said, "You'll never be president, Mr. Ramsdale. You're dirty. Filthy with crimes you know about and even those you don't. How many more people are you going to torture on your way to the White House? Are you going to let a hospital full of people be blasted to bits so you can play president?"

The limo headed slowly toward the Holland tunnel, but Steve and Ramsdale were oblivious to their location.

"I don't know anything about bombing a hospital," Ramsdale finally offered. "Where did you hear that?"

"Mrs. Langston overheard her kidnappers mention abortion clinics they were going to blow up and blame on the Christians."

Ramsdale rubbed both eyes with the balls of his fists, then said, "I don't believe that."

"Well, you'd better believe it quick, because you're probably the only one who can stop it. You've got to come with me to the FBI."

"You're crazy," Ramsdale said.

"And you're a murderer."

"I can't do anything about these clinics. I don't know anything about them." Ramsdale seemed to be crumbling into desperate little attempts at survival. "I can't be seen talking to the FBI."

"Oh, my, yes. What would people think? That you cavort with criminals, that you're a despicable liar and a mass murderer? Wouldn't want them to think that! Not when everyone will soon discover it was really Dominick and Cort Peterson."

"How do you know about Peterson?"

"Your drugged-out buddy from the good old commune days?" Steve paused for a slow, deep breath. "Mom told me all about you and Dominick and Cort. The only thing she didn't regret about those days was loving you."

The muscles in Ramsdale's jaws rippled as he clenched his teeth.

"And now you can finally honor that love by stopping these bombings."

"How?"

"You'll have to start with Dominick. I'll take you there."

"I'm not going anywhere," Ramsdale said coldly.

"You're going with me to the FBI. I'll bring you to justice all by myself if I have to."

Ramsdale looked viciously at Steve.

"Got any thoughts about knocking off your own son, Father?" Steve taunted.

"You would ruin me for revenge?"

"You're already ruined. For greed. For power lust. The question now is, can you redeem any portion of yourself by saving a few hundred lives?"

Then Steve added with a smug grin. "That would make your next life a little grander, wouldn't it? Polish up the karma, and who knows, you might come back a king. Isn't that the kind of stuff you believe?"

Ramsdale looked stricken. "Do you hate me this much?"

"Forget me. The whole nation will be clawing for your blood if you do nothing to stop this bombing."

The phone on Agent David Hutto's desk rang. Jake was sitting nearby.

"Hutto."

"This is Steve Michon."

Hutto motioned for Jake to pay attention, then hit the speaker button on his phone. "Where are you, Steve?"

"I'm on my way to your office. I have someone with me and was wondering if we could get into the building without being seen."

"Who is it?"

"I'd rather not tell you right now, sir. But if this person could talk to Dominick, there might not be any bombings."

Hutto considered his options. "What if I brought Dominick to this person?"

"That's even better."

"Why can't you tell me who it is we're meeting, Steve?"

"Just trust me, sir. Jake does."

An hour later a New York Power utility truck pulled into a parking garage in midtown Manhattan. It spiraled its way to the top floor and stopped in front of an enclosed garage. The driver got out and opened the door, returned to the truck and drove inside the three-car facility. Fifteen minutes later, a black Honda Civic pulled alongside the truck, and the garage door closed.

Before anyone stepped from the Honda, the side door of the utility truck flew open and five armed FBI agents, including Hutto, jumped from inside. They surrounded the small car and flung open its doors. Steve and Ramsdale were immediately jerked outside and searched. Then the agents recognized Ramsdale.

"Sir?" a bewildered Hutto addressed Ramsdale. "I don't understand."

"Who are you?" Ramsdale asked curtly, "And where's Dominick?"

"Agent David Hutto, sir. And what do you have to do with Dominick Swain?"

"It's a very long story, and I don't think we have time for it all right now, do we? There's a matter of bombs going off. Let's address that first. Now, where is he?"

Steve was surprised by Ramsdale's sudden command of himself and those around him. He had no way of knowing that his father had come to a curious peace within himself over the last few hours while preparations for this encounter were being made.

"We couldn't take a chance that this was an ambush, sir." Hutto glanced reproachfully at Steve. "But I'll arrange for you to meet with him if you'll tell me what this is all about—and I'm satisfied with what I hear."

Ramsdale looked at Steve with a yielding in his countenance, a calm resignation that took Steve by surprise. "This is my son," Ramsdale said with unmistakable pride.

Hutto was startled.

Ramsdale continued. "He's the reason I'm here. He knew Dominick would listen to me."

While the other agents remained on guard, Hutto, Steve, and the senator climbed into the truck and shut the door.

"Tell your story, Senator Ramsdale," Hutto said.

For the next thirty minutes, the senator unburdened himself of his terrible secrets. Afterwards, Hutto closed his eyes and rubbed the back of his neck.

"I've never seen a man come to greater ruin than this," Hutto remarked sadly. "Nor have I seen greater courage than you've just shown me, Senator."

For the first time, Steve felt sorry for the broken man sitting next to him, the man he'd never known as a father, and probably never would, he thought.

"Sir, you know what will happen to you."

Ramsdale didn't respond.

"I'll hold off the announcement for as long as I can. But you're now in custody. You understand that, don't you?"

A tight smile stretched across Ramsdale's face. "Maybe now I can get some rest." Then he turned to Steve.

"You have your mother's mouth, do you know?"

Steve just looked away.

Hutto radioed a signal from the truck, and within moments another utility truck approached the garage and was let inside. Once the garage door was lowered again, the door of the second truck opened and a haggard Dominick appeared. He was handcuffed and chained at the waist and ankles. It took four agents to lift his bulk from the van and set him on the ground.

Hutto led Dominick to the truck and opened the door.

"Linc!" Dominick gaped in horror. "What are you doing?"

Ramsdale sadly shook his head. "What I have to do. And, by the way. . ." Ramsdale motioned toward Steve, who was seated in a back corner of the van. ". . .I'd like you to meet my son."

As Dominick turned quickly, the chains jerked against his ankles, and he lurched forward into the van. Hutto and another agent grabbed him in time to cushion his landing but not before he saw Steve.

Dominick managed to raise himself to a sitting position, all the while glaring back and forth between father and son.

"He's mine and Angela's, Dominick," Ramsdale said quietly.

Then, something Dominick had been trying to retrieve from his memory sprang forward. "The blue Grand Prix was yours!" he blurted. Dominick now spoke rapidly in fragments. "The picture in your apartment. You on the hood of the car. You followed me, didn't you?"

"When were you ever in my apartment?" Steve demanded.

A slow, malicious grin crept across Dominick's face. "It seems you aren't the only one who likes to spy on others. But you were better than we, I admit. You concealed the most important thing of all. Your identity. Why?"

"I knew about you and the senator. Mom told me all about you. She said to watch you both. That one day you would do something to hurt Ramsdale, and she didn't want that to happen."

"She's dead, Dominick," Ramsdale said in an oddly restrained voice. "My Angela is dead, just like the security guards at the casino. Just like the Langstons would have been. But no one else is going to die because of me, Dominick. So tell us about the clinics."

By eight o'clock Monday night, the FBI had a full description and background on Cort Peterson. After a long and bitter exchange with Ramsdale, and after realizing there was no longer a presidential office

to be gained, Dominick had finally revealed his plans for the bombings in Atlanta and Chicago.

Detonations in both cities had been scheduled for the following
morning.

CHAPTER 38

"Any time now. It'll stop."

Cort Peterson watched the steady rain wash over the windshield of his truck as he sat in the parking lot of the Days Inn on I-85 south of downtown Atlanta. One of his people had left the panel truck for him in the airport parking lot—complete with a surprise package for the Strathmore Clinic for Women, ready for delivery the next morning.

"Rain or no rain," he said aloud, adjusting his wig, "this show's about to begin."

He rested his chin on the steering wheel and looked into the dark sky. "It's more spectacular at night. But you're right, Dominick. There'll be more casualties in the daytime. I can wait."

He started the engine and drove slowly out of the motel parking lot. After checking in that afternoon, he'd taken a shower and a nap. Now it was nine-thirty, and he was ready for a late dinner and a few last moments of leisure. That dark little bistro near the High Museum would do nicely, he thought. No one would know him. He had been to Atlanta twice before, to scout the clinic and again to meet his contact and arrange for the assembly of the bomb. He merged with the traffic headed toward town on I-85 and mused about the coming headlines.

Langston was a bust. *But wait 'til the news crews arrive on the scene of carnage in downtown Atlanta and Chicago. Wait 'til I call and claim responsibility in the name of the Soldiers of the Cross and threaten even more reprisals for the slaughtering of unborn babies.* "The Soldiers of the Cross? Who are these evil people?" everyone will demand. "Is Raymond Wellon one of them?"

Peterson chuckled out loud. "You'll be glad we did it, Linc. Trust me. Then I'll have you right where I want you."

He laughed some more. "And poor Dominick. Prison's no place for you. But don't fret, old man. I'll get you out. You know I have my ways." He began to hum contentedly to himself.

Just then, a bright yellow compact car suddenly darted in front of Peterson, and he hit the brakes, glancing fearfully into the rearview mirror and bracing for a rearend collision.

"You idiot!" he yelled, but no one heard him. "Don't mess with me!"

At once, the soothing thoughts of dinner and music in the dimly lit bistro were dispelled. Now he was unsettled and sullen. Suddenly, the vision of a five-story brick building burned into his head. The clinic. Something's wrong. The truck lurched into the passing lane and gathered speed.

The Strathmore Clinic for Women was northeast of downtown in an area largely populated by urban professionals. The peaceful old neighborhoods where generations of families had raised their young had been recycled. Now, homeowners roller-bladed and drove sports utility vehicles through the quiet streets.

Peterson exited the freeway and raced for the clinic. It was still raining, and pedestrians dashed across slick streets carrying umbrellas. *Careful,* he warned himself. *Don't kill anyone before you have to.* He lifted his foot off the gas.

He was beginning to feel foolish. Clutching the mangled ear, he scolded himself. *You're flying around like a panicked old woman. There's nothing wrong. What could be wrong? Dominick's not going to tell the feds about the clinics. No one else but me and my man in Chicago knows. And he's scared to death of me. So everything's fine. I'm a fool to let a near-miss in traffic unnerve me.*

He decided he needed a relaxing dinner more than he thought. Only blocks from the clinic, he turned around and headed for the bistro just off Peachtree Street.

Just then he heard a siren and saw flashing lights coming toward him. He pulled to the curb and watched a fire truck rush by, heading in the opposite direction. He'd just eased back into traffic when he saw more lights coming and heard another siren. Then another. He swerved into a driveway off the street and watched. Three more fire trucks sped past him, their horns screaming at him. A knot tightened in his stomach.

Don't be ridiculous, he scolded himself. *No one knows! Even the ones who assembled the bombs had no idea what they were for. You're just an old woman!*

He turned on the radio. Light rock filled the truck. He watched the flashing lights disappear and decided to do the same. For now, anyway.

He tapped the steering wheel to the beat of the music, all the while suppressing a warning deep inside. But soon, he couldn't ignore it any longer. *Trust your instincts,* he told himself as he changed directions again and chased after the trucks.

The sounds from the radio had filtered to the background of his mind until suddenly he locked on two words: ". . .Cort Peterson. . ."

In stunned disbelief he listened as the announcer continued: ". . . believed to be in the Atlanta area. The clinic is being evacuated and persons with any knowledge of Peterson are asked to contact the FBI at. . ."

The truck lurched around a corner and pulled into the driveway of an old Victorian home. Two blocks down the street Peterson could see clearly what was happening. Patients in hospital gowns wrapped in blankets were being helped out of the Strathmore Clinic for Women by the staff. An assortment of emergency vehicles were parked in the street. Police were everywhere. A road block was being set up in every direction from the clinic.

Why did you do it, old man? Peterson seethed, watching fifteen months of planning evaporate before him.

He thought of Chicago and grabbed the phone on the seat next to him. The conversation was quick and forceful. "Get out of there now," Peterson ordered his man. "Stash the bomb. I'll be in touch. One day soon, I'll need you again. We're not finished."

Moments later, as Peterson watched the spectacle at the clinic, another news bulletin caught his attention: ". . .and this just in. After canceling several public appearances in New York today, Senator Linc Ramsdale was seen entering FBI headquarters in Manhattan where, sources say, he may be providing information about Dominick Swain and the motive for the bizarre events at the Hotel Internationale this morning. The senator has been unavailable for comment, and it is believed that he is still inside the FBI building. One Ramsdale aide indicated that the senator was distraught over the Langston kidnapping and the growing threat to religious freedom."

"Linc!" Peterson shouted into the windshield. Then he noticed a police car cruising slowly toward him.

Time to go.

He backed carefully out of the drive and headed down the street away from the clinic. In his rearview mirror he saw the cop end his patrol at the corner and turn around.

Looking for me? Peterson scowled as he headed back to I-85.

He picked up the phone again and dialed long distance to a marina on the Gulf of Mexico. Again, the conversation was clipped and direct. "I'll be driving. Airports will be watched. Have the boat ready."

He thought of the bomb on the floor behind him. *What a waste.* As he drove, a vision took shape in his head, and his eyes narrowed. As the vision grew, his mood lifted. *Yes, indeed! Why waste a perfectly good bomb?*

Neal MacElroy had spent his last few quarters on cigarettes. They and the half-empty bottle of gin in his frayed pocket would have to warm him through the coming night. He crouched low in the doorway of the closed Atlanta Sunrise Travel Agency, shielding his book of matches from the blowing rain.

After three tries, he managed to draw in enough flickering fire to light a cigarette. As he took the first long drag into his lungs, he gazed up at the magnificent new sanctuary of the Bethany Presbyterian Church across the street. With this new addition, the church now covered most of an entire city block, and its congregation still spilled from the aisles at two services each Sunday morning.

Neal marveled at the soaring gables and brilliant stained-glass windows as he curled against the hounding rain. Life on the street was hard enough without the rain soaking the thin coat he'd worn through too many winters.

He'd taken the bottle from his pocket for a quick swig when he noticed a truck stop quickly in front of the church. A man got out and looked up and down the street. Then he walked to the back of the truck, opened the door, climbed inside and closed the door behind him.

Neal thought he was in there a long time. Then finally the door opened and the man got out. He picked up something from inside the truck—a large package of some kind. Neal watched the man climb the steps of the church and lean the package right up against the front door. Then he ran back to his truck and took off.

A donation. Neal decided the good man had dropped off a box of clothes, or maybe food. And who better to receive such a gift than old Neal MacElroy. In seconds, he repocketed the gin bottle and ran across the street to the church.

The package was heavy. That was good, Neal thought. Probably a ham and some potatoes. Maybe a bag of peanuts fresh from the Georgia clay. Even shoes. A coat, maybe. Neal was terribly excited about his good fortune and ran with it to his hideout.

For the last month, he'd been living in the basement of an abandoned building down the street from the church. Inside the basement was a mattress he'd dragged through a broken window, open cans of food, and candles—which he now lit to explore the contents of the package.

He tore off the brown wrapping and tape, made a slit across the cardboard with a knife from his pocket and pulled open the box. He looked inside and screamed. His brief tour in Vietnam hadn't taught him much he wished to retain, but he knew an explosive device when he saw one.

Neal lunged through the open window, shredding his thin coat and scraping flesh against the broken glass, but never slowing his frantic escape from the basement. He crossed the street and dove into an alleyway just seconds before the three-story wooden structure that had been his home blew into the streets of downtown Atlanta.

CHAPTER 39

"You're not going to believe this!" exclaimed the agent rushing into David Hutto's office just before midnight.

Hutto was on the phone with the Denver office. Dominick had confessed to kidnapping the Patterson girl and told Hutto she'd been left in an old silver mine in the mountains. Denver was calling to report her rescue and fair condition.

"What is it?" Hutto asked the agent, putting Denver on hold.

"Atlanta just called. They've got a building blown to bits downtown and some homeless man jabbering about a guy with a bomb at the church down the street."

"Go on."

"They're waiting for the old guy's alcohol level to drop so they can make more sense out of what he's saying, but so far they've determined that the guy saw someone leave a package at the church. Then the old man stole the package, thinking it was food, took it to the basement of this old abandoned building where he'd been sleeping, discovered it was a bomb and ran just before it went off."

"Think it's Peterson's bomb?"

"Yeah, I do. Too much of a coincidence."

"Could he describe a vehicle?"

"A dark truck, he said. Said he didn't know one from another. But they're combing the neighborhood for anyone else who might have seen what happened."

Hutto remembered Denver still holding. As he reached for the receiver the agent in his office casually added, "Oh, and something else. The building that just blew? The church the old guy was babbling about has been trying for years to get the city to tear it down."

"Why?" Hutto asked.

"They want to put a pregnancy counseling center and adoption agency there."

CHAPTER 40

The frosty mantle of winter had fully melted into spring, and Lake Tawanee was cascading with new life, its waters replenished and rising.

Now at home in the sprawling mountain lake, *The Abbey* glided regally from her new berth at the marina. Joanna eased the throttle forward as the boat cleared the last buoy.

Jake had pulled the fenders in from the sides and had just finished securing them in their racks when he felt the boat's sudden surge of power. *The Abbey's* long graceful bow rose from the water, then leveled off on plane.

They cut through the early morning silk of the water's surface heading for Thieves Nest. Approaching the ancient bluffs surrounding the cove, *The Abbey* slowed and passed in review between the monolithic cedars still standing sentry at the entrance.

"Spooky as ever," Jake admitted, throwing the anchor into the cobalt waters.

"Not to me," Joanna said. "It's like a womb." A brief pain flickered over her face, and Jake knew she was thinking of their mother.

But she brightened quickly. "It's nice to have you home for a while, little brother," she said. "Papa's beside himself with both of us here."

"I wish you'd bring him to see me sometime. I'd love to show him around campus."

"You know he doesn't travel well. He's just now getting over the trip to New York. It's best you come home and bring Carol with you next time. I'm glad you two are dating again."

Jake grinned and winked at his sister.

They sat quietly gazing about the watery chamber.

"I'm going to see Dominick in prison," he suddenly announced.

Joanna frowned. "Why? Hasn't he caused you enough trouble?"

"I just want to talk to him. Dr. Langston has been there a couple of times. But Dominick won't even see him."

"What makes you think he'll see you?"

"Curiosity. He'll want to know how I escaped from the farmhouse, for one thing."

"Surely you won't tell him about Theresa."

"Of course not. By the way, I got a call from her. She's in Mexico. She ran from the others just before the FBI grabbed them behind the hotel. I tried to talk her into giving herself up. I know David Hutto would help her after what she did for me."

"Will she do it?"

"Not any time soon. I told her she'd get tired of living the fugitive life and to call me when she was ready to give it up."

"Good advice. I'm sure David will do all he can for her." She glanced away at the fern-draped granite walls surrounding them.

Jake noticed a softness about her he hadn't seen in a very long time. He watched her play with a lock of tangled auburn hair that had escaped the clasp at the back of her head. Then something suddenly occured to him. "David Hutto made an impression on you, didn't he?"

The blunt question startled her, and color rose in her cheeks.

"And what's that?" Jake teased. "Could it be a blush on the face of the iron maiden?"

"You know, Jake, you're just more trouble than you're worth." She pretended to be annoyed.

"You like him, don't you?"

"Who?"

"Hutto."

"I heard this conversation on the playground in third grade," Joanna snapped. " 'Oooh, Joanna, I know who you like. You like that new boy, David, don't you? Do you think he likes you, too?' "

Joanna got up and lightly punched Jake in the arm on her way down the cabin steps.

"Have you heard from Steve lately?" she called, changing the subject. She gathered cold drinks and sandwiches as Jake answered.

"He called me last week. He and Molly are getting married."

Jake baited a hook and set a line in the deep water. Joanna emerged from the cabin and handed him a soda. "That's great. What about Ramsdale? Has he seen him?"

"Only once," Jake said popping the top of the can. "Steve says he just feels sorry for him now. That's all he feels."

"That's no basis for a relationship," Joanna remarked.

"I don't think Steve wants a relationship with his father. But that may change. Langston's been visiting Ramsdale, too. He's told me the man is desperate to reconcile with Steve."

"You've gotten really close to Dr. Langston, haven't you?"

"I'm just overwhelmed by his forgiveness. He nearly lost his family, and I was partly to blame. But he calls me to come visit all the time. I play ball with his son, and his wife feeds me. I just can't get over it."

"I bought a few of his books," Joanna said. "I figured someone worthy of Dominick's rage must have something important to say."

Jake looked away and shook his head. "Do you know Langston was ready to quit his writing, his whole ministry just before the kidnapping?"

"Why?" Joanna asked with surprise.

"Something about the opposition wearing him out."

"And now?"

"He says, I quote, 'It's dangerous to leave the world uninformed.'"

Joanna and Jake sat quietly gazing about the hooded beauty of the dark cove, grateful that they had even narrowly escaped the danger.

"Are you worried about Cort Peterson?" Joanna asked, her expression grave.

"No, are you?"

She didn't have to reply. Jake read her concern. "Look, Joanna, just because he escaped doesn't mean we're in peril. He's got nothing to gain by coming after any of us. He's probably on a mountaintop in Tibet right now settling down for a life with Dravian, or whoever."

Joanna quietly munched on her sandwich until she grew restless. Jake took a huge bite of his corned beef sub.

"Well," she said, finally, "I feel like dropping some big news on you." She cleared her throat. "I bought the Lake Tawanee Marina."

Jake's eyes grew wide as he struggled to swallow. "You what?" he garbled through the corned beef.

"The couple I bought it from are retiring to Florida. Ironic, isn't it? We're trading places."

Finally clearing the sandwich from his mouth, Jake said, "How do you come up with the things you do?"

"Sheer genius."

"Sheer madness. What do you know about running a place like that?"

"I'll learn. Besides Lucy's going to work part-time as my business manager, and I'll hire whoever else I need to help me run the docks."

"So you're really going to stay."

Joanna looked surprised. "What did you think I was going to do?"

"Go back to the big time. To Miami."

"And what's the big time, Jake? A status job, prestige, yacht parties? That's empty stuff. I'll go back and visit my friends. Shake and Marlene and Pete—they're too good to lose—but my home is here with Papa."

Joanna stood up and stretched her long frame. She clapped her hands once high above her head. The echo ricocheted around the stone walls of the cove.

"I've finally come to life, Jake, and nothing looks the same. I don't see narrow little minds in Deer Creek anymore. I see freedom from what the world says we should be. And I feel relief from the terrible burden of anger."

Jake wasn't sure what she meant.

"I don't understand why Mom and Dad had to die," she said, "but one day I will. For now, I've finally laid them to rest."

Two weeks later, Jake drove through the massive iron gates of the federal penitentiary in Calhoun, Maryland. It was Sunday afternoon, and the receiving hall was crowded with friends and families of inmates.

"Name," snapped the admitting guard.

"Jake Gaddy."

"Address."

"420 Ivy Park Road, Charlottesville, Virginia. I'm a professor at the University of Virginia."

"Well, that's real nice, but I just want to know where you live. Zip and telephone?"

If you only knew what it took to get back on the faculty you wouldn't be so cute about it, Jake thought as he supplied the necessary information.

"Arms out, feet apart," the guard demanded.

Jake was searched high to low then sent through a metal detector as others waited their turn for clearance. Word was sent to cell block six that Dominick Swain had a visitor named Jake Gaddy in reception. No message was returned. Jake took a seat at a long receiving table flanked by armed guards and waited.

It had been almost two months since Jake saw Dominick handcuffed and hauled away by the FBI. He wasn't sure what to say to him. He wasn't even sure why he was here.

After a long wait, Jake glanced at the clock. It was nearly three. Visiting would end at four. He searched the open doorway, but no one was there. He looked down at the Bible he'd brought, the same one Dominick snatched from him in the basement of the Connecticut farmhouse. Jake was remembering that encounter when a sharp voice startled him.

"Just a scared little rabbit!" Dominick blurted as a stern prison guard led him to a chair across the table from Jake, forced him to sit down and warned him to keep himself under control.

The shock of seeing the man momentarily rocked Jake's composure, and he couldn't speak. The once formidable and always elegantly groomed "master of his own destiny" was frail and hollow about the eyes. He was hunched inside the orange prison-issue jumpsuit and seemed pained by the steel cuffs at his wrists.

"Are you happy to see me like this?" Dominick growled. His voice was coarse, and his gaze unsteady.

Jake finally found his voice. "I'm sorry for your suffering."

"I hope that's not all you've come to say," Dominick said. "I was rather hoping for something like, 'I was wrong to betray you, Dominick. There's still hope for the cause.' Can you offer me something like that?"

Jake paused before answering. His hand was on the worn Bible in his lap, beneath the table where Dominick couldn't see. "There is no hope for your cause, Dominick."

"Don't be so smug. Being confined to this place doesn't make me powerless. There are those who will do my bidding for me."

"You mean Cort Peterson?"

Dominick grinned triumphantly.

Jake lifted the Bible from his lap and placed it on the table. "Recognize it, Dominick?"

"Well, well. The boy evangelist brought along his primer."

Jake smiled slightly. "I imagine at one time, Dominick, you were like me, searching for truth, for what was good in life."

Dominick regarded Jake with cold indifference.

Jake continued. "And I guess you found someone who captured your wandering thoughts and molded them into something that thrilled you. That's what you did for me."

Dominick cocked his head contemptuously to one side.

"But it wasn't truth you showed me," Jake continued. He opened the Bible and turned to a verse in John.

"And you think that is," Dominick growled, glancing at the open page.

Jake ignored this. "Jesus said, 'I am the light of the world: he that followeth me shall not walk in darkness, but shall have the light of life.' "

"Means nothing," Dominick sneered.

Jake turned to 2 Corinthians. "Did you know that 'Satan himself is transformed into an angel of light'?"

Dominick was about to speak when Jake cut in. "You made the same mistake I did, Dominick."

The older man raised his eyebrows.

"You ran to the wrong light."

Dominick locked his hands about each other in a double fist cuffed by steel. Sweat trickled down his brow, and the rage mounting inside him slowly colored his cheeks.

Jake saw it coming. He quickly closed the Bible and dropped it to his lap, placing his empty hands casually back on the table. "Try to remember when we were friends, Dominick. When we shared a good laugh, a good time."

Dominick tossed his head back and stared at the ceiling.

"You're different people in one body," Jake continued. "Remember what it was like between us in Washington? You wanted to teach, I wanted to learn. We respected each other. Then came Chinatown and Cort Peterson, and suddenly you were someone I didn't know. At the hotel with Langston, you were like a raging demon. And right now. . . who are you now, Dominick?"

Dominick relaxed his hands and dropped them into his lap. He slowly leaned against the back of his chair and crossed his legs. A self-assured smile spread unevenly across his face as he spoke. "The only one who can save you from Cort Peterson."

Jake felt a chill race down his back. "Why should I be afraid of him?"

"Because he hates you. You're his enemy, and he destroys his enemies."

It was Jake who now fidgeted in his seat.

Dominick continued. "Your escape was an accident, a mistake we made. Cort hates mistakes. Ever wonder what happened to his ear?"

"No, and I don't—"

Dominick cut him off. "He made a mistake one night in a drug run at Bimini."

Jake grew suddenly still.

"Had himself a little boating accident down there. Ran full throttle into a dark cove, like the careless young fool he was, and hit another boat. He killed the people on board the other boat and his buddy riding with him. He didn't make any more mistakes, until you came along. He knew you were trouble and wanted to get rid of you. But he let me talk him out of it."

Dominick looked curiously at Jake. "What's the matter with you?" he demanded. "You look sick."

It took a moment for Jake to respond. "When was the Bimini accident?" His voice was low and unsteady.

"About twenty years ago when—" Dominick stopped abruptly. He stared suspiciously at Jake. "Wait a minute. Didn't your parents. . ." He paused to remember the few things Jake had told him about the tragedy. Then realization turned slowly into a satisfied grin. "Well, well. What do you know?" Dominick's words almost drooled from his mouth. "I do believe we have ourselves a juicy piece of justice here."

But Jake wasn't seeing or hearing Dominick. His mind raced away with the vision of Cort Peterson at the helm of the boat that killed his parents. He saw two boats burst open, spilling human remains into a dark, consuming sea. He heard his sister cry. He saw Eli's ashen face at the funeral. He grew numb and cold.

"You never told me where your parents were killed, just how. It was Bimini?" Dominick's expression wavered between disbelief and vengeful pleasure.

Jake finally focused on him, and a question tumbled from his lips. "Where is he?"

Dominick laughed out loud.

"Where is he?" Jake's angry outburst drew a warning glance from a nearby guard.

Jake rose slowly to his feet, then leaned into Dominick's face. He was shaking. He opened his mouth to speak. The words didn't come, but the guard did.

"Mister, you better sit down and behave yourself before I kick you out of here."

Jake turned to face the guard. He nodded and sank to his seat, smoldering eyes locked hard on Dominick.

"What would you do if I told you?" Dominick asked slyly.

Jake sat quietly working through a torrent of emotion, ignoring the gratified smile creasing Dominick's face. After a time, he breathed deeply, seeming to reach some point of resolution within himself.

"It's revenge I see in your eyes, Dominick, and it's ugly and futile. I'll have no part of it."

"No, it's sweet. And if you ever find Cort, you'll want it for yourself. You'll want to claw away his other ear, pierce him with steel, and throw him into the same dark waters." Dominick grinned wider. "You'll want it, all right."

The heavy metal door slammed behind Jake as he left the prison. It was good to be in the sunlight again.

He walked through the grassy yard toward the parking lot and stopped. A breeze blew in from the rich farmland across the road, and he inhaled the warm essence of the earth. Raw and vital.

But without the light, he thought, *the land would be barren. And all upon it.*